Books from *Sphere of Compassion*

THE MAIN CHARACTER!

Hero's Epic Journey Arc

1. *The Hero's Epic Journey Begins*: The Main Character!

2. *The Hero's Epic Journey Continues*: The Main Character! (Fall 2019)

The Main Character: Legendary Origin Stories!

1.5   *Guardian Angel:* Stalker (Summer 2019)

2.5   *Broad Spectrum Assassin*: Assailant (2020)

OF THE EXPS

Rebellion Arc

1. *Exp 8*: Rebellion of the Exps

Resurrection Arc

2. *The Hero of Sel*: Resurrection of the Exps

3. *Sellum*: Res. of the Exps

4. *Destruction, Creation, Absence*: Res. of the Exps

Rise Arc

1. *Eternal Rival*: Rise of the Exps (Fall 2019)

Table of Contents

Disk 1: Reality Check

Disk 2: The Terror of CatBoys!

The Main Character!

THE HERO'S EPIC JOURNEY BEGINS!

SEASON 1 PART 1

Director: Alexander J. McCarty

Editor/Cover Designer:

Gabriel McCarty

THE MAIN CHARACTER! Season 1 Part 1 The Hero's Epic Journey Begins!
Copyright © 2019 by Alexander J. McCarty

ISBN 978-1-943733-08-8

Published by Sphere of Compassion, Inc.

https://sphereofcompassion.com

authoralexandermccarty@gmail.com

https://facebook.com/alexanderjmccarty (Updates often with character art)

http://www.instagram.com/gabriel_of_the_exps

http://www.instagram.com/alexander_j_mccarty

https://twitter.com/of_the_Exps

http://www.tumblr.com/oftheexps

Front Cover design by NobodyMono

https://NobodyMono@facebook/twitter/instagram/tumblr.

https://nobodymono.artstation.com

Back Cover design by Valignar Malrune

https://www.deviantart.com/valignar-malrune

EXTRAS

Acknowledgments

This wouldn't have been possible without the continued support and help from my brother: Gabriel McCarty. We created this series and its characters together. He is always willing to help plan out scenes with me, brainstorm and brings these characters to life with his art. Oh, and did I mention that he edited this book too!

Special thanks to Ivan, Gabriel, Val, and Ken, who read and supported me way back when I wrote the first draft nearly seven years ago.

Next, I want to express my gratitude to my friends and fans who supported this book by providing feedback on the beta and the subsequent weekly chapter releases. In particular I want to thank Michael, Drew, Andrea, Cameron, and Adrian. Thanks to Drew and Michael again for inspiring me with their stories, worldbuilding, advice, and dedication to writing.

Also want to thank everyone who has helped us at conventions! Random Ramblings Productions is a YouTube group that we are proud to sponsor and they're super helpful at spreading the works of Sphere of Compassion. Robby, Monica, Riley, Chris, Oscar, Rosemi, Gus, and Adrian have also helped us set up and manage our booths at conventions.

Extra shout-out to NobodyMono who designed the cover and Valignar Malrune who drew Best Friend for the back cover of the print version of *The Main Character*.

I thank my id for keeping me vital and driven, my ego for keeping me positive and critical about my work and my super ego for directing my creative energies toward a better world for all living beings.

Lastly, I thank you, the reader, for purchasing this book. I hope you enjoy it and continue to support me and my future books.

Thank you! =(:3)* (That's a bunny, by the way.)

EXTRA SPECIAL THANKS

Patreon Subscribers:

Drew Markowitz (writer of *The Planetoids*; a fun sci-fi fantasy animestyle novel series that blends Avtar style characters with Miyazaki style worldbuilding); see link. https://www.amazon.com/Planetoid-One-Forest-D-P-Markowitz-ebook/dp/B07PZ8ZPJX/ref=sr_1_3?keywords=planetoid&qid=1553976302&s=gateway&sr=8-3&srs=17964632011

M. W. Arita (writer of *Demi-Girl*; an urban fantasy novel that explores the vast mythos of Japan in a modern environment!); see link. https://www.amazon.com/M.W.-Arita/e/B07NBZCW6M/ref=dp_byline_cont_ebooks_1

Introduction

A long time ago my brother and I saw a parody video by Egoraptor called Girl-Chan in Paradise. We found it really fun and thought, hey we know tons of anime, we could make our own parody series. A couple years later on vacation, my brother and I made our own mock anime opening song about Main Character, Boobs, Best Friend, Glasses Kid and Stalker. It wasn't until I saw Akikan, a fun ecchi comedy series about a corporate conspiracy to pit living soda cans against one another, did I find my true inspiration to start writing *The Main Character! series*. Kakeru inspired Main and he's one of my all-time favorite anime protagonists.

Naruto also heavily inspired *The Main Character! series*. The whole dynamic between Naruto and Sasuke was so interesting and I wanted to know what it would be like to explore this hidden attraction through the closeted thoughts of an outwardly heterosexual anime protagonist.

Of course there are countless other series that have given us clever ideas, fun jokes and inspiration for *The Main Character*: Monty Oum's RWBY; Director Hayo Miyazaki's films (particularly Nausica and Mononoke); the BlazBlue, Xenosaga, Danganronpa, and Disgaea video game series; the Bobobo, Future Diaries, Dokkoida?!, Eden's Bowy, Bleach, and Puni Puni Poemi animes, and the mangas of Seikon no Qwaser, Deadman Wonderland, Buso Renkin, Berserk, Needless, Jojo's Bizarre Adventure, Yu-Gi-Oh! and Brandish were all pivotal in inspiring the characters, settings and story of *The Main Character!*

More recent inspirations include: Shera and The Princesses of Power, with its fun, diverse cast and adorable character interactions; Dragon Prince, it's take on dark magic inspired us to look deeper into our own lore; The World God Only Knows, one of the smartest and best psychological animes and convinced us to make our heroes ViralTubers. Fairy Tail, whose interconnectivity of characters and story arcs set a new standard for Shounen anime; Digi Charat, with its plethora of cat honorifics and bizarre humor; Girls Bravo, a superbly written ecchi comedy anime

I discovered recently that inspired both Banana Man and Harem C, a character you'll see in the next *The Main Character!* book.

Infinite thanks to the godfather of anime: Osamu Tezuka.

Oh, and Terra Formars, just because it's our favorite manga! READ IT!

This book is dedicated to every anime, movie, book, and manga creator that has ever inspired me and to you the readers for whom I write for! May you enjoy this metaphysical journey into the tropes of anime. I hope this story bring you many laughs!

DISC 1:

REALITY CHECK

THE LEGEND RE-BEGINS ONCE AGAIN

Episode 1 Part 1

There I was, standing face to face with my archenemy. Blood dripped out from our wounds and down to out fingertips like the way paint drips down a grimy wall. We stared at each other with a single drowsy eye. Either of us could slip into the next world at any moment. I wasn't about to give up. Everyone was counting on me, even if they weren't aware of it. But let's pointlessly go back to a time before this. Now that I've got your attention, let's go to a time where I was just an average kid armed only with bravery and dreams of adventure! This is the story of how I became the world's greatest hero!

Oh, crap! I just spoiled the ending. Damn it. No wait, does that make it edgy? Maybe I should rephrase it.

This is the story of how I became the Main Character King!

"I look into the sunlight…ow! I burnt my eyes. And now I'm running down an endless path pointlessly…pointlessly. Now there's a slide show of a bunch of people I don't know. And it's ruining who joins up on my team. Damn Spoilers! Then my hand is reaching out to the sky. That's so deep! Now all the villains are taking up my screen-time! But then I jump in and punch them with my spiky hair. I'm now clenching my fist on top of a mountain of graves. Holy shit that's some awesome symbolism! I'm then knocked back. I wipe off the blood off my cheek and then I run forth and punch with all my might! No matter what I won't die! And there is only one reason why. It's because I'm The Main Character! Me me me! The Main Character! Hell's yeah! I'm The Main Character!"

"Stop right there. How much longer does this go on?" asks my best friend, looking up at me from the comfort of my lap.

I comb back my sexy spiky hair and respond. "Thirty more times. I needed to fill it in so it was a whole two and a half minutes like the new One Place openings!" I exclaim in a confident, charismatic and subtly sexy voice.

"And what is the significance of all this?" asks my best friend in a dark, whispery and depressed voice.

"I've been dreaming of another new world. One where I totally kick ass! Wouldn't it be awesome to inexplicably be transported to an alternate dimension?" I ask with shimmering eyes.

"Whatever keeps you going…I guess," says my best friend before cutting his wrist with a straight razor.

"Hey man, what's bothering you?"

"Nothing of importance," he says with quivering eyes.

"Put that frown away." I bend over and tickle his sides.

He cackles demonically as he squirms around. "St-Stop," he says, blushing a deep crimson.

Aww, he's like a clawless kitten when he's like this.

"Sorry for being so negative." He smiles at me. "How can I help?"

"Do you think that song will work for our ViralTube opening if I spice in some clips from previous episodes?" I ask, scrolling through our past anime reviews.

"Your devotion shall give it new life," he says, beaming at me with those gorgeous intense red eyes.

Damn, I kind of just threw my audience in the middle of a scene without any exposition. My name is The Main Character. You're probably wondering if that's my real name. Well both my parents are gone, so I don't know what my real name is. I chose this name and hopefully that will also give me the power to choose my own destiny.

Now you get to hear about what I look like because I don't have money for an animator. I look about as Asian as most anime heroes. I have bright orange spiky hair and an insatiable appetite. My eyes are…hazel, I think. I wear a fashion forward pink and blue ahego shirt. Let's see, what else? Oh yeah, I'm a sadomasochist and a delinquent. I'm also an epic otaku Neet virgin! I believe in justice. I have a starfish shaped birthmark at my power center. I love going on aimless bizarre adventures. Oh, and I'm really laid back and cool. You may be wondering where I got these sexy muscles from. I'm always sparring with my best friend just like a certain brotherly duo of alchemists so I'm both ripped and experienced in combat.

Best Friend sat up, his shoulders still drooping. His sleek jet-black hair has droplets of blood in it and covers one of his eyes. Don't ask me how he got permanent blood stains in his hair. Every time I ask him…he just smiles. It's kind of scary. He wears a black pleather jacket with chains and metal studs. His torn jeans have impractical zippers and belts all around it. Oh, and he's a whole five inches taller than me! My best friend is sixteen years old and we've been together ever since we were babies. He doesn't use his real name because it reminds him of that fateful day. "What are you thinking about?" he asks, tilting his head and staring at me fondly.

"I'm thinking about what anime to watch next," I say, picking up the remote and scrolling through the new hot trash to find a hidden gem. "Any suggestions?"

"Blood, gore and family bonding," he says with a gentle smile.

"Well there's another new Devil Man-child! Let's watch that!"

Best Friend rests his head in my lap. "Perfect choice."

My senses went on high alert. An adult had entered the room.

"Main, breakfast is ready." The woman's name was Linda, but I had my own nickname for her. Since she's slightly relevant I'll give her a character description. She has long locks of red curly hair, eyes of an unimportant color that always look down on me through her rectangular spectacles.

"Yeah, Old Hag. I know it's ready. But I'm busy," I say, putting my feet up on the adjacent sofa.

"It would be good for you to spend time with the other kids. It's Jeremy's birthday," she says, trying to wound me with a guilt drill.

"You know how much I hate birthdays," I say in a voice teeming with angst.

Here's the thing. I am actually only four years old! I know, I'm hot. The reason I don't look four is because I was born on a leap year. And because of that

I've always had less presents than the other kids. Being unique and awesome has its major downsides sadly.

"It would mean a lot to him if you showed up. We are going to have some cupcakes after breakfast," says Old Hag with a big smile.

Holy shit, they have cupcakes!

My eyes light up but Best Friend gives me an intense look.

"After the opening song? Okay?" I say, putting my hands behind my head like a carefree badass.

Best Friend pinches my sides. "You've been cheating, haven't you?"

I can't bear to look into those disapproving eyes.

"You thought I wouldn't notice," he says in a solemn tone.

Eeesh! Unlike her, he knows how to guilt trip me.

"I can't help but like sweets. I'm a teenager," I said, sinking into the couch.

"Tsunderes and muscle men love sweets. You're neither, so don't pretend it's part of your larping alias," says Best Friend, grabbing my cheeks and turning me to face him. "Your health is a serious thing."

I turn around to see Old Hag was still standing there. "What do you want, woman?"

"I want you to respect me and the other orphans," she says, turning off the TV.

Oh crap! Did I mention that I'm at an orphanage? Well I am. This place is my only home. Lost Keys Orphanage is a rundown ugly grey building where kids get dropped off as often as they leave. I don't have a freaking clue which generic kid Jeremy is and frankly I couldn't care less. Side characters come and go so why bother making friends?

"Don't ignore me," she said, sticking her finger in my face.

"I want you to get off my back, Old Hag. I don't care about a bunch of normies. I already said I'll be there after the opening." I snatch the controller from her hand with my Saiyam-like reflexes.

"We have to cut the budget, Main. I know how much entertainment means to you but we can't keep paying for your monthly streaming service," she says with a sweet smile that betrayed her cut-throat words.

My blood froze like the panoramic action shots from Very Tail.

"Anime is life not mere entertainment! This isn't one of your wannabe 80's style Netfilms series; this is legit storytelling with plentiful panty shots!"

"I'm not punishing you. We took it to a vote and Netfilms won out. We only have enough money in our budget for one service. They still have your Japanese animes so what's the problem?"

Oh my god! Only total noobs call them Japanese animes. I feel tainted being under the same roof as this plebian.

"So what? I'm supposed to Spike Seagull with illegal odd jobs so you don't pull the plug on me?" I ask her with a grimace.

Not that he ever ends up making money without Bae Valentine spending it.

"Drop the attitude, kid," she says with a stern look.

"Eight dollars a month, right?" Best Friend stood up before walking out of the room.

Eight times twelve equals…a shit ton more money than I have!

I follow him. "Are we going bounty hunting?"

"You're staying home to set up our queue for the month." He ruffles my hair but doesn't smile.

"You've been training me! I'm ready to go out crime fighting with you."

"Martial arts are for self-defense not gaudy tournaments or vigilante work," says Best Friend, checking the sharpness of his throwing knives.

"Hey, you always shower when you come back. You're in there for hours and you never let me in. You don't have to shoulder the burden alone. We're a two-man Supah Sentai," I say, putting out my hand.

He places his hand atop mine and his pale cheeks light up. "I will return."

The old hag comes out from behind us. "Hold up!"

"Anime is our only escape from a world that sees us as discarded trash. Taking that away is like taking a child away from their parents." He turns to me. "I'm going to get you that money," says Best Friend with that intense gaze that makes me tremble.

The doorbell suddenly rang. Something inside me told me that the person on the other side would change my life forever.

Oh yeah. That's how you build suspense!

Old Hag swung open the door. "Welcome to Lost Keys. How can I help you?"

A man in a cozy sweater and his sexy brunette wife light up upon seeing me.

"Well, my lovely husband and I were hoping to have a little one to keep us company."

"The orphans are in the kitchen," says Best Friend, pointing with a throwing knife.

The woman bends down and looks at me with hope in her eyes. "You're a Scorpio, aren't you?"

She's absolutely right. Since it was my favorite celestial spirit, I had decided to be a Scorpio. I honestly had no clue what my actual astrological sign was.

"You dare tarnish his name with your toxic labels?" asks Best Friend, giving the woman a murderous stare.

Whoa! This is escalating quickly! Time for the Main Character to diffuse the situation.

17:00

"You guessed right! I'm a Scorpio! We are!" I exclaim, doing a rocker pose and sticking my tongue out.

The woman wiped her eyes. "Rover was our child…and a Scorpio. The home is just too lonely without our dear Rover around. Miss, we'd like to take this one. Money is no object," says the lady, taking out her husband's wallet from his pocket.

Yeesh. Marriage ain't like it is in anime, that's for sure. That guy is more whipped than Dracula from Castlemania!

Best Friend's gaze lightens. "Rover wasn't your child. He was a dog that filled the gap in your life. There are plenty of dogs at the local shelter. It's called Paws for Peace, I can escort you there."

The wife's eyes flare up with justice. "How dare you assume Rover's sex and species! She's a cat for your information!" She turns to her man slave. "Tell him, honey bun."

"Rover was an angel. A gift from god," says the man in monotone.

We get all sorts of weirdos showing up here but these two are special.

Old Hag waves at the couple to get their attention. "Maybe a cat is more what you're looking for to replace Rover."

"Nothing could replace Rover! She was so pure!" wailed the wife, sobbing on her husband's arm. "We only want the boy to lessen the pain."

What am I a freaking pillow!?

Old Hag turns to the ruckus in the kitchen. "Sorry. If you'll excuse me." She rushes off to check on the side characters.

Best Friend flicks his wrist to reveal a hidden blade. "If you don't want to join Rover prematurely, follow me to the pet shelter. Main isn't going with you."

The husband grabs his wife's hand. "Don't you threaten my wife." He unfolds his hands and shows off that he's missing a pinky. "You don't want to mess with me, little boy."

Great! He's a freaking gangster! This is so not good!

"Got in trouble for treachery, eh? I wouldn't flaunt your mistakes." Best Friend points his hidden blade at the man's other hand. "You know, I could make you symmetrical."

The wife shoves her man aside. "We'll come back later. We shouldn't miss Gerald's barbeque."

They walk out, hand in hand.

Best Friend put away his blade. "Disgusting hypocrites. Care so much for dogs while feasting on the flesh of other animals."

"You're not going after them?" I ask, mostly relieved.

"If they return, their tomboy cat will be reunited with them." He spins the blade on his finger.

A tomboy cat-girl would be so hot!

"Main, you there?" asks Best Friend, tapping my forehead.

Old Lady came returned, smelling like cupcakes. "Those two were certainly interesting," she says with a chuckle. "I'd never let my little orphans be pets." She pats my head. "You're humans not animals, after all."

Best Friend walks off.

"What are you so happy about, Old Hag?"

"Well, I just checked the mail and there was a letter written to you. There's exactly ninety-six dollars inside the letter. That's exactly the amount you need to cover the price of your SquishyRoll subscription!"

"You searched through his mail?" asks Best Friend with dark eyes. "Also, look here." He opens up a biology book. "Humans are from the kingdom Animalia. We are animals, period."

"Oh, you know what I meant." She crouches down and smiles at me. "Looks like you'll get your anime streaming, after all."

Okay so she's being all secretive about this but I bet you anything the old hag is the one who put the money in the envelope. The timing and the amount are both too perfect.

19:00

Best Friend snatches the envelope from my grip. He turns it around and inspects it. "No name."

"Relax, Old Hag obviously did it," I say.

"She's done many good things, but not once has she given us actual money," says Best Friend, peeking outside the windows.

"So, how about breakfast?" asks Old Hag with a smile.

"No need. I'll feed him," says Best Friend, putting a stick of celery in my mouth.

I wish he wouldn't baby me all the time.

"We gotta go if we don't want to miss the bus." I went in the fridge, put a piece of bread in my mouth and ran off.

And now for a quick commercial break. Just kidding! This is my story and I don't want you missing half of it because of a shopping impulse. No product placement allowed. Let the program resume.

You're probably wondering what kind of cool school the Main Character goes too. Well, sadly it's nothing special. No teachers who teach elite kids how to use their super powers; no ninja exams and sadly it's not an all-girls school where I'm the only boy. It's a boring normal grade school called Watson Elementary. I think the board room that came up with the name thought they were comedians or something. Anyways, I'm currently repeating the third grade.

My eyes glaze over as the teacher repeats what he says like a freaking Pocketmon.

I've lost track of how many years I've been stuck in this stale classroom. I hardly fit in this tiny desk. The only thing unique about the class room is the seven-year old college student we have for a teacher. He's currently teaching us to how get a grant for having multiple internships or something. The moron doesn't realize he's speaking to a bunch of grade schoolers.

"Pay attention Kenneth, you aren't special," he says, tossing a piece of chalk at me.

How dare he use a fake name to address me!

I catch the chalk in my hand and flick it back at him.

I am special! Just like the OG Black Swordsman, I was born an orphan. My mother gave birth on a train and I was shot out the window by her at conception. Luckily my supposed parents gave me a third of a heart shaped amulet. I guess they wanted me to always keep false hope that one day we'll be reunited. My circumstantial birth is the beginning of my story, unless you count past lives of course. In which case I was absolutely a wolf searching for Paradise!

The teacher stands on his tip-toes to address the class. "School won't pay the bills. You'll need a job so I'll be giving you tips on how to breach into joining a business."

My teacher has a real name, but it's no more significant than he is. He isn't a magical European boy who can flip skirts just by sneezing. He's not an ex-biker gang boss, a bored smiley-faced alien or even a ditzy boobtastic bombshell. He's just a quirkless normie that scored high on an IQ test because of his Ultimate Luck talent. I call the little twerp Glasses Kid. You can't see him behind that large podium, but he has short white hair and light blue eyes that look really huge because of his oversized glasses. He wears a stupid graduation hat and a buttoned-up midnight blue business suit. Look at that smug little smile. He thinks he's so damn smart!

Eh, but enough about the short stack. Let's talk more about Best Friend - the only one besides me who actually matters! He's kind of suicidal. In fact, he's told me numerous times that he lives on only because of his tragic past. Until he fulfills some vague goal, he won't be able to die in peace. I have a feeling his goal is to finally graduate from the Third Grade. That's why I've stolen his text books and set fire to his scantrons.

Man, I'm really a great friend. But I can't take it anymore! I have to escape this place. I've tried to burn down the school several times, but I always get caught. If I had the Escape Diary it would be no problem, but until Murmur shows up, I'm stuck here. That's why I decided to finally study. This is going to be the year I graduate and fulfill my dream of going to Tokyo U! Best Friend and I made a promise to pass together! We're going to do it! And then we're going to get married and have a ton of kids!

Holy crap, I just jumped the gun.

Let me introduce you to the final important character.

21:00

"Sticky Fingers!" I exclaim with a dramatic pose.

I unzip my backpack and place my hand on my girlfriend.

Sure, she's grafted onto a sticky hug pillow, but that doesn't change that we've watched fire-works, sunsets, snuggle every night and best of all she never tells me about her feelings. I don't actually know what anime she's from, probably something really niche but awesome like Assault on Titan. I don't know her real name, but her tits are so massive that they completely cover her face and most of her torso. Being the master wordsmith that I am, I've decided to call her Boobs. She's eighteen because I say so and her hair is blonde. She always whispers sweet nothings to me whenever I need her and by that, I mean she doesn't say anything. She is a pillow, after all. One day I will have to abandon her sadly. I must grow more powerful if I am to defeat the NHK.

"Breasts and women should have no power over Main Character!" I exclaim, standing up from my desk.

The other kids laugh at me and I sit down with embarrassment.

Best Friend shoots them a dark glare and they stop immediately.

Everyone else here is so insignificant that my mind doesn't even see the point in making out their eyes. I normally just see a blank face and a mouth when they talk. Why should I waste brain power animating extras? They're all a bunch of stupid little brats anyways. No eye candy here unless you're Adam Blaze, or Gogo Shiojji.

Oh crap! Glasses kid is calling out our final grades! I better pay attention.

"I believe in you Main. I know you studied hard," says a random classmate in front of me.

Wait, she believes in me…I need to introduce her. I'm animating her eyes in. Okay, she has hair covering her eyes and its color is

Oh crap, the teacher just said Best Friend's grade.

"An F+…I've improved. I'm now a slightly better failure." Best Friend grips his face and chuckles to himself. "I need some new razors. My blood has made these ones too rusty." He removes his hand and beams at me. "Looks like we'll be spending another year together."

What if I pass? I don't want to graduate without him! Who will give me kisses goodnight? Who will wash my back with his tongue? And who will massage my ego!? Damn it, I won't even have a warm body to cuddle naked with when the orphanage gets cold.

I get out from my tiny plastic chair. I run up to the teacher and pick him up by his collar. "Alright, Glasses Kid, tell me my grade, or the suspense will kill you!"

"You got a D-…you almost passed. I gave you a C in effort though. I could tell you actually sorta tried this year," he says with a stupid smile and a nerdy, goofy, phlegmy voice. He pats my head, embarrassing me in front of everyone.

I toss him back down and run to Best Friend. I bend down and grab his soft hands.

"Let's promise to graduate together… and actually do it this time!" I exclaim with awesome conviction.

"Alright, after all… there's still something I must accomplish," says Best Friend, clenching his chest.

We stood there locked in each-others entrancing gaze like the queer hetero ice skaters from Yaoi On Ice.

The nice girl from earlier pops up behind me like a Fuuko projection. "Don't worry, I know you can do it! I've watched you study and I know you'll make it next year," she says with much admiration and a bit of drool.

She may be taking up my screen time, but she is talking about me. I guess I should give her a name. Something about her feels kinda familiar.

"Um…who are you again, girlie?" I ask, scratching my head.

"I'm your childhood friend." She clasps her hands together and leans toward me. "I won't ever forget the promise you made that day. I've done everything so I can become someone worthy of your feelings," she says before hiding her face under hands.

Who the hell is this girl? She says she's my childhood friend, but she seems more like a stalker. Good thing I always have a gun with me inside Boobs.

23:00

"So, Stalker, what was the promise?" I ask her while taking off my Kamia shades.

"You do remember!" She squeals before running off back to her seat.

Wait her seat was right in front of me! And it's facing me! How long has she been here? Either way it looks like she's going to graduate. Lucky little bitch got an A.

I guess I should add her to the character roster. Alright, she has curly red hair, tan skin and light pink lips. She's wearing the light blue school's uniform and has a Mokuuna backpack. I don't mind having another adoring fan, especially one who acts like a typical girl from a romance anime. Yeah, I know I'm far beyond common tropes, but the fact that she's acting this way in real life makes her unique in my eyes.

"So, do you want to walk home together again?" asks Stalker in a cutesy wispy and mumbly voice.

Wait, we've done that before?

"Yep. Every day since the First grade."

No. That's not creepy at all.

"Where do you live?" I ask with a nervous look.

She tilts her head and her eyes go vacant. "Why with you of course, darling."

She lives with me? This is insane! Just who the hell is this girl? Geez she's like Yuno Goresai but the non-legal version, which deletes the only reason to make her my girlfriend!

"When did we meet?"

"You're a legend! The Main Character! I've watched all your videos and I'm always the first to comment."

Thank goodness she's just a fan girl. I can handle this.

"Are you AngelLolipop8?" I ask with wide eyes.

"Yuppers!" she exclaims, leaping into a hug.

Awww, she's not so bad. She's my number one patron. She's been a fan since our very first video. It's actually really cool meeting her in person. Too bad she isn't a total hottie with a sexy burn mark.

"Thanks for all the support."

"You're welcome. This is so awesome! Awesome! Awesome! Awesome! Awesome!" she cheers, swinging around as she hugs me.

"What was your favorite video review?" I ask with a confident grin.

She smiles at me warmly. "Kodomo no Chikan!"

I pull her arms off and set her back in her chair.

"Hey, master. Guess what…I'm not wearing any underwear," says my Stalker in a super innocent voice, making it all the more unsettling.

What is cute in anime is really creepy in real life.

Deep breaths Main, focus your Nen. She's just a kid…ugh but that's the problem! Alright, just a few minutes left and then its summer time. Best Friend and I are so going to the beach tomorrow. We'll splash each other with water while giggling like little girls. Then we'll rub oil on each other's backs with our bare bodies. After that we'll chase all the chicks in swimsuits! And when that's over we'll spend the night in a hotel. We'll be pillow fighting till the sun comes up. This summer is going to be awesome!

Well, well, look at the time. The bell should ring any moment and then it's the start of my vacation! I just hope the ominous swirling stormy clouds outside aren't a premonition of what's to come. Oh well, there's only a minute left of class. What could possibly happen?

25:00

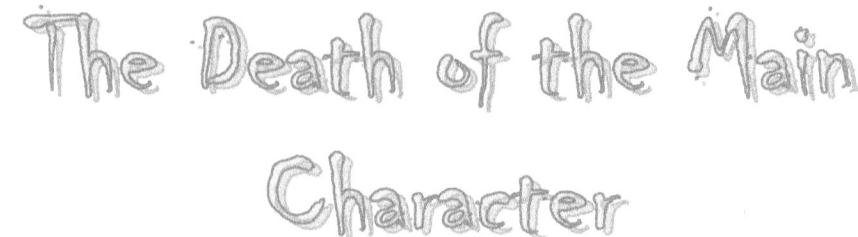

Episode 1 Part 2

That title is really making me uneasy. It looks like the letters are outlined with blood. If that wasn't bad enough, it's in Chiller font style. Some bad shit is going to happen, I just know it.

The ominous clouds outside became even darker and more foreboding.

"Main, don't worry. I'll protect you, Nyo," says Stalker, snuggling up to my arm.

"It is my duty to protect him, not yours," says Best Friend, tearing her off me.

"Why didn't you act sooner?" I ask him with a look of concern.

"I was examining her intentions. She seems harmless enough." He turns to the girl. "If you try to take advantage of him or kidnap him, you'll lose a finger. I'll let you pick which one."

She giggles and slugs him playfully. "I'll be a good girl."

Oh, I should check the status of our newest review.

I reach behind Boobs and pull out my tablet. It was a gift from Best Friend on my second birthday. I freaked out when he gave it to me because there was someone's severed hand clenching it. Thankfully, after we broke the grip with some pliers and cleaned the screen, there weren't any fingerprint stains on it.

I open up our new video to see a big red flag.

"Did we stir the pot too much?" asks Best Friend with a curious look.

Sure Seven-Hundred Deadly Plot Devices is treasured by newbie weeaboos, but that usually just nets us a couple thousand dislikes. I praised the fun characters and backstory but Best Friend nitpicked it to hell and brought our rating down to an 'only watch once'. Why was our video review taken down? I

26:00

know we said Lizabeth is not consent, but the anti-SJWs shouldn't have the authority to remove our hard work.

I go to our archive.

Flagged, they're all flagged. It's over.

"Is everything alright, darling?" asks Stalker, patting my head with a crazed grin.

Article 13…did it pass? Is the world of free streaming over? This can't be real.

"It passed on the 26th. It's been less than a week."

"Tell me this is an April Fools' joke."

"Regrettably it's as real as the Devil's Will Cry 5 Blood Palace DLC update. I look to forward to conquering that challenge when we return home."

"I don't want to back." I turn to Best Friend. "You know, double suicide doesn't sound like such a bad idea."

Yeah! That's it! I have a knife; he has a knife. We both try to plunge it in, but I love him too much. Then I confess my love to him as I blank out. Then the two of us meet up in heaven and lose our virginity in an X-rated OVA! It's not ideal, but it's our only option.

"I know what will cheer you up. We can watch Brigadoom together!" exclaims Stalker with a girly twirl.

"No! What's the point of watching things I love if I can't trash them in low budget video reviews? What's the point of love without hate?" I ask, clenching my sides in tears.

The title was right. This really is the death of the Main Character. My ViralTube channel persona is dead. I've been living as him so long…I don't know how to be anyone else! Is this what Rorshank felt when his world crumbled?

The bell rang and the lights went out.

"Everyone remain calm," says Glasses Kid before screaming out in agony.

The lights came back up and a hooded figure was holding Glasses Kid's head.

It was so surreal. Like an overly gruesome chapter of Battle Royalty. His vacant eyes still looked smug to me.

I'm dreaming right? Wouldn't be the first time I dozed off in class. Of course! It's April Fools', that trickster teacher must be going all out this time!

The figure turns its attention to me. Under the hood was a collection of stars.

This thing was unearthly.

Okay, there are two options! One: he's going to select me to be in the next Queens' Blade. But considering the newest reboot and the fact that I have a penis, that seems unlikely. Option two: he's going to kill me!

A dagger shoots out from its long white sleeves. Best Friend jumps in front of me and grabs the knife.

"I won't let you destroy my life," he says softly as he drags the knife across his chest.

"Do you trust me, sensei?" asks Stalker, looking directly into my eyes.

What the hell is going on? What do I say? Should I trust her? I hardly even know her!

Am I going to die here? Well at least I'll make the headlines. Wait, Glasses Kid was already killed. What if his death is the highlight of the news report? Shit, he's a kid! Those always get the spotlight in these kinda scenarios, hence the Lost Child arc. I can't worry about that. Right now, I need to make sure no one else dies. I can't allow them to steal my flair.

"Hey Red Man, stay away from my little chick!" Best Friend tosses the knife right back at the creature. It absorbs the knife in its cloak. It then put out its sleeves. Knives shoot out faster than my fear could seize me. I watch in futility as my fellow classmates are slaughtered. I still can't make out their eyes, but their blood is as clear as crystal.

This isn't a joke. This is real. They're dead. No. They can't all be dead.

I turn to see that a few of them are bleeding but still alive.

What is this horrible feeling? Is this what people call a conscience? Damn it, seeing little kids suffering makes me think of Uchio! She was too young to die! My eyes are watering up. I can't see shit!

I wipe the tears from my eyes.

I wanted to be a hero, right? Well now's my chance. These kids need me.

I toss two tiny desks at the assailant. "You want the Azure, right! Well it's right here!" I pound my fist against my chest.

"You're incredible," says Stalker with love-struck eyes.

"I'll distract him. You save the kids, alright?" I ask, deflecting an incoming tentacle blade with a chair.

"I won't abandon you," she says, reaching for my hand. "Will you accept my help?"

For some reason I feel like I'm about to make a contract with a cute but deadly otherworldly entity.

"Watch out!" yells Best Friend.

Oh shit! Four blades are coming straight for me.

Best Friend leapt in front of me. His body was suspended in the air. serving as my shield. The blades had pierced him, but it wasn't fatal.

Stalker was still staring at me, waiting for my response. I turn to her, mustering up all my bravery.

"If I die now, I'll just be another statistic. If you can save my life, I will entrust it to you," I say with incredible firmness.

Am I going to end up becoming a magical girl because of this? Whatever, I'll gladly wear a frilly skirt it if it can save my best friend!

Stalker smiles and then takes out a Taser. The bitch fries me while still giving me a warm smile.

I try to get up, but it's no use.

She walks straight up to the cloaked figure. "Dad, he's the one you want. No one else here matters," she says, pointing right at me.

That thing is her father. W.T.F. seriously! This has got to be one f'ed up dream I'm having. Please Lord Madarara, let this just be a Sharingun hallucination.

Best Friend slices the tendrils that pierced him and rolls out of the way of the next attack. "So, you finally reveal your true feelings. I had a feeling you would strike today. I already warned you, Stalker."

Why does everyone know what's going on but me?

"Let's do it, Cerberus!" Best Friend pulls out dual handguns, one red and black and the other black and white. "I said that if you tried to kill Main, I'd murder you like I did my parents." He shoots her right in the chest.

This all feels so wrong. I know he was defending me…but, she's just a kid. Ugh, why am I getting flashes of Riika's tattered corpse.

"Big brother is mine! Once he's dead, we'll be together forever!" she exclaims, crawling up to me and leaving behind a smear of pink blood.

"Best Friend, what the hell is she?" I ask him in horror.

"She's your enemy and I am your ally," he says, tossing a gun to me. Best Friend shoots a tendril, ducks under a second one and then throws a knife right at Stalker's head.

Just before the dagger could make contact with her skull, the girl was sliced in half by the cloaked man. Her two severed halves reached out to me before collapsing into a puddle of blood.

"What do you want with me? You just killed your daughter, you sick bastard!" I point the gun right at him. "Leave now and I'll let you live."

My hands are trembling. Why can't I pull the trigger? Heroes are supposed to be fearless, goddamn it! Goku, please lend me your energy or give me a goddamn sensu bean!

"With your death…salvation!" exclaims the attacker, raising his sleeves.

Tentacles shoot out and pull in the bodies of my fellow classmates.

30:00

Damn it. These tentacles are being wasted here. There's an all-girls high-school just up the road. Okay seriously, I'm really freaking out here. Why are the faces of my classmates materializing now that they're twisted with fear and pain? I have to do something. I have to at least try to save them!

I fire the entire clip into the tentacles, saving a handful of kids instead of ending the life of the enemy.

My mind flashes to a moment when Best Friend and I were sparring shirtless.

"Remember, Main. A true hero should try to save the most lives, not everyone. Following Shirow Emiya's footsteps will only lead you to ruin."

He looks so radiant, like a Hamom master. How could he be dying?

Metallic wings sprout from my assailant's arms before they shoot out toward me.

The impact shakes me back to my senses.

"Main, live on." Best Friend smiles lovingly as he pulls off his shirt. He was strapped from head to toe with grenades. "I've always been ready to die for you. It was living for you that was truly painful. As long as you're safe, my life has purpose. I'm sorry, you'll have to graduate without me."

What is he doing?

Best Friend rushes toward the assailant, beads of sweat making his chest sparkle.

"You cannot die! You are the source of his power!" exclaims the assassin.

His tentacles sharpen as his bladed fingers grab onto Best Friend's neck. Another bladed tentacle slices the grenade vest off.

No! No. This wasn't supposed to happen.

I pull the trigger but there aren't any bullets left. I spent them saving a few kids and for what? This monster is going to kill them all anyways. I tried to be a hero and now I'm going to lose him.

In the end I'm just a dumb kid playing dress up.

Best Friend fires a final bullet into the assailant's cloak.

Purple blood sprays out from the wound, melting the ground as it touches it.

"Run." My best friend is cut to ribbons before my eyes. Even in death he has such divine elegance. Each shred of him glistens in the sunlight and waves in the wind like a beautiful red snowflake.

Killing off characters in the first episode is just a cheap edge-lord technique. There wasn't time for the viewers to get attached. He deserved a better death, like Itachii, instead he died like human fodder from Goblin Scalper. Oh god. He's really gone.

I felt my face. It was drenched in tears.

My best friend is dead and I'm still making anime references. It's the only way my mind knows how to process all this crazy shit. But it's not enough. Shit I can't see anything with all these tears.

It's just me and the murderer now. I'm not going to just stand still and die. I have to use the legendary Joseph Jostar's secret technique!

My legs move me away from my enemy at incredible speed.

If I can get him away from the school then I can save some of those kids. Best Friend won't have died in vain. Yeah, I'll give his death purpose and I'll kill the one who did it!

I toss my ridiculously heavy textbook at the window, smashing it to pieces. I then crash right through it, just barely dodging an incoming blade.

Where do I run? Come on what would Joseph do? There aren't any volcanoes nearby. How do I beat this guy? Of course, a gas station! There's one just down the road!

As thousands of thoughts bounced through my head a car was thrown right in front of me. I run on top of it and jump off.

That's it, ride the adrenaline!

I make it to the gas station with the assailant hot on my trail. I reach into my backpack and pull out the pistol behind boobs.

If only I had remembered sooner. My mind was in a blur. No. I can't dwell on that. Every second counts.

I pull out my heft AGL Arms .45 Long Cult. "Everyone, get out of here!" I yell, raising my custom replica and firing a shot.

These goddamn morons are crouching down, not running. Do they want me to blow them up?

It's too late. The assailant arrives and still only a few people actually flee. The rest are frozen in terror.

I can do this. Forget about these people. They're just side-characters, strangers. That thing killed my best friend and it will die!

I aim the revolver at the gas tank, but notice a baby in the car.

Sorry, Best Friend. I'm doing this my way.

I fire a round into the assailant's lower cloak.

The creature's purple blood sprays on the car, but stops before it can melt all the way through.

Metal spider-like appendages come out from the creature and it races toward mc.

Sorry Best Friend, I can't stop the monster who killed you. I'm a damn failure.

I run as fast as my legs will carry me.

I need to go home. If I make it to the orphanage, then I just know I'll be safe. Best Friend wants me to live. I won't betray his last request.

I jump onto a car and feel it flip beneath my feet. I kick off, seeing bladed tendrils zoom by me. As I soar through the air, I feel a strange sensation. Blood is now gushing out of my arm. No...there is no arm, just blood.

I'm going to die. The title was absolutely right.

I look as far as I can, seeing my orphanage in the distance. It radiates with a beautiful light, beckoning me.

"You son of a bitch! I'm going to make it! I'm going to live!" I yell as I fire blindly behind me.

I keep running but then suddenly trip and fall.

What the hell!? Glasses kid is the klutz, not me!

My leg is gone and blood is gushing out from the wound. The assailant approaches me as I try to crawl away from him.

This is where a deus-ex machina is supposed to show up, right? Preferably a cute girl from another world in tight clothes.

A girl in a futuristic outfit then appears in front of me.

Sooo predictable! The tropes I've hazed are now saving my life. This irony is thicker than Handzo's futomaki rolls. It's over. I'm finally safe.

"If you come with me, I promise you'll live," she says, creating a portal out of thin air.

Wait, where have I heard that before.

(Note: Insert Flashback of Stalker Girl here. Side Note: have an extra unrelated minute of runtime in order to save on the episode's budget.)

Should I trust her. It turned out badly last time. Oh shit, that thing is moving toward her. I have to do something.

"I'm not going to be some pawn for your revolution! Solve your own problems, beyotch!" I yell, shooting at her feet with my pistol.

She pulls the gun out from my hand with her telepathic powers. She digs her heel into my nuts and then leaves into a portal.

In hindsight, maybe that wasn't such a good idea. What if she could have fought that thing? This is no anime. Being a hero is going to get me killed.

The hooded figure looms closer and closer, building up unnecessary suspense.

I aim my gun at him, ready to fire.

One final bullet. A single headshot should end this.

A girl with black hair riding a bicycle comes from out over the bend and runs right over my neck.

"What a shitty death," I say before everything goes dark.

Yeah that's it, I died from a Kagomi wannabe. Turns out I'm not an Aijin after all. Shit! Oh well, at least I'll share the top spot with Yoshigake Killa for the most pathetic death.

Here comes the ending song. I suppose it's the ending in multiple ways.

A cheap panoramic image of me descending into darkness is shown. Sad piano music plays.

Awesome dreams. Greater failures. Lesser beings killing greaters. What the hell just happened to me? Who the hell ruined my script? There was no explosion. I just died. Damn that sucked. The hero's journey came to an end. With everything loss and nothing to defend. The hero died. I only wish it was a lie!

Now for the prequel to the next episode.

What the hell, it's just dark black fog. Is this really it? Shit, could I really have died for good? Tune in next week for the start of a new adventure of The Main Character!?

The self-fulfilling prophesized hero

Episode 2 Part 1

Last time on The Main Character: an assailant chased after me and I'm killed by a bike. What, not comprehensive enough for you? Well then, maybe you should have been supporting my debut, asshole! Anyways, back to the show.

Where the hell is Bowtan!? She's supposed to come out and make me a spirit detective by now! When I die in my dreams, she always comes. And then I become an action hero out of nowhere, just like Yusuuke. Damn it Bowtan, where are you? She isn't coming, is she? Then I really am dead. Run over by a bicycle, what a let-down. How could Main Character die like this? I'm supposed to get killed by some bad ass OP misanthrope and then I'm supposed to come back in the next episode with demon powers. Ugh, whatever...cue the opening.

I look into the sunlight. Shit, I got run over by a bike. And now I'm running from an assailant fruitlessly...fruitlessly. Now there's a slide show of a bunch of people I still don't know. And now I know that none of them will ever join my team. God Damnit! Then my hand is reaching out to the sky. Grasping for life! Now all the villains are taking up my screen-time! And that son of a bitch isn't even there! But then I jump in and spontaneously combust! I'm now clenching my fist on top of a mountain of graves. Holy shit those are the graves of my classmates. I'm then knocked back and then I get run over by that stupid f'ing bike! I then get sliced to ribbons by Assailant. Yeah, that's his name. No matter what, I am dead. And there is only one reason why. It's because of that bastard guy! He killed The Main Character! Me me me! The Main Character! Hell no! I'm The Main Character and now I'm dead!

Alright, now what? A black void, really? The prequel was right? Damn it! Wait, in the distance I can see a light. So there really is a light at the end of the tunnel.

I stand up and run towards it. I then realize it's a train.

Shit!

I turn around and run the opposite way. But it's too late. It smashes right into me, killing me a second time.

Well, at least it's cooler than a bike.

Oh my God, I'm being materialized. I'm arriving in another world. And I'm freaking naked. There's a big black ball in front of me with something written on it: "Your life is over you bastards. Now it belongs to me. So, there you have it".

Oh great, I'm having the Gantzo dream again.

After telling me to kill Kananade, the Angel Beasts alien, the ball opens up and reveals a rack of guns. I take the gun and aim it at the sleeping guy inside the ball. His head blows up. I really need to have some free domain dreams or my viewers will get lost.

My eyes shoot open and the assailant is hovering over me. He takes a thermometer out of my mouth and lets out a sigh of relief.

Great. This dream is even weirder than the last one!

The creature held its forehead. "You almost gave me a heart attack. I hardly killed you in time. You should rest, space-time-matter-gravity-dimension travel can be rather stressful."

I swear, the spiky stars in the black void of his face became less jagged.

"Good morning, Main!" exclaims Stalker, right on top of my lap. Her sparkly drool lands right on my bare chest.

Wasn't she dead? Oww, that hurts so much!

I try to curse at her, but words just came out in a jumble.

"So, nurse, will he be okay?" asks Best Friend in the corner, slitting his wrist.

There he is. With those gorgeous caring crimson eyes! I don't want this dream to end!

"My husband will be fine. Dying can be stressful but thankfully none of the wounds he suffered are fatal. He just needs rest and some TLC," says Stalker with that same airy smile. She wipes her drool-soaked hand up my arm.

This girl is freaking nuts! Wait, why does her saliva actually feel good?

I turn my head to Best Friend, trying to say something, but all I can do is open and close my mouth like a freaking fish!

Best Friend turns away from me with flushed cheeks.

Seeing me so pitiful must be an embarrassment. But when he looks so vulnerable like that my mind can't help but wander.

"You need to rest," says Stalker, drooling in my mouth and dispelling my fantasy.

This is ridiculously weird. Even as a fan of Mysterious Girl X, I do not approve of this!

Assailant places a stool on the ground and stands atop it.

This guy has no social graces.

"Listen, I owe you all an apology. I'm a broad-spectrum assailant. I'm no good at taking out single targets," says Assailant, covering his flustered face.

"Are you kidding. You did a great job, poppa! You didn't even kill everyone in the whole school. It was only a classroom of casualties. When you first became an assailant, you killed a whole city's worth of people and you let the hero get away!" she exclaims before giggling childishly.

Assailant joins in the laughing as well. Best Friend then joins the laughing train, freaking me out with his demonic cackling. I leap on at the last moment, letting out a very frightened awkward chuckle.

Even metaphorical trains are unsettling to me. The only exception being the Cole train!

"Dwelling on your failures will only hold you back," says Best Friend, looking miserable.

Wait! My arm!

I look to my side to see I haven't become a handicapable hero.

I feel more confused than when I first finished Evengelion! What just happened? And why do I feel like this is real? Real or not, everyone is looking at me. Even as a dying patient I seize the spotlight! I am so freaking awesome.

"You probably want to know what's going on, don't you?" asks Best Friend, abruptly looking up at me. His shimmering blood red eyes were staring deep into my bright hazel ones.

"I…um…yes!" I exclaim, finally grasping the power of speech.

Strange my throat doesn't hurt anymore.

"Well yeah, but I don't feel like explaining it. My job is to stand here and look cool. Isn't that what you said that fateful day?" he asks, turning away like a total badass.

Shit, this isn't good. If he's this awesome, then I'll lose the popularity poll again!

"We should at least introduce ourselves. I'm Assailant, the village's chosen murderer. And this is my lovely daughter…Stalker. She was chosen to look after you and make sure nothing ill befell you."

"Well she's as successful as Yuko Suckaki. Your little princess electrocuted me! And as for you! You murdered all those kids. What the hell is your problem?"

Stalker's cheeks puffed out. "Hey, my Big Daddy tried his best! I know you're shaken up, but please don't pick on him."

"Your pops is a damn murderer! He's as irredeemable as Minene Uryuu!"

"When you're angry like that, your nose twitches like a bunny's. I can't bear to watch," says Best Friend with wide eyes.

Shit, now we're both embarrassed!

Assailant makes an otherworldly wheezing sound, which I think is him clearing his throat. "My little strawberry told me all about you. Not many boys rub bars of soap on their nipples; you're very unique. She also told me about the promise you made that day. And just know, if you break that promise I'll kill you personally. Oh, but I already did kill you, how ironic!" he exclaims before laughing again.

Great. Asshole thinks he's a comedian. To make matters worse I never made her a damn promise! If I had, then I'm sure a flashback would happen to remind me.

The area shifts and gets coated in a sepia tint. I see myself showering.

Why is my flashback in 3rd person? Why are they always in 3rd person!? Wait, there!

I notice a girl peeking at me from the window outside. She's muttering to herself.

"Yeah yeah yeah!" I cheer, holding an imaginary mike to my mouth.

She blushes and then faints.

No way does that count! I was clearly singing to myself and there's no way she thought I could hear her! This is some grade A human shit!

Assailant leans over me. "Is he dreaming while awake?"

"He's having flashbacks," says Best Friend. "He experiences them often, but thankfully not as often as Noruto. They are no doubt caused by the terrible thing that happened to him."

"Father dearest, you dropped your name tag." Stalker hops on the stool and places a sticker that says 'Hi, I'm Assailant' on her dad's robe.

"Wait, your name really is Assailant, and she is Stalker?" I ask with baffled flabbergaspism.

Yeah, I don't care if it's not a real word, I'm that freaking surprised right now.

"Our names are whatever you deem them to be. As long as you live, we are in your debt. But don't worry, just in case you fail, we've already dug you a grave. My cupcake paid for it all by herself." He squeezes her cheeks with the blades that came out from his hand.

"Pops, stop. You're cutting me," says Stalker, giggling as she pulled away.

"My apologies, sweetums."

Well at least I know where she gets her strange nickname giving quirk from.

Assailant turns to face me. "You are hero number thirteen thirteen thirteen thirteen thirteen thirteen thirteen thirteen thirteen thirteen thirteen thirteen. Wow, thirteen thirteens…you won't last long," he says with a nervous chuckle.

"Don't say that, Papa Bear. I was chosen as his Guardian Angel, after all. Come to think of it, you're my thirteenth hero," says Stalker with a smile.

"My name is Main, Main Character. Don't you dare just slap a number on me!" I yelled furiously.

"Then that makes it fourteen thirteens, hence breaking the misfortunate hex," says Best Friend.

"My love puppy is right!" Stalker stands tall, pushing out her washboard of a chest. "Giving him a number makes him even more likely to have a horribly painful and gruesome death. We have to believe in the him that believes in himself." Her eyes were sparkling like a beautiful blond shirtless vampire boy but she totally whiffed that reference.

"Throw your concerns into the furnace. Main's the most reliable person I know," says Best Friend with a smile.

Glasses Kid rushes into the room. "You all didn't explain everything to him yet, did you?"

"To do so would be to deprive you of oxygen. The floor is yours," says Best Friend, hoisting the kid up onto the stool.

"What are you doing here!? You were decapitated! I saw you die. How are any of you alive?" I ask, glaring at him.

Glasses Kid adjusts his glasses. "It must be so hard living with such a simplistic mind. Worry not, plebian! I've written a whole four-page Times New Roman double spaced A.P.A. format report all about it. It will answer every question you never had about Main Character. Oh, and Glasses Kid is not my real name. I'm Four Eyes, the Seven-Year-Old Uber Genius!" he exclaims, literally patting himself on the back.

"You're Glasses Kid now. Let's hear your report," says Stalker as she licks the scratched-up soles of my foot.

Can't let her find out that my feet are my weak point. I don't trust her a smidge.

Glasses Kid fixes his glasses and clears his throat. He turns to face me with an arrogant look. "I've simplified the document so that your still-developing mind can grasp its concepts. First off, the train you were hit by in your dream is a mental manifestation of your ill feelings towards your parents."

"How can you know what I was dreaming about?" I interrupted.

Stalker covers her face. "Sorry. I kinda said it to everyone while you were sleeping."

I shake my head. "Then how do you know!?"

Glasses Kid taps my head. "Let me finish! You asked what happened, after all."

"Fine, whatever. Ramble on," I say with an annoyed look.

Glasses Kid nods. "You've never been able to forgive your parents for your remarkable, yet inconvenient birth. Because of this you always dream up fantasy worlds that are just cheap knock offs of the anime you watch. Lacking creativity and possessing below average intelligence, you focus all your brainpower into your drive. You lack direction, which is where I come in."

The arrogance exuding from him is palpable.

"I am the object of your envy, as well as your mentor. In this sense you are my apprentice."

"If you mock him once more, your head shall slide off your shoulders," says Best Friend, whipping out a knife.

Oh, I get it. Glasses Kid is like that arrogant incompetent character that calls the main character his sidekick. Those are always the worst, except for Kaido Momoda, that man is a freaking legend!

"His words are empty. Proceed, Glasses Kid," I say, calming my best friend.

"Sure thing. Best Friend is more than your shield though, he is your right arm. He acts for you and only you. And he has decided to carry the burden of the truth by himself. He is carrying all of your misery and his own. Oh, and the reason he cuts his wrist is because it releases endorphins. It's not because he's suicidal, that's a complete coincidence. You know Main, the feelings you have for Best Friend might be more akin to family than friendship. He's like a brother…isn't he?"

Best Friend rolls his eyes.

Glasses kid's face relaxes. "After finding out that your mother planned to shoot you out the window, he swore vengeance against your parents. You see, they didn't want to get swept up in the controversy of abortion so they decided to improvise. Anyways, once he finally tracked them down, he took the second third of your heart-shaped amulet and…"

"You've said too much." Best Friend looms over Glasses Kid. "If you wish to keep your tongue, you will end my story there."

"I'll uh, jump to the next character then," says Glasses Kid, wiping away a bead of sweat.

I turn to Best Friend. "Is what he's saying true?"

"As if that arrogant child knows more about me than you," says Best Friend with a calming smile.

He's right. The kids just blowing hot air.

"Now to continue on." Glasses Kid reaches in my backpack and pulls out Boobs.

Thank goodness. She's still alive.

He looks at the pillow and shrugs. He then turns to Stalker. "Let's focus at the matter at hand. Stalker, you're up!"

"That's me!" exclaims the girl, rubbing her glittery spittle on my legs.

"Can you stop spitting on me?" I ask with a glare.

"But I'm your nurse," she said, pointing to her nurse cap.

Glasses Kid claps his hands together to get my attention. "Stalker is your assigned guardian angel. She was chosen by this village in order to locate and protect a new hero. Guided by the aroma of your baseless drive, she found you showering. Seeing your bare body and your overflowing confidence caused her to fall madly in love with you. This is where the promise comes into play. While looking in the mirror you said to yourself: 'No matter what, I will become a great hero. Oh my God, I am so sexy. Just look at my muscles. Oh, and I am not going to die a virgin! Yes, I'll get laid and have a ton of kids! That is a promise!' Since she was behind you, unbeknownst to you of course, she assumed you were talking to her. In truth, you were making a…" He looks over at Best Friend, who is sharpening his throwing knives "…manly promise to yourself, so you would find the power to keep on living."

That flashback I had was wrong. Now that I think back, she wasn't muttering to herself. She was just breathing heavily. I'm the one who made the promise.

"Why is he crying?" Best Friend held his dagger to Glasses' Kids scrawny throat.

"You don't need to shed his blood. These are happy tears. Stalker, you really want to help me fulfill my promise to myself."

"Wrong. It's a misunderstanding," says Glasses Kid.

"No, you're wrong!" yelled Stalker, with a pointy figure of objection. "I know he was talking to himself, but I absolutely will help him fulfill his promise," she says with eyes shining like green rupees, no wait, gold rupees.

Glasses Kid, no longer feeling threatened, continues to ramble on. "Stalker tried to prolong your life for as long as possible, failing the third grade as many times as it took to stay by your side. But then you made the promise to Best Friend that the two of you would graduate together. This of course caused her to study. Poor girl, she really believed in you. Once she got an A, the horror on her face was palpable. She knew that she would be separated from you. Which of course meant her father was going to come and kill you. The reason you never noticed her is because the hero's guardian angel is invisible to the hero they are protecting. Best Friend never mentioned her name so the empty desk facing you was never questioned. Knowing that the day of prophecy had arrived, hand-picked by Assailant himself out of a jar of a bunch of rolled up papers, he decided to dispel the cloaking hex around her. This is why you were able to see her that one day only. Moving on. She zapped you in order to give you super speed. That is why you were able to almost outrun Assailant."

Okay. How good is this little brat? What he's saying makes sense…I think.

"Focus, Main. Your teacher is talking. Now that you know her true feelings, you must be wondering how you got here. The answer is Assailant, our final character. He is a very specialized assassin. Anyone killed by him outside of this dimension will be magically teleported to this village. So, to protect his daughter from Best Friend, he killed her. Thus, bringing her home safe and sound. It's rather admirable actually. He sliced her in two…what a great father! Taking into consideration that he looks nothing like his daughter, I presume he was transformed into this bizarre entity. He was most likely chosen by the village to be their assailant. To become one, he had to sacrifice his humanity. By seeking to escape his own reality, his body transformed into a tool of inter-dimensional travel. The mind is the most powerful force in the universe, after all." Glasses Kid taps his forehead and hops onto the stool. "Once his daughter was three, she was sent to Earth to locate you. She gave him updates every night, telling him how much she loved you. She always asked him why you had to die. But the village did not permit him to tell her. So, he merely says. 'He must die so that we can attain salvation.' So-"

I glare at the arrogant kid. "No way you can just assume what they said in the past."

"Of course not. I'm paraphrasing. We're nearing the end of the story. For years Stalker betrayed her entire village for your love, how romantic. And yet you still died. She was furious when she heard the news, but delighted once she saw you here. The reason the information was kept from her was to strengthen her trust with her father. This village was founded by trust and thus trust sustains it. And don't worry about your classmates, they were all returned back to our world. The only condition being that I stay here and provide you assistance."

45:00

Why didn't he start with that? Well, I guess I didn't really save anyone. Still, I'm relieved. Those lucky little twerps get to return home their loving parents.

"Tasty." Stalker licks my tears.

"Happy tears! Happy tears!" I exclaim as Best Friend readies his blade.

Stalker turns to Glasses Kid. "That's not all correct," she says softly. "I zapped him to knock him out. I didn't want him to suffer. I realized he wasn't going to run at that point. I just…I didn't know what to do." Her eyes release a torrent of tears.

"Dai-jo-bu. I'm fine. No need to cry." I made a funny face to make her giggle.

Glasses Kid points at Stalker with a slight blush. "The cuteness of that giggle won't make me ignore the hole in your logic. How can Main outrun a trained assassin?"

"Well, Daddy Death is kinda heavier than most of the assassins since he has so many weapons. And he was wounded. As for that incredible speed…that was from these thick thighs," she says, putting saliva on her face before using it to rub my legs.

"Does that mean, everything else he says was right? How did he figure it out?" I ask with wide eyes.

"Come now. All this is mere conjecture. Anyways, I gladly accepted their offer. After all, no award is greater than knowledge. This entire world is a collection of new facts and ideas. I can't help but yearn to investigate it. I also want to see how you develop, Main. And that's the gist of my first hypothesis. I have eight other equally lengthy and just as possible assertions if you would like to hear more," says Glasses Kid, adjusting his big circular glasses.

This little bastard talks more than Ishiduh Uryu! He read me like a Wykipedia summary.

"That's quite alright. You've made an exceptional analysis. We haven't told you anything yet about this world. How do you know so much?" asks Assailant in awe.

Glasses Kid hops off the stool. "That was a mere string of connected inferences. They are backed up by evidence, not facts. Truth is relative, so, in the end it's all sloppy speculation. I hope I adhered to your customs. I made my entire report centered around Main, as a sign of respect to your beliefs," says Glasses Kid with a bow.

"So, are you my brother?" I ask Best Friend.

"Ask yourself that question. Blood is irrelevant when compared to bonds," says Best Friend, sucking the blood out of his wound.

Always so mysterious and sexy.

"Alright, so this is another world then? And I was transported here, right? I want to know about this place," I told Assailant.

"The village chief will be back soon. He will explain exactly what you need to know when he arrives. For the time being, all you need to know is that you are our prophesized hero," says Assailant with a bow.

The guy who killed me is now bowing to me…I can't even think of a reference for this. Oh no, my head hurts. How can I process all this madness?

"If you didn't save Main's life from that drunk biker, I'd cut you down where you stand," says Best Friend, glaring at assailant.

That's right! He didn't kill me. He teleported me. This follows plenty of tropes and it solidifies my role as a hero.

"I'm not going to give up on your promise," says Stalker, giving me a sweet kiss on the cheek.

You know, looking at her with a new perspective…she's rather cute. And she really does care about me. If I play my cards right, put on a little charm and lower my standards a bit…I might be able to make her my friend.

47:00

The Perks of a Hero

Episode 2 Part 2

Stalker's mouth is agape. Her eyes are rolling in the back of her head and she was giggling like a drunk.

"Is she okay?" I ask, pointing to my fangirl.

"It's not something you said…" Best Friend's eyes intensify. "Was it something you thought?!" He picks up Stalker. "Are you psychic?"

"Maybe," she says, fluttering her eyelashes at me.

"Relax. She's on our side. So, Stalker, why don't you give your new demon king a tour of his castle?" I ask with a wink.

She gives me a blank stare.

"Kyou Karoh Maoh!? It's only the greatest Shounen-Ai in history! How can you not know of it?"

"Well, when did you watch it?" she asks, tapping my chin.

"Let's see. I think I was two and a half, so roughly six years ago. Why?"

"Well I've only been watching anime with you for four years. I found you on your third birthday."

"Apparently she was invisible to both of us when she spied on you. I felt a presence but I assumed it was a ghost. I didn't mention it because…"

I leap out of my hospital bed and cower at the corner of the room. "Where's the ghost! Keep it away from me!"

I'm not really afraid of ghosts, but since Ranga the Blood-edge freaks out over them, I'll proudly take up his fears.

Best Friend held himself in his embrace. "I'm terrified of ghosts."

"Wait, you're actually afraid of something? But you always seem so fearless," I say.

"I live in fear," he says with a face beaming with courage.

48:00

I turn back to Stalker. "You said you found me on my third birthday. Did you get me a gift?"

"Of course I did!" she exclaims, leaping into my arms.

"Then that heart-shaped amulet I got…wasn't from my parents?"

There was no hiding the utter look of despair on my face.

"Wait!? No, um…your parents gave it to me! I uh, found them and they wanted me to pass it on to you!" she exclaims, licking my tears as they poured out my eyes.

"You're a kind girl," says Best Friend with a deranged smile.

"You met them!? Hey, when I get back home, can you take me to them?" I ask, brimming with hope.

"I uh, lost track of them. But I'm sure we can track them down…" she grasps my hand and wiggles her hips with a dazed look, "together."

"We're here now so we should make the best of the situation. Main, what's the plan?" asks Best Friend with a salute.

I toss Stalker onto my shoulders and grab Best Friend's rough hands. "Let's go sight-seeing."

"An excellent idea, Oni-chan," says Stalker, patting my head.

"You haven't earned the right to call him that," says Best Friend, shooting her a murderous look.

"Better that then master." I lift her from my shoulders and hand her to Best Friend. "Can you carry her? Boobs gets jealous really easily," I say, scratching my head.

I know inanimate objects don't get jealous but if pretending they do makes me feel less lonely, then what's the harm. Too bad Boobs didn't magically come to life like Seira Orgal.

I pick up my pillow pal and walk out of the hospital tent.

Civilians walk down the grassy streets of a feudal village. The Houses are made of wood and the people wore simple grey and ragged clothes.

This looks like just a generic Inuyasha filler village! There aren't even any signs indicating what building is what. Is this really going to be my hub world from now on.

We walk down to the bazaar and find an exuberant man selling bananas. He points to Boobs. "Young man, looks like your girlfriend is hungry! Why not treat her to the healthiest food in all the lands! Potassium, protein and deliciousness all condensed into a portable edible delight! Did you know that bananas were once the food of kings?"

I absolutely do. Girl Bravo episode 2. Who says anime doesn't teach you history? Morons who haven't seen Hentalia, that's who. You know what, I like this guy. I dub thee, Banana Man!

"I'll take a bushel of them," says Best Friend, pulling out a wallet from the pocket of a passerby.

"Do any of these shops sell ramen?" I ask.

Banana Man scratches his head. "Nope. Never even heard of that. Is that some kind of foreign food?"

"It's a Neet's lifeforce! How do you not know that?" I ask, rolling my eyes.

"I can cook ramen for you," says Stalker with pride.

"I appreciate the offer but we really need a ramen shop here. If I choose to defend this village, then it has to have a ramen shop. No exceptions." I cross my arms.

Best Friend plops a banana in my mouth. "We can discuss the construction of a new shop later when the village chief shows up. For now, enjoy what you have."

Stalker downs the whole banana with an absurd erotic look before pulling it out and only licking the tip. "Are you impressed?" she asks, winking at me as her tongue moves about.

50:00

"Ah, I see you watched Girl Bravo as well. Your technique is a bit off and you need to look more innocent or else it ruins the fantasy aspect. Stand right there, Best Friend."

"As you wish," says Best Friend, doing as instructed.

I crouch down so my face is at the Banana Man's crotch level. "Behold!" I open the banana, looking at it curiously. I giggle, tap the tip and then wrap my hand around it. After giving it a few pumps, I lightly lick the tip down to the base. I pull up and kiss it, leaving a thin trail of saliva as I pull away with flushed cheeks. I then begin to suck the banana and finally swallow the piece. "It's really soft and very sweet. Thanks for the banana. It was good for me too," I say, batting my eyelashes with innocence before playfully nibbling the tip.

Stalker girl's eyes had rolled back and she was muttering to herself.

Seductive banana eating done properly can score you a free meal.

The man at the shop had a big smile. "Glad you've had a change of heart!" he exclaims, slamming his hand into my back and nearly making me choke on the banana.

"Is that it? Aren't you going to monologue about your love of bananas?" I ask, eyeing another tasty treat.

Banana Man stood in front of the barrel of bananas. "One free banana per customer. I keep my passion in check to preserve the stock. This entire village is dependent on my potassium rich produce!"

Best Friend comes up and whispers in my ear. "You shouldn't act lewd in public. Their gazes are tainting you with dark fantasies. I'll have to tear out their eyes, which will make staying here rather tricky," he says, taking out small hook-like blades.

I grab his hand. "Relax, they're all guys. No harm done."

Wait, why are they all guys?

"I'll never forget what you taught me," says Stalker, copying my technique perfectly.

The crowd's faces twist in terror before the voyeurs disperse.

Huh, that's odd.

51:00

Something taps my shoulder. I turn to see Assailant.

"Why are you humiliating my daughter in public?" he asks, exuding a dark aura that brings panic to those around us.

I take a step back. "I was just teaching her a technique to get free food. Survival skills are of the upmost importance."

Best Friend stands in front of Assailant, wielding six knives. "If you have a problem, I'll be happy to help you get over it."

"Stop! Both of you! You're scaring Banana Man!" I turn to the frightened salesman. "My apologies."

"It's alright. Business has been dipping as of late, anyways," said Banana Man with a solemn tone.

I grab Best Friend's hand. "Hey, let's see what other shops are here," I say, waving Banana Man farewell.

"Hold up. In the Forest of Scary Name, there's a legendary banana bushel says to have twice the potassium of regular bananas," says Banana Man.

"So what? I can just eat two bananas if I want that," I say, waving him dismissively.

Best Friend abruptly spun to face the man. "We accept your quest."

"He hasn't even told us what the reward is," I say.

"It matters not. Accepting the side quest has absolutely no repercussions. It simply gives us more options. What are the rewards?" asks Best Friend.

"A free bushel of bananas every breakfast," says Banana Man.

"We'll pick them up if we're in the area," I say before walking down the rest of the market place.

"Is there a bookstore nearby?" asks Glasses Kid to a strong lady selling jewelry.

"There's a library but it is for the Chief's eyes only. Would you like this necklace? I think it would really complement your glasses," she says to the boy.

52:00

"I'm not dumb enough to derive value from impractical material possessions," he says before walking off.

"Sorry about him. His parents didn't beat him often enough," I say, bowing before walking off. I flick Glasses Kid's forehead. "Hey, twerp. Are you sure the other kids got home safely?"

"Oh, I didn't know you cared about anyone but yourself," he says with a snide look.

"Hold up. I just don't want them on the front of the paper instead of me."

"So, you want your bicycle accident to be on the front page?"

Oh shit. He's right!

I grab his shoulders. "Okay, this is serious. They're all okay? Every last one?"

"Of course!" he exclaims, poking me between the eyes. "I am their teacher; my credibility relies on their safety."

"Get that stick out of your ass. I saw their bodies! I just want to know they're fine!" I yell.

Side-characters or not. They got put in danger because of me!

Glasses Kid hops on a crate and pats my head. "Relax, my ignorant pupil. The news of a resurrected classroom of grade-schoolers will completely bury your embarrassing and pitiful death."

Okay. I have to get back home, fake my death, come back and claim to be the messiah. That's the only way for me to get back the credibility I've lost.

"There's a brothel," says Best Friend, pointing to the large fortress of a building with neon lights and vigilant guards.

Well, it's clear where this village's budget went.

"Let's go check it out," I say, elbowing my BFF.

Best Friend stood in my path. "I will personally take you once your twenty-one but until then, I forbid it."

53:00

"Come on. I'll be an old man by then," I say with a pouty face.

"I've made up my mind. Glasses Kid, you'll have to investigate it in our stead."

"Hello. I'm only seven years old. I can't go in there," he says, blushing like a tomato.

"Fine then, let's continue exploring the village." Best Friend stops in place when he turns the corner.

There was a large ranch with animals I've never seen before. It was like a Prehistoric petting zoo.

"Want to ride the baby mammoth with me?" asks Stalker, reaching for my hand.

"These animals. Where are their parents?" asks Best Friend.

"Huh, I never thought about that," says Stalker with a curious look.

"Of course you haven't. You see them as rides at a theme park or mere exhibits to be enjoyed at a museum. They don't exist for your entertainment. They are individuals who love their parents just like you do," says Best Friend with intensity.

Stalker burst into tears. "I'm sowwy! I'm weally weally sowwy! Uhuhuhuwaaa!"

"I forbid you from crying!" I exclaim, pointing at her dramatically as if I had a Geass.

"Huh?" Stalker wipes her eyes.

"Your saliva heals wounds, so that likely means your tears can resuscitate someone at the brink of death. Save your tears for when I need them. Your duty is to keep me alive, right?"

She smiles. "You're right. No more crying," she says, making a zip sound as she closes her eyes.

Holy shit she's cute! That cuteness can definitely come in handy if we need to create a distraction later on.

The civilians take out bells from their robes and shake them. "The chief has returned!" they chant.

Stalker hops off Best Friend's shoulders. "I'll tell him the hero has arrived. Head back to the hospital tent, okay?"

"What about the poor animals?" asks Best Friend.

"We can go see the owner another time. This is Main's moment," says Stalker.

"You're right. We'll see you then. Glasses Kid, were leaving. Where did he go?" asks Best Friend.

"He probably assumed we were meeting back at the tent. I can't believe we're really in another world," I say, putting my arm around his shoulder.

"Don't let the excitement get the better of you. They may try to swindle you. Best be wary," says Best Friend.

"So, we swindle them back?"

"Maybe."

"Ha! You didn't even care what Banana Man's reward was."

"He is a good person. He sells produce and he didn't look at you with deviant eyes. It would have been wrong to try and swindle him."

"Well, we're here."

Best Friend rushes ahead and opens the flap of the tent for me to enter.

"Watch a master at work." I get back on the bed and put on a pissed off look. "We have the upper hand let's make use of the situation," I say, twisting my arm so it looks broken.

The village elder came in the room. He sat atop a levitating water lily. His wrinkles formed the word wisdom around his tree-like face and bushy leaf beard. Hmm, I'm going to call him Old Dude.

Two men accompanying Old Dude carry in a massive stone slab. They set it down with a loud crash at the foot of my bed.

I look at the drawing to see that it shows the prophecy of another hero. It ends with him dying from what looks like an angry cat.

The old man's eyes open the slightest bit. "When the past and future are in danger, a hero from the present will come unwillingly to save them both," says Old Dude, projecting his voice with the strength of his mind and the motion of his wrinkles.

"Unwillingly is an understatement. I was murdered! There had better be a good reason you brought me here, Old Dude," I say harshly.

Wow. I didn't expect to have such an outburst. But if you think about it, this whole situation is really messed up.

Assailant pops out from behind the bed. "How dare you speak to the village chief so disrespectfully? He is the only reason this village is still standing!" he yelled, the stars making up his face becoming red and jagged.

"Do not speak for me. We are all of equal insignificance." Old Dude looks up at me with a smile. "Whatever name he bestows upon any of us must be accepted graciously and semi-permanently. I find it rather clever how he names each of us based on our role. His egocentric perspective of reality is truly fascinating."

I cross my arms and give him a yakuza grimace. "And how do you know I'm the destined hero? Most prophecies are incredibly vague. I had a life and you took it from me. I'm not going to just die because of some false prophecy. Maybe your village wasn't meant to survive!"

I won't accept some slipshod plot. I demand my prophecy have some credibility!

"Rest assured, I leave nothing to chance," says Old Dude.

Using just three fingers he picks up the massive stone slab and shakes it vigorously. The image of the doomed hero vanishes, leaving a blank prophecy. He releases the slab, but it continues to float in the air. His two assistants, strong men wearing black shirts that say 'assistant 1' and 'assistant 2' bow and give him a high-tech magic marker.

I watch in confusion as the prophecy unfolds before my eyes.

"There is an ancient legend. A legend exactly as old as time. It tells of dark ominous times. It tells of a great era of oppression after a catastrophic event. But when all hope seems to be lost, a single hero will be brought from another time in order to save the world. His name is of his own choosing. Born on a leap year, he is free from planetary influence. He is The Main Character!" exclaims Old Dude, writing the prophecy as he spoke it. "He is a young boy, only...how old are you?" he asks, momentarily pausing.

"I'm four," I responded with pride.

Old Dude raises his eyebrows but then continues. "He is a young boy of four years with yellow spiky hair. His eyes are the color of...silver!" he exclaims, squinting at me.

Wait, they aren't hazel?

"That sounds like Main," says Stalker in awe.

No way she's that clueless.

Old Dude smiles and switches to his other hand. "Main was but an average boy in his world. But here he is a great and powerful hero. He is roughly six feet tall and has great strength in his arms. He however cannot conquer the darkness alone. By utilizing the skill and drive of each member of his team, the hero shall outwit the darkness and usher in a new age of temporary peace!" he exclaims, flipping the stone slab around so all could see.

It was remarkable, the hero looked just like me. I'll give the old guy some credit, he's quite the graphic artist but he's a terrible con artist.

"Wait a minute Old Dude. How can a prophecy you just created be true?" I ask him with great cunning.

"The hero shall question the prophecy, but in the end, he shall fulfill it!" exclaims Old Dude, rambling on.

"Main asked you a question. It would be best if you answered him," says Best Friend darkly.

"What difference does it make? A prophecy is a prophecy. It is as sure as death itself," says Old Dude with a smile.

Glasses Kid adjusts his glasses before speaking. "It's absolutely genius! I never trusted age-old prophecies. Many of them have already been fulfilled or are grossly taken out of context. By creating your prophecy now, he has given you a specified goal. Besides, if it really makes a difference, he is technically making the prophecy in the past."

"How is that?" I ask, turning to the little nimrod. "I'm standing right here. If he thinks some two-minute old prophecy is going to convince me to risk my life, he's absolutely wrong. He can save his own damn world!" I exclaim, getting up like a badass.

Every moment I spend here is another moment that I lose potential subscribers. I have to return home and get my videos back up on ViralTube.

"Alas. I cannot. I have already exerted all my energy defending the universe from the wrath of the pale purple tranny alien. I am too worn to save us now," says Old Dude, acting frail and resting on his cane.

"Sir, with all due respect, that was centuries ago," says Assailant with a bow.

"Yes, and I've been enduring vigorous training to prepare for the next interstellar crisis. Only Main can free us now," says Old Dude, playing paddle ball.

"Save your own damn planet. I'm going home," I say, walking out of the room.

"You still don't get it. This…is our planet," says Glasses Kid, about to go on a tangent.

"Just what the hell does that mean!?" I exclaim, grabbing him by his collar.

"The past and future of your world were smashed together," says Old Dude, squishing an apple and orange against each other for metaphorical significance. "They have become a single planet, seamlessly molded as one." He drank the mixed juice. "You live in the present world, which is on a separate plane of time than this planet. They are both interconnected though. If this world is destroyed, your present will vanish along with it." He shatters the glass for impact. "That's how I know you can save this world. The state of your present planet is proof in of itself. However, the future is not set in stone. You must rise up to defend the past and future of your planet."

"Main, isn't this what you always talked about? You've always dreamed of another world," says Best Friend, making a rainbow motion with his hands.

"This isn't that world! The world I always dreamed of was just a cheap rip off of M.A.A.R. without the tournament. Besides, heroes are supposed to stand up to fight on their own! I will not be their pawn!" I yell with great strength.

"I don't think you fully understand. If you decide to help us, we will be forever indebted to you. You shall be hailed as a king throughout the land. Whatever your wish is, it shall be granted. You could even find the One Place and become the king of the ninjas," says Old Dude with wide eyes.

Did he seriously just say that? He's just using references to get me to agree to his badly written plot. I won't fall for his cheap Overpowered Player One gimmick!

"And what if I refuse?" I ask coolly.

"Then we'll have to send you in as a sacrifice to appease The Love Dictator. And I'll have to completely redo the prophecy," says Old Dude with a sigh.

Love Dictator? Those words should never go together.

"Help us, Main. You're our only hope," says Stalker with shimmering eyes.

"Not even quoting Jedi Wars will change my mind! I do whatever the hell I want!" I yell, pushing Stalker out of the way.

"We'll let you name the planet," says Old Dude, getting desperate.

"I've already decided on that. This is the world of SteamPunk!" I exclaim firmly.

Assailant tilts his body in a spiral of confusion. "Um, is that just a coincidence? How did he know?"

Old Dude slams his cane against the ground. "A hero knows what he is protecting. Please Main, both our worlds are in danger. Only you can save us!"

"I want a ramen shop and free ramen for protecting the village," I say.

Old Dude nods. "Decide which shop to be taken down and it will be so. We'll have our best chef's work on your exotic meal if you accept."

"Do I get a harem?" I ask bluntly.

"Of course!" exclaims Old Dude.

"I'm in," I say, shaking his hand.

And so, another episode is completed. I milked the scene like it was a MILF. It was obvious that I was going to agree, I just wanted to make things a little more dramatic. Plus, I wanted to see what I could get out of it. Damn I'm smart. Anyways, it looks like it's time for the ending song.

Lighthearted music fills the air. Best Friend and I are starring out at the sky. Random pictures of us doing stupid shit goes by. And then they all suddenly combust into flames. Stalker is dancing for no real reason. And then my neck is slowly getting run over by a bike. Wow, what a stupid song. Why do some ending songs just suck? Who the hell needs a serene environment in an action show? It's ridiculous. And now it flashes the shadow of a villain at the end to have some sort of relevance.

Anyways, next time on M.C. That's Main Character for short. Some tribal lady is teaching my team how to fight the enemy. And awesome, it looks like I get a freaking rocket launcher. Why is Stalker naked? And why does Best Friend have his shirt on. All this and more on the next heart-pounding episode of Main Character. Don't miss it!

THE TRIPLE THREE
TRIALS OF TRINITY

Episode 3 Part 1

How predictable. Before I can become a hero, I have to pass some stupid test. This is freaking ridiculous. They want my help and now they're going to treat me like a freaking guinea pig. Whatever, it will be a great way to show off my awesome skills. Just like my man Kiito, I have real world combat training! Time to pwn some noobs! Cue the theme-song.

"I look into the sunlight...ow! I burnt my eyes. And now I'm walking down an endless path pointlessly...pointlessly. Wait a minute last time I was running. Now there's a slide show of a bunch of people I don't know. Is Assailant really going to join my team? Hell no! Then my hand is reaching out to the darkened sky. They just made it darker with a filter, that's so cheap! Now all the villains are taking up my screen-time! But then I jump in and shoot them with a pissed off rocket launcher. I'm now clenching my fist on top of a mountain of graves. But wait, my classmates aren't dead anymore. I'm then knocked back. I wipe off the blood on my cheek and then I run forth and punch with all my might. And now I see that it's a tribal man I'm fighting. I look at my side to see Stalker and Best Friend. Glasses Kid is in the back crying. I jump up and punch, creating the title. I'm The Main Character! Me me me! The Main Character! Hell's yeah! I'm The Main Character!"

Well the song got a bit longer, but I still need to add more. Oh well, it's a work in progress. Anyways, back to the show.

Last time on Main Character. After using the seven dragon balls to resurrect my fallen allies, I took a spaceship to a distant planet. Desperate for a hero, the people of the planet created a dark tournament to decide who is the most fitting. After defeating Assailant in the final round, I am told that there is one final test I must overcome. Eager to prove myself worthy, I graciously accept. I am ready for whatever challenge they toss my way. I wait in the greenhouse training room, suited in leaf armor. I see the trees beyond the glass, which is likely where we will be tested.

"Is this really supposed to protect me?" I ask Best Friend, checking the sturdiness of my leaf greaves.

Maybe they harden on contact or something. That would be cool.

"It's supposed to camouflage you. Running and hiding is all you need to worry about," says Assailant, attaching a cannon to each side of his cloak.

"If you need us, then why do we have to be tested?" asks Best Friend.

"It's so that you feel more like heroes. Is it working Main?" asks Stalker, beaming at me.

"It sure is. Plus, it will be a good warm up for the battles to come," I say, clenching my fist in anticipation.

"Is there a reason I have to come along? A scholar belongs in a library not a battlefield." Glasses Kid crosses his arms.

"Stop whining!" I yell. "Hey Assailant, you never did tell me why we had to leave Boobs back at the medical tent."

"I only did as instructed," says Assailant, loading cannon balls.

"What's the deal, Old Dude?" I ask.

Old Dude appears before me.

Can he teleport?

Old Dude combed his fingers through his beard. "It isn't safe for her here. We returned her back to your world."

"That's for me to decide. She hates being left out of fun stuff! I'm never going to hear the end of this because of you! She's my girlfriend, after all."

"The lies we tell ourselves," says Old Dude solemnly.

"Speaking of lies. The little kids this psycho killed…" I point to Assailant "are they safe at home?"

Stalker pops out from behind me. "Aww, you're so caring. Don't worry, they're all with their families. After their memories were wiped, they were returned back to the present," she says while stroking my leg.

I grab her hand and toss it aside. "You don't have to lie to me. I saw them die. I will fight in their memory," I say, dramatically looking toward the stars. A projection of faceless children appear in the night sky, which is also technically a projection since it's daytime.

Old Dude dispels my fantasy with a wave of his staff. "I assure you they're quite alive. I escorted them back myself."

Ugh, these idiots can't get a clue. If I'm going to be a hero, having someone to avenge is super important. If I pretend they're all dead, I can use that to push me forward.

"Assailant, I need you to go back to my world and kill Boobs. If she isn't here, my team won't have any eye-candy."

Stalker looks up at me with eyes full of shock.

I give her a little smile and turn to Assailant. "Only you can do this. I believe in you," I say, putting my hand on my greatest enemy.

"I only do hits for my village. Besides I'm a broad-spectrum assassin. Many innocent lives would be lost if I tried," says Assailant before I slapped him across the face.

"Have I displeased you?" he asks in a vulnerable voice.

I need this guy gone so he doesn't steal my thunder. Time for a heartfelt speech.0

I grab his shoulders. "Don't talk like that you idiot. You're always taking the burden for everyone. You surrendered your life in order to assure your daughter had a bright future. You don't own your own body and I'm the hero! I'm telling you to go kill my girlfriend, are you really going to deny me?" I ask, grabbing him by his neck.

"You're right. She'll be dead in no time," says Assailant with a shaky salute.

"Thank you, my loyal vassal," I say with a smile.

"You are our salvation," he says before sinking into himself and vanishing from sight.

Finally. I'm getting some respect.

Glasses Kid glares at me. "You just got rid of our strongest ally. How vain can you be?"

I turn to the little know-it-all. "The guy is a giant friendly fire hazard. I did us a favor."

"Such wisdom," says Best Friend, sharpening some throwing knives while balancing a cook book on his knee.

"Thanks. Hey, Old Dude. Why does Best Friend get a crossbow and armor while I get leaves and a boomerang?" I ask upset. "Where did he go?"

"I have an anti-air cannon if that helps," says Stalker, attaching it to her back.

I catch her as she topples over. "Maybe you should stay home and give me your cannon."

Glasses Kid examines the strange device in his hand. "I don't want to hear your complaints, Main. I have to wear this giant bull's-eye on my chest! And my only weapon is an automatic magnet. In other words, I'm a moving target!"

"Was this your doing?" I ask Best Friend.

He smiles.

Yeah so viewers note. Best Friend met with Old Dude beforehand to decide what weapons we would get. Is that why I have these leaves? Does he expect me to succeed without any help?

Stalker pats Glasses Kid on the back. "Don't worry; I'm the team's guardian angel. I'll protect you too," she says, wearing a full body shield.

"Oh…uh…thanks," says Glasses Kid with a deep red blush.

Don't tell me…Glasses Kid has a crush on Stalker. This is ridiculous. He has no love. Plus, she totally has the hots for me. All I need to do is convert that admiration into friendship. I'll make you my friend, Stalker. That is my promise to you.

"Assailant was supposed to be your team's warrior, but it looks like that won't work out now. But enough stalling. It's time for your training to begin," says Old Dude before de-materializing himself again.

The ceiling drops and arrows suddenly rain down.

Stalker jumps in front of me, only guarding my legs with her little body. Best Friend knocks me out of the way, taking the arrows head on. Glasses Kid dodges them with ease.

That little twerp has learned much from me. No, actually how in the hell is he dodging them?

Best Friend picks up his quiver and slowly tears the arrows out of his skin. He licks the blood off of them and then shoves them in the quiver.

"More ammo, lucky me," he says with a warm smile as blood gushes out of him.

Is he okay?

"Congratulations. You have passed the first trial," says the rough and gritty voice of a warrior woman.

"I'm the one who is supposed to be tested, not him. I'm the hero damn it!" I yell at the ceiling.

"I'm sorry, I'm a useless shield," says Stalker, tending to Best Friend's wounds with her sticky saliva hands.

"Don't, they're my mistakes. I will wear them proudly," says Best Friend, putting her spittle back in her mouth.

"Looking for this?" asked Glasses Kid, picking up what looked like a conch shell. "Maybe I can use this to triangulate the current position of our instructor slash adversary."

The ground suddenly parts. A platform rose up from the hole. A limbo stick, a tire and a hurdle all stood in a line.

Is this a test of humiliation.

"Your reflexes…bad. See how athletic ability fairs. Difficulty set to third grade," says the woman on the speaker.

Stalker walks right under the stick but trips on the tire. "Help me, hero," she says with a desperate look.

65:00

At least someone's trying to make me look good. Oh, I know what to do.

"Glasses Kid, you're up," I say.

"But P.E. is the only class I ever failed," says Glasses Kid worriedly.

He went under the limbo stick before it violently shot down.

"Damn magnetism! It's crushing me!" he yells, squirming in agony beneath the pole.

"Sorry, but I only help out my friends." I say, putting my arms behind my back.
"How about this: if you promise to be my friend, I'll save you," I say with my hand already on the heavy limbo stick.

"I'll do whatever you want, just don't let it kill me!" he yells as blood gushes out from his shirt.

I lift the stick and help him to his feet.

"You saved me," he says with teary eyes before coughing up a wad of blood on my jeans.

"What are friends for?" I responded coolly, while wiping his mouth clean with a leaf.

"It's my turn now," says Best Friend, stepping up to the plate.

Jets came out of the sides of the limbo stick, causing it to shoot out of my hands.

"As long as he lives, I won't be stopped," says Best Friend.

All his wounds collect around his wrist. Blood then gushes out, forming into a freaking katana. He slices the limbo stick in half, making sure to duck under it.

Okay, so when the hell did he learn how to do that!?

Missiles suddenly shot out of the hole between the tire, all zooming toward me.

Even projectile explosives can't resist me.

66:00

"I've got this!" I yell, tossing my boomerang.

The five missiles all lock on to the boomerang, following its lead.

"In the end, everything comes full-circle," says Glasses Kid, spouting some philosophical bullshit he likely got from a TED talk.

The boomerang was heading right back to me.

Why couldn't it have been a Frisbee!?

Best Friend shoots an arrow into each of the missiles, blowing them up in mid-flight. "Good work distracting them," he says with a nod.

I walk up to the hurdle and then jump over it.

"Aright, that's two trials down! Bring on the last one!" I exclaim.

"Had to cheat even to pass a simple challenge. Not impressed. No matter. Two trials down! Prepare for final first trial! Test intelligence," says the Russian lady.

"Wait, intelligence! Shit, we're screwed!" I exclaim.

This isn't fair! Most Shounen heroes are total idiots! It's part of their charm! That and being gluttons who bounce back like a punching bag with a vengeance!

"Let me handle this one," says Glasses Kid, polishing his spectacles.

"First question: how teach four little children as warriors?"

Glasses Kid holds his side and cringes.

"We're you hurt?" asked Stalker, checking for wounds.

"It's her grammar. It's so bad," he says, falling to his knees.

Great our weakest member has a really easy to exploit weakness.

"No answer means failure!" yells the Russian lady.

I look to Best Friend.

He smiles. "It's up to you to encourage him."

"Lean on Stalker," I said with a wink. "You know the answer and she's counting on you."

Glasses Kid blushes as Stalker helps him to his feet.

"You got this, Nyu," she said, giving him a thumbs up.

Glasses kid smiles at her and then turns his attention to the speakers. "Your question should have been stated as 'how do you teach for little children to become warriors". Here is my answer! You use arts and crafts to get them engaged. You make an occasional joke to lighten the mood. Then you keep them intrigued with interesting facts and give them a star for their cooperation."

"Discipline! That is only answer!" she yelled.

A log attached to a rope comes down from the ceiling and slams into Glasses Kid.

Stalker rushes to his side. "He's knocked out."

Ugh. He's really dragging us down.

"Next question. How answer if are unable to catch breath? Yahahaha!"

Stalker raises her hand. "Ummm, you uh, write it down." She winces and braces for impact.

"Correct! Final question. Doesn't need oral answer. Are willing do anything to be a hero?"

I turn around and raise my pointer finger and thumb proudly.

"Splendid. Now move to second trial. Everyone fight everyone. Survival of fittest. Last one gets to live. Battle royale bloodbath begin!" she exclaims as the walls of the room open up.

Wait a minute, we all have to kill each other! This is ridiculous. What was all that talk about teamwork for? Old Dude said I must utilize a team in order to save this world. Does this mean that I'll need a new team? I am so freaking confused.

Stalker turns away from my gaze.

"Do you know about this? Has this happened before?" I ask her.

Best Friend turns my way. "She's only a child. You're her first hero, Main." He raises his weapon against Glasses Kid.

"Hold up! Don't shoot him!" I yell.

My buddy turns to me with vacant eyes. "You shouldn't have to bloody those gentle hands."

"Hey, it's my life so I want her to do it," said Glasses Kid, pointing at Stalker while hiding his flushed cheeks.

"Nobody is killing anybody," I say.

Stalker stops fiddling with the rope in her lap. "Aww man, no double suicide?" She lifts up the rope.

It's two nooses that come together to make a heart shape.

That would be so cute if it wasn't creepy as hell.

"Nope. No suicide. It's against the law," I said.

"Actually, we encourage suicide in our village," said Stalker.

"Well it's against the law now because I said so!" I yell, snatching the rope from her hand.

"Suicide is a cowardly way to go out. Either way, my journey ends here. What are you waiting for? Kill me and claim your dream," says Best Friend, tossing me his crossbow.

"You're joking, right? Do I look like Grimmith?"

"Come now. If you want to achieve your dream, blood must be shed."

"I'm not going to kill you. If you're dead, then I'll be all alone," I say with a tear.

"You'll never be alone. I'll always be right here. Presuming this is where they burry me, that is," says Best Friend, pointing to the ground.

Damn him. Getting me to chuckle in such a shitty situation. Well two can play at that game.

69:00

"Dead people give shitty advice. I'm not going to do this without you!" I yell.

"Fine then, what do we do then, Captain?" he asks me.

Since when did I become the leader? The hero is supposed to just go out, spout bullshit about justice and friendship to his enemies and go out and kill monsters and animals. He's not supposed to be responsible for his whole team, is he?

"Main, don't worry. I've already made prearrangements. Our graves will be side by side," says Stalker, jumping on my back and checking the dimensions of my neck.

"Hey, why don't we all stand on these four platforms?" proposes Glasses Kid.

Look who woke up. I won't let him take this moment from me.

"I've decided. I'm not killing anyone. I'm the hero and you guys are my nakamas!" I exclaim.

"Hello, the platforms," says Glasses Kid, trying to get my attention.

"I've got an idea. Let's stand on these conveniently placed platforms," I propose, already on mine.

Stalker jumps off my back and goes to her platform.

Considering what the angry lady said and now the platforms, I'm getting Hungry Games vibes and that is not good. Then again, they already told us to kill each other, so it can't really get worse.

"Congratulations. Passed trial. Understood could not do alone. Almost impressed. Almost, but not quite. Time for final three tests…me," she says, somewhere in the thick bushes.

"Main, get down," says Best Friend.

"Must survive. Must locate. Must defeat. All without casualty." An arrow wrapped in vines shot out from the bushes, heading straight for me.

"Can keep teammates alive? Can even survive yourself?" asks the hunter lady.

70:00

Best Friend steps in the path and is hit in the chest. "Stay vigilant," he says before tearing out the arrow and wrapping his wound.

I shove my hand in Stalker's mouth and then place it on Best Friend's wound. "Stop taking all the pain for me. We share the same bed, the same toothbrush and even the same stuffed animal." I place the saliva on his wound. "Why won't you share the pain with me?"

"I'm a glutton for punishment. Always have been…ever since I saw that you were alive. We're connected Main. Your life matters more to me than anything," he says, putting his arms out in front of me.

I punch him in the face.

Yes! The fujoshis will eat up this brotherly angst!

"You idiot! Our lives are only temporary! The thing that really matters is our friendship. It's the only thing that can be immortalized!" I exclaim as the arrow zooms past me.

I'm such an idiot. I assumed that just because I'm awesome that all the arrows would come after me. I let my completely justified arrogance delude me of the truth. Now Glasses Kid is going to die.

Stalker runs in front of Glasses Kid, bracing for the attack. She makes a heart sign with her hands, creating a Valentine barrier like the legendary Cutey Honey!

"You don't have to protect me. I'm your teacher. I'm legally responsible for your safety," says Glasses Kid as the arrow battled with the barrier.

"You still act like were in the present. This is the past-ture. I'm not your student. I was always just a spy. Now stop standing there like an idiot and move!" she yells as her barrier starts to break.

"No, I may not be strong. But there is still something I can do," says Glasses Kid, putting his hand on Stalker's shoulder. He got lost in thought and started massaging her.

"What are you doing!? I can't concentrate like this! Stop! I only like tall guys!" she yells as cracks sprout throughout her barrier.

"I'll save you both!" I exclaim to them.

71:00

"There's no time. Be ready to run," says Best Friend, pointing above us.

Ten arrows were rapidly heading toward us.

"To be a hero…I have to have faith in my friends and myself. But Stalker isn't my friend…can we really trust her?" I ask Best Friend when I should have been running.

"If it's any consolation, she's my friend. We talk about you for hours after you fall asleep at the Orphanage," says Best Friend with a smile.

Yet he never once mentioned her to me. Why does my life have such obvious plot holes!?

I take a deep breath. "Alright then. She's a friend of a friend then…that's good enough for me."

"You're my best friend. I get that it's your duty to protect me. But you have to let me protect you too," I say as death looms closer and closer.

"Fine, but if I die…promise me you'll live on," says Best Friend, holding my hand.

"I promise," I say before Best Friend pushes me out of the way.

I watch in horror as the arrows zoom toward his tender body.

"Blood Barrier!" yells Best Friend, tearing off the wrap and scraping his wound open.

His chest wound sprays out blood like a fountain. The arrows pierce the barrier, and dig into Best Friend's sexy chest. He reached out his hand to me as he collapses to the floor. "Run!" he says with a fatigued look.

No need to tell me twice. Got to get her away from my friends and finally win some hero points.

I zoom out of there as fast as my toned legs will carry me. I suddenly trip and my head slams into a jagged rock. I look below me as my blood drips down my forehead. My ankle is caught in a wooden bear trap. I struggle to get my foot free, but this only tears it up further.

Damn it! I hate feeling helpless. They're all counting on me, I have to break free. Every second I waste is one more second my best friend bleeds out.

72:00

I hear Stalker's voice nearby. I move my head to the side to see her shaking Glasses Kid. The little guy is completely knocked out.

"Forget about him! He's a side character. The main character needs your help right now!" I yell with great persuasive power.

"As you command, Captain!" she says, tossing Glasses Kid aside. Stalker runs up to me and then stops to look at my bleeding foot.

"I can break out anytime I want. It's just that having you break me out will strengthen our bonds," I say reassuringly.

Ugh! This is not good for my street cred. I really gotta step up my game.

"I understand," she says, eating up my clever lie with a sly smile.

You know, I think I can work with her. She seems reasonable enough.

Stalker takes off her shirt.

Here I am bleeding out and she decides to strip! This loli needs to sense the goddamn mood!

"What the hell are you doing!?" I ask, almost choking on my own disbelief as she removes her bra.

Why does she even have a bra and why is it black lace? Strawberries are the best undies hands down.

"I'm getting ready. Come on, take off your shirt," she says, folding her clothes in a neat pile.

Tell me this isn't happening! I'm way too young for this! She's like twice my age! And worst of all, our potential friendship will be ruined. No…this isn't just an end to friendship. It could kill me just like it did Kamia! Come on Main, believe in the you that believes in you and get yourself out of this mess.

What fate awaits your new favorite hero? You'll have to stay tuned to find out!

Episode 3 Part 2

Did my editor forget to add "and" in-between "Friendship" and "The"? Either way I still am going to get a freaking bazooka! Man, this episode is going to be kick ass! I don't want to waste any time.

I look at the tiny terror looming closer to me.

"I mustn't run away. I mustn't run away."

Oh wait. Little girl trying to force herself on me. Thankfully her ero-zones are being blocked by what must be some sort of light-based ninja technique. Who knows how long that will last? I have to find a way out of this mess or my book will get blacklisted by those purist liberals! I have to stall her.

"Think about what you're doing," I say, while covering my eyes.

"You think I like this. You turned out to be a major disappointment." She took a deep breath and then looked up with a shaky smile. "But…I won't lose sight of my goal."

Aha! I see something poking out of the grass. It looks like a stump but maybe it's actual a trigger of sorts.

"Step a little to the left," I say, motioning with my hands.

"Like this?" she asks.

A massive log on a rope swoops down and slams into Stalker. She is flung like a rag doll over the cliff side.

It looks like I'm the only one left, and I never got that bazooka.

At least I avoided this becoming a hentai. That was waaaaay too close. Still, purposely getting my ally hurt is bound to hold back our friendship.

Just then something big and bouncy appears before me.

Boobs is here! Yes! Her uselessness will give me the misogynistic drive needed to save the day. Whoops. I mean yay! A strong female lead is here to save the helpless male! Is that politically correct enough for you purists?

"Where is Stalker? Is she safe?" asks Assailant all serious-like before slicing down several arrows.

I peek over the edge of the cliff. Stalker was naked and unconscious in a small puddle in a pond.

"She'll be fine, don't worry," I say as professionally as a real doctor.

Assailant slashes a tree down in the blink of an eye. "Where are you, Static Huntress? I'm not going to let you just get away with hurting my daughter!"

"Know nothing of world. Cannot manipulate. Won't find me. Assure that," says the Static Huntress.

"I don't need to find you. I'll just cut down every tree in the forest! You'll be sliced to ribbons for sure!" yells Assailant.

Ugh! Why am I on the sidelines? Damn I have to steal the spotlight in some way. Of course!

"He's using the secret Forest Slicer technique. This technique is passed down only to assassins who have abandoned their clan and using it drains the life of the user."

Heh. Eat that Glasses Kid. You're not the only one who can spout nonsensical exposition.

Knives pierce out from Assailant's sleeves. "Don't presume to know so much."

Boobs was lying next to me, her voluptuous lumps radiating in the sunlight. Wait a minute…sunlight?

"Master, don't stare at me," she said, hiding her face in her breasts.

Did a pillow just talk to me? Well no? It's called IMAGINATION! Watch ToeQger and you'll understand. But I can give you my short list of live action recommendations at another time. I have a victory to steal.

75:00

"Assailant, this isn't some arena! We are outside! That means that Static Huntress could be anywhere! But wait another minute, her arrows came from a certain location. I'll go check it out," I say assertively.

Oh yeah. My strategy will save the day! For Brittania!

My neck stretches its limits as my eyes regrettably move further away from Boobs. I go through the bushes, careful to not step on any bear traps. Arrows suddenly shoot out from the ground before me. Even my lightning fast reflexes weren't quick enough. The arrow shot into my left arm, sapping it of all its energy.

Great! Now I'm even more useless. Think Main. What would Detective Koman do?

I close my eyes.

Okay so she's triggering the arrows from somewhere. That means she is watching our every move. But where the hell is she!?

I look around and hear nothing. No birds, insects chirping, not even leaves rustling.

I'm all alone, just like that fateful day. But I have to be strong. Everyone is counting on me. With that much pressure, I'm bound to succeed.

"Hey, Hunter Bitch! I figured out your little game, now come out!" I yell, strategically giving away my position.

I crawl further along, evidently triggering a mine. The mine shoots up before releasing a net. The net zooms above me, carried by leafy green birds. The balls along the sides of the net then open up, revealing arrows. The tips of the arrows came off, shooting darts forth. The darts then open up, becoming suction cups. Every single suction dart hits its handsome target.

"Poison suction cups! What an insult! Does she think I'm not man enough to handle real darts? That's it, this bitch is going down!" I yell so furious that I actually spoke my thoughts out loud.

A voice then appears from above me.

"What the !@#* is your problem you little $#!+? I was trying to catch a god+@%^ nap. Do you always !@#$* with people who are sleeping? I ought to blow your !@#*ing brains out you $#!+ munching (=^+bag!" yells a furiously grouchy thing in an androgynous and robotic tone.

I look up at the above tree to see it…my freaking awesome bazooka. The title never lies, this proves it.

"Hey jackass? What do you say I help you down from there?" I ask it, rather politely I might add.

"I'm not some !@#*ing princess in distress you $#!+head. I was trying to sleep!"

"Sorry I woke you up, uh, fair maiden," I say with a grimace.

"For your information I identify as an attack helicopter and go by the pronoun 'Ultima!' So, you best be respectful or I'll murder your misogynistic @$$!"

"Here's the truth. I'm kind of in a bad spot. See, my foot got caught in a bear trap and I…"

"Well maybe you shouldn't have been outside the village walls then. There's no law here $#!+ for brains! You're not the first !@#*tard whose wanted my help but I pray to the !@#*ing almighty Source that you're the last."

"Please, I'm just a kid really. I…I want to go home." I add a sniffle for extra pity.

"Go cry me a sympathetic river, build a bride of pity and then jump off of it you @$$hole!" yells my future rocket launcher.

I punched the tree with all my might. Ultima fell down, right at my feet. My god Ultima was beautiful! Ultima glowed with a golden glow. Ultima's metal exterior felt as sleek as a new car. Ultima smelled like Best Friend's homemade muffins! Ultima tasted like metal and sadness. I press Ultima to the grass and hoist myself back to my feet.

I never realized how much I used pronouns until now. This politically correct shit is really bringing down my story.

"What the !@#* are you manhandling me for you @$$hole?" Ultima asks quite rudely.

"There has to be a mute button somewhere," I say mostly to myself as I check every angle of Ultima's sleek body.

"I'm not some !@#*ing tool you $#!+face! I'm a living creature with feelings and $#!+!"

"You don't have a name, do you?"

"What kind of ridiculous assumption is that you (-#*sucker?"

"Alright, so then what is it?"

"It's none of your !@#*ing business, $#!+head!"

"In the name of myself, I dub thee Friendship!"

The title is always right after all. This time I had finally shut Friendship up. If you can't find a mute button, you make one!

Steam poured out of Friendship before everything went silent. The next moment, tiny pieces of bark flooded the sky.

Wow, this part would look great in 3-D. All I can hear is this beeping sound. But it wasn't telling me that my toast was ready, it was my ears popping.

I looked through the smoke to see that a whole row of trees had been blown to bits.

"How did that happen?" asks Friendship, finally cooling down.

"That my friend is our power. It is the power of Friendship!" I lift Ultima into the air.

"!@@#$%^)*#!%*)^)#!*%))%!"

All I hear are beeps as I blast everything in sight.

I pat my newest buddy. "Calm down buddy. Do you know where the Static Huntress is?"

"Brawny %!+(# is in the !@#*ing sky dumb@$$! How else could she be following your every !@#*ing move!?" asks Friendship, all pissed off again.

"Why do you curse so much? Do you realize that all I hear are bleeps?"

"I don't !@#*ing care what you hear. I curse because I was designed to be child friendly and I !@#*ing hate it!"

This little robot has more rage than Bokugo. What could have happened that made Friendship like this? Oh shit. I gotta stay focused. She's above me.

I look up. Now that those useless trees were out of the way, I notice a small helicopter. It was covered in leaves so it was hard to make out its exact shape. Standing on the helm was the Static Huntress.

"Boy finally found enemy. Now, must find way to...what the?" she asks before Friendship blew her out of the sky.

"Nice shot!" I exclaim, giving my gun a sorta high five.

"Unlike some people I can shoot a moving target," Ultima says, rather proud of Ultimaself.

The burning leaf-copter plummeted down. It landed mere meters before me, blanketed in a fiery blaze. The Static Hunter calmly walked out, her entire body aflame. "Good hit," she says, drinking a whole bottle of vodka and smashing it against her muscular chest.

Here's hoping the extra fire will burn her to dust.

Wow, she looks like a man.

Oh crap! That sounded sexist! I'm an otaku damn it! I know appearances mean nothing!

What I meant to say is she looked like a strong well-rounded female character. Okay seriously, the chika had muscles like Toeguro, eighty percent not one-hundred percent, and her face was battle worn and boxy. One look at her moss-covered bod was enough to put most men to shame. She had eight pack abs and incredible thighs wrapped in vines. She was like a body builder and a sprinter all mixed up in one. Her flaming body was covered in scars old and new. Her brown, muddy hair was singed but already short. Somehow the Bureau of censorship found a way to keep her leafy clothes from burning away in the fire.

Yeah, you heard me right. Inflammable leaves!

"You've made angry. Not good move," she says, spitting out all the vodka she had drank.

It rained down on her, somehow putting out the flame. How the hell did she keep all that vodka in her mouth, this bitch was tough.

"Nothing about you makes any sense!"

I can feel my grip on my viewers weakening. The reality I established thus far is under attack. I won't let this go the way of Utwawarerumonono!

"Not here to amuse you?" she says, placing a handcrafted arrow on her biceps.

The arrow shoots off like a bullet and hits my already limp arm. The pain rides up all the way to my neck. I crack my fingers and rip out the arrow, my arm was now back in business. I lick the blood off the tip of the arrow and then collapse.

I was trying to be cool and now I'm back on the ground. What just happened!?

"Poison tips. Stupid boy," she says as she walks toward me.

No, I can't die again. This sucks ass! I'm The Main Character, how can I lose!?

"Friendship, help me out!" I yell as loud as I could.

"Simple child," says Static Huntress, pulling a string that was apparently connected to Friendship.

Friendship's muzzle points upward before firing and the rocket shoots into the sky.

"This jungle mine," she says.

"Forest!" I yell, swiftly correcting her.

"Wild my jungle. Understands her. Understands me."

"No. I really don't understand you. But you'll be in trouble if you kill me. There's a whole village worth of fans who will come at you and burn your precious 'jungle' to the ground!"

"Village won't save boy. Lost faith in feeble heroes. Life mine. No-one left to protect. All alone," she says, allowing me to crawl away.

"Enough! Is there any reason you have to rub it in!? I know I'm going to die, just get it over with. I don't need a whole explanation, do I?" I ask rhetorically.

Yeah, I know that word. Impressed, aren't you?

"Always talk to prey." She sits on a burnt stump "Who else would listen?" she asks, with a hint of sadness.

"What you need is a friend," I say, completely right of course.

Whenever the hero is cornered it's time to try the friendship angle. Fists come first but if they fail then just keep spouting friendship speeches till you win your enemy over. I'm not afraid. I saw her in the opening song and she was on my team.

"Use every part of catch. Insides are dinner. Skin be blanket. Clothes…make good rugs," she says, as if she actually lived somewhere.

"Did you hear me! I could be your friend."

"Have many friends. All on vacation."

Sure they are. Damn it, where is Glasses Kid when you need him? He could easily talk until my paralysis poison wears out. He could have this jumbo babe on her knees, begging for a reprieve from his blabbering in a mere twenty-three minutes.

"Slowly raise foot. Adds to drama," she says as she lifts her foot up instead of just smashing my brains out.

"You don't have television, do you?" I ask, but not cruelly.

"Jungle only thrill needed," she says, still not killing me.

I look around very slowly and took a deep breath. "Forest."

Not at the last moment, a furry of knives shoot toward the Static Huntress. She picks me up and uses me as a shield.

I have so many great uses.

I scream out, but not in a girly way, as the knives make my back their temporary residence. She tosses me aside. And may I add that I traveled quite far indeed.

I land, thank you God, right on Boobs' legs.

"Who is she?" asks Boobs with a piercing and invisible glare and an airy high-pitched voice.

"She's my enemy!"

"Why is she practically naked. Don't you love me?" She looks at the enemy's muscular build. "Am I not manly enough?"

"Now is really not the time!"

My focus then shifts to the battle before me. Assailant's tentacles grab onto his knives before slicing Brawny Bitch furiously.

Yeah, I think I'll keep that name for her. And by the way, I'm just bitter she's my enemy. I'm not sexist, okay?

The bad-ass woman leaps over the tentacle. She grabs the knife and then slices it all the way down his slimy appendage. The knife is now at his neck.

"You lose. Not big surprise." She shoves the knife straight through his cloak.

Is he dead? I hope not, that would really be anticlimactic. If he wants to die, he should at least wait till the end of the season or at least do it to save my life.

His other tentacle grabs hold of the knife and tears it out.

Brawny Bitch is already a few meters away from him, holding a high-tech cross-bow, complete with laser sighting.

"Already lost. Mines everywhere," she says, lowering her crossbow.

It was a stalemate, that's a Checkers term by the way. He was stuck and she could shoot him at any moment. Yep, a true stalemate.

"I hope I don't offend you." Assailant bows to his enemy. "I can kinda float," he says, awkwardly scratching his hood as he rose from the ground.

My Godoka he was right! In fact, I don't think I've ever seen his feet touch the ground. Does he even have feet?

"Traps proximity. Like birds. Never catch them," she says, firing three arrows at once.

Assailant strafes to the side, dodging the volley. He rushes up to her as she fires. Each of her shots completely miss their mark.

What was she planning?

Once reaching her, he thrusts a knife into her chest. It shatters like the hopes of an otaku when they learn that Earth-chan is flat.

"Jungle is mother. Make Huntress strong," she says, even though it was clearly a forest.

His tentacle became razor sharp, zooming right for her head.

She moves her head to the side and fires another arrow at her stationary opponent.

The tentacle only nicked her face, while Assailant was pumped full of arrows.

"Daddy!" yells Stalker, running to his side.

You'll be happy to know that she was fully clothed now.

"Stay away Sugar Plum, it's dangerous!" he exclaims, before his cloak opened up. "My hatred for this world gives me the power to protect it!"

A miniature black hole shoots out from his chest. The gravity vortex pulls everything around it towards its insatiable void.

Brawny Bitch plants her feet in the ground, as stubborn as a fundamentalist.

Okay, I don't know what that is, but Glasses Kid uses the phrase a lot to insult me.

"Made amused. Time got serious," she says, pulling a mine out of the ground. With those ungodly thick muscles, she punches the mine at Assailant. It zooms right past the black hole and hits him head on.

The dark warrior falls to the ground, smoldering. That's when I realize something. Friendship is still in my hand. I'm armed and ready to fire. I aim the gun at Brawny Bitch as she walks toward her newest victim.

Suddenly something warm yet firm grips my left hand. It's Best Friend and O.M.G. his shirt is off and so are his pants.

Thank god I don't suffer from nosebleeds! I can have as many pervy thoughts as I want and no one will know. Mmmm, look at those booty shorts.

"If Stalker can strip for you, then so can I," says Best Friend, pulling off his underwear with a single finger.

Wow…that was so freaking hot. For some strange reason I want to binge Freed! right now!

"Go ahead Main, finish this," says Best Friend, grabbing my hand as if he was in labor.

"Hasta la vista baby!" I exclaim before Friendship's rage got the better of him.

Ah, sweet sweet silence. And what do you know? Brawny Bitch is on the ground, completely out cold with smoke coming out from her mouth. She miraculously survived like a One Place antagonist! Which means she can still join my team! Victory!

Alright, time for the ending song.

Best Friend and Stalker are side by side. They both turn their heads, beaming at me in their own ways. They then start to strip, very slowly. The shirt comes off first. Then Best sensuously takes off his pants. Oh, and Stalker removes her skirt, I guess. Now they both take a pair of scissors and cut off their own undies. Skulls and valentines, what a contrast. They are both only wearing socks. Now they lean up to the screen and blow a kiss. Now that is some smart two-sided fan service. Very Tale has taught me much. They then turn around and leave. Best Friend struts away, his bare butt glistening. And Stalker, she kind of just bounces. Then it zooms out and I'm knocked out on a bike alongside Friendship. We're both in a puddle from our massive nosebleeds. Alright! Now that is my kind of ending. I don't know why Stalker has to take up the other half of the screen, but if I re-watch it with one hand over my eye it's absolutely perfect! Anyways, time for the preview.

84:00

Next time on The Main Character. The main villain appears. This is the man who I will have to beat the living shit out of at the end of the season just so you know. It looks like Brawny Bitch is up and about, sorry for the obvious spoilers. And hey what do you know, Stalker has her clothes on. Wait, who is that rainbow colored figure? Find out on the next potentially stimulating episode of The Main Character.

FLAMBOYANT VILLAIN'S DEBUT

Episode 4 Part 1

The time has finally arrived. The final battle is here! I'm not going to let this bastard get away! I'm going to kill him now! Wait, then won't my journey end? Who am I kidding? I'm sure to get renewed for another season. Another villain will emerge out of nowhere and some major plot twist will be revealed. After Madarara got beat Noruto got a whole new series, after all! Oh yeah, this is going to be epic! Hurry up opening, I'm ready.

I look into the sunlight…ow! I burnt my eyes. And now I'm jogging down an endless path of fire! Now there's a slide show of a bunch of people I still don't know. Now to introduce the team. This is my Best Friend! He is really cool and he controls blood apparently. This is Stalker! She is a creeper and can make shields. This is Boobs! She has really big boobs…that's about it! This is Assailant! He's a psycho murderer and I'm going to make him my friend. This is Glasses Kid! He talks a lot. But none of them really matter. I'm The Main Character! Me me me! The Main Character! Hell's yeah! I'm The Main Character! And I'm going to kill this bastard. Why…because I'm The Main Character!

Alright, it's getting longer. Just got to keep this up and gain an actual sense of rhythm. This is going great! I've got a real team now. My importance has gone up three levels. Okay, time for the recap.

Last time on Main Character: After a very emotional and melodramatic speech, I convinced my allies to let me face the Static Huntress on my own. Stalker of course didn't listen and instead took off her clothes and tried to sleep with me. Luckily, a single flex of my amazing muscles was enough to knock her out cold. Damn, I am so sexy! Anyways so I found a vulgar rocket launcher in a nearby tree that I decided to call Friendship. The bazooka begged to join my team. After Ultima's tragic story swayed my heart, I had to accept the vulgar bazooka's membership. Assailant and Boobs were both defeated by the warrior woman, leaving their hopes and dreams with me. I hoisted up Friendship and with our combined power, I beat Brawny Babe with a single attack. After that she bowed down and vowed to join my team. Since my team was a good size, I decided to split us up once we arrived at Forest of Scary Name. Stalker, her dad and Hunter Babe went looking for the super bananas in one location. While me, Best Friend and the little twerp went looking in the opposite direction.

The trees in the forest bend in unnatural ways and their leaves are extra shiny. It's a mix of "I wanna touch 'em!" and "what will happen if I touch them."

Glasses Kid turns around. "Hey Mark, you're dragging us down. Pick up the pace."

Another fake name. How dare he?

"Is something wrong?" asks Best Friend, lifting up my shirt to check for wounds. "Why didn't you get this healed?" he asked, applying his saliva to my ankle injury.

"Hey if I just rely on other people to heal me, then I'll take my powers for granted like One-million percent boy," I say with an awkward smile.

The real reason I didn't heal is so Best Friend will have to carry me bridal style! Oh yeah! Think of it as a prelude to our future wedding. Oh, but no homo, of course. Main Characters must be hetero, even when they don't want to be. Poor Heartfillya.

Glasses Kid examines my foot. "This looks like a good time to reveal my latest invention."

"Cough! Cough! Plot device. Cough!" I exclaim.

Glasses Kid reaches into his pack and pulls out a small metal device. It unfolds into a mechanical prosthetic leg. "If you just discard your injured flesh, we can attach this little helper."

"Wait a damn minute! That's handicap appropriation!" I exclaim.

"Um, what?" asked Glasses Kid with a confused look.

"Pretending to be handicapped when you aren't is super offensive. Plus, real handicapable people don't get weaponized legs. It's offensive. I outright refuse."

Glasses Kid rolls his eyes. "Nobody is watching. You're not some hero with plot armor. You're my student and it's my duty to safely return you home. I won't have my teaching's license revoked because of your forced schizophrenia!"

"I don't know what you said, but you had better take it back!" I yell.

Best Friend motions me to sit down on a nearby stump. "I found some ointment," he said, crushing up some leaves and applying their natural blood to my wound.

"Why is it red?" I ask.

Best Friend takes out a small book and shows it to me. "The great giant of genesis supposedly died in this forest. His flesh turned into these leaves, thus they are red."

"Haha! Absurd," said Glasses Kid. "The pigmentation is from the unique weather in this region. They absorb the nutrient rich rain water and assimilate it."

"Does it still hurt?" asks Best Friend, looking up at me.

As much as I'd love him to carry me, I can't lie to that gorgeous face.

"I'm fine now.'

"Hey guys, I spotted the bananas!" exclaims Glasses Kid, pointing all the way up.

At the very top of a tropical palm tree look alike was a bunch of bananas.

This side quest is nearly done.

"Get behind me," says Best Friend, ready to tear open his wound as he rushes to the foot of the tree.

Something grabs my leg. Apparently, the vines here are mobile. They suddenly drag me across the grass.

"Oh, the trees eat humans! That explains the pigmentation. Even in a fantasy setting logic still thrives," said Glasses Kid as I being pulled up into a hole in a scaly tree.

A figure slides all the way down and lands in front of us. It's wearing a gas mask and has our bananas in its hands. "They're wood wyverns." The figure tosses a Molotov cocktail into the hole in the tree and the vine releases me.

The tree screeches before rushing off.

I brace for impact but am caught in Best Friend's arms.

So close. If I stole a kiss, would he blame me?

Best Friend sets me down and approaches the figure. "State your purpose."

The figure takes off the mask to reveal a familiar face.

Best Friend smiles. "Didn't expect to see you out here, Banana Man."

"Well I decided it didn't feel right sending a bunch of youngsters out to get some bananas for me. Sorry for all the trouble," he says with an awkward smile.

"Sorry? Dude, your sabotaged your own side quest." I glare at him. "Now it's going to be marked as not cleared forever! Why didn't you trust me to do what you asked for?"

"My daughter was ten when they took her," said Banana Man, preparing to steal the scene with some sad backstory.

"Wait, your daughter was an actual girl?" asked Glasses Kid.

What kind of dumb question is that?

Banana Man nods. "She was the treasure of the village. Had hair like a bowl of fruit, long blond locks shaped like bananas and little orange buns above her braided grape extensions."

"It's been eight years since then, hasn't it?" I ask.

Banana Man's eyes widen. "It has. How did you know."

"Well it would make her eighteen, which means I can hit on her if we find her without pissing off American audiences who think seventeen-year olds are lolis."

"Fruity was like the princess of our village. She had powers to peek into the past."

"Don't you mean the future?" I ask.

"Nope. She wanted to be a fortune teller and used people's pasts to predict the future. But she couldn't predict what would happen the day the village was attacked. Little bells ringed throughout the night followed by screams. The girls were all taken and the men who tried to protect them had their stomachs clawed open."

"Then why aren't you dead? You should have protected her."

Banana man lifts up his shirt, revealing a scar that reads "REGRET". He lowers his shirt and looks to the ground. "I tried to, but tossing fruit and small rocks at highly trained warriors isn't as effective as you'd think."

Unless you're a Jackson hobbit, that is.

Banana man holds back his tears. "My miserable life was saved by the villages guardian angel. And now she protects you. After losing my daughter, I didn't care about the lives of others. I've sent out several heroes before you, none of which understood the greatness of bananas. I rationalized that without proper potassium they would have died soon anyways. Nine of them died. When I realized you were the tenth one, it made me think of my ten-year old daughter. I didn't want to lose anyone else."

Best Friend embraces Banana Man. "Don't worry, Papa. We'll get her back for you," he said in the voice of a little girl.

Well that was odd.

Banana Man smiles. "All I want is for you to get out of this forest safely. Meet me at the village and I'll find a way to bring you back home to your family," he said, holding Best Friend's hand.

Best Friend turns and smiles at me. "My family is right here."

Glasses Kid starts laughing. "You two are way too gullible. Thankfully you have a chaperone with you. Banana Man is using reverse psychology to get you to go after his daughter."

Hold up.

I turn to Glasses Kid. "You mean he's one of those generic village dads who tries to turn in the heroes for his daughter's safety and were supposed to save his daughter even after the betrayal because good guys are idiots?"

"Precisely," says Glasses Kid.

"Shut up," says Best Friend softly. He shoots Glasses Kid a murderous glare. "I don't care if this is a trap. His suffering is real." He grips my hand. "We have to help him."

I'm pretty sure he's stealing my lines. If he wasn't so hot, I'd be seriously pissed right now.

The forest suddenly becomes foggy.

Banana Man places his gas mask on Best Friend. "Get out of here. The spores will mess you up."

"That's right!" exclaimed Glasses Kid. "This fog is actually cinema microscopic, small enough that you can see, spores that eat away your memories."

I can't forget about all the epic anime I've seen. Oh geez, if I forget about One Place, I'm going to have to do one helluva binge to catch up.

"Hand it to me. I'm the most important one!" I holler.

"Adults should always put on oxygen masks before helping out the kids. Hand it over! Knowledge is my power!" yells Glasses Kid.

"No." Best Friend says softly. "I can't lose them." He grips his chest. "I need them!" He rushes at me.

I swipe my leg and he jumps. This gives me the perfect chance to grab hold of the mask.

He slams his face into mine.

"Stop fighting! The spores just make you cry! He's lying!" yells Banana Man.

"Your daughter didn't get kidnapped. She left your village willingly, didn't she? You wanted her to be a fruit girl. You never supported her dream!" exclaims Glasses Kid.

"Bite your tongue you little brat," said Banana Man, knocking out Glasses Kid with a single punch.

I roll along the ground with Best Friend. "Dude, hand it over. You know how important I am."

"Anything you forget, I can remind you at your bedside. We can re-watch every anime together. It's inconsequential."

Just what the hell is he so afraid of forgetting?

Banana Man pulls me off of Best Friend and shoves the Forest of Scary Name's plant guide in his face. "The spores only make you…cry," he said, breaking down into tears.

"I'm sorry for not trusting you," said Best Friend.

My vision becomes foggy as tears overwhelm me.

I felt a soft wet thing remove them.

"Your tears are delicious," he said, removing the gas mask and revealing a big smile.

Sooooo hot!

"I'm sorry." He says over and over as he places the mask on my head.

"It was Glasses Kid who did this," I said, glaring at the knocked-out pipsqueak.

That little prankster went too far this time.

"He's not the only liar," said Banana Man as he hoisted the boy onto his shoulders with a face full of tears.

"The only way I'll forgive you for lying to us is if you tell us where your daughter is," said Best Friend.

"She won't want to come back. I should have supported her," said Banana Man, falling to his knees in misery.

"As long as you draw breath, your happy ending is within reach. You simply have to seize it." Best Friend grabs my hand and pulls me against the tree. "Please, woodland creature. Get us out of here."

The tree topples over and sprouts legs. Those little legs then rush out of the forest with the four of us riding its back.

"You don't think the extra weight is hurting him, do you?" asks Best Friend with a look of concern.

Awww. Take note ladies. If you ever want to find a good partner, find one who is kind to animals. But not Best Friend, because he's all mine.

"I doubt it's more than an inconvenience," I say, patting his back.

He pulls away and hugs himself with shivering arms. "I don't deserve you."

"Yeah, yeah you punched me. I'm not happy about it either. You're going to have to snuggle away the pain tonight if you want me to forgive you." I give him a big smile.

The smile he returns to me is quivering.

"We're in the clear!" exclaims Banana Man, patting the head of the Woodvern to signal him to stop. "Thanks for helping us out," he says, plopping a banana into the woodland creature's camouflaged mouth. He then hops off the tree beast. "I should head back to the village."

Best Friend bites his thumb and solidifies the blood into a needle. He points the needle at Banana Man's throat. "If you don't tell us where she is, I'll kill you."

"Oh, and thanks for lending us the mask," I say, handing it to him.

"My daughter is in Glam castle. Nobody who enters ever leaves. Well they do leave, but they always return."

Not sure if this is supposed to be scary, but I can pretend it is.

"Then we'll set a new record," I say with a grin.

Best Friend lowers his weapon. "Safe travels."

"Hey, don't forget these," I say, handing the produce procurer the banana bushel.

His face becomes stiff like a manikin. "Quest completed," he says monotone.

Haha! This guy is hilarious.

Banana Man drops some coins into my hand robotically and gives me two bananas from the bushel.

"Thanks," I say.

"Thanks for what?" he asks, his face becoming normal. "Well, see you around." He leaves the area.

"I don't think he was acting. Could have been possessed?" asks Best Friend.

I unfurrow his brow. "Relax, man. He was just messing with us. Well, now that we completed the quest it's time to look for the others," I say with a smile.

Best Friend grabs my hand and raises it. "There's a reason I told Stalker to go with the other group."

Was it so we could be alone? Am I blushing? Oh, I hope he doesn't notice.

I lean in to kiss him without thinking.

"Main!" Stalker tackles me from behind.

Cock blocked! Damn it; she's really getting on my nerves.

"With her diary she can find you no matter where you are," says Best Friend.

"Wait, you have the Yukki Diary, colloquially known as the Stalker Diary?"

Stalker shakes her head. "Nope. Even better. You'll have to frisk me if you want to find out."

Not sure if I'm more afraid of not knowing what her diary does or finding out what she'll do if I accidently turn her on. I mean, she did try to molest me when I was unable to fight back. That gave me Sword Art Onedge vibes and not the fuzzy kind.

Stalker puts some spit on her hand and rubs it on my bruised face. She puffs out her cheeks and glares at Best Friend. "I'm not leaving him alone with you ever again."

"I don't blame you," said Best Friend softly.

Assailant pops out from a shadow on the ground.

He can hide in shadows. Good to know.

"The mushrooms are ready. Static Huntress made a fire too. It's nice and warm," he says, pulling me and his daughter along.

Brawny Babe looks at me and then turns away. "Your team is victor. Claim your prize."

"Oooh!" Stalker takes some vines from the ground and ties her arms up into a bow. "I can be your reward," she says, leaning into me.

"I want you to help me with a rescue mission," I say to Brawny Babe, skillfully ignoring Stalker's advances.

She shakes her head. "Led team wrong way on purpose. Was testing you," she said, nearly knocking me over by pushing her finger against my chest.

"Well I succeeded regardless."

"Take back weapon," she said, unfastening Friendship from her back.

"Did you keep them safe?" I asked the bazooka.

Ultima didn't respond.

Maybe it's asleep. I mean the only gun I know that sleeps is Lassoo, oh and the two blond cutie pies who serve Death Jr.

"So Static Huntress, how has your life been?" asks Assailant casually.

"Don't act like know each-other," says Brawny Babe, crossing her arms.

"So Big Brother-sama, how did you beat her? I knew you were amazing, but she's like a mythic warrior!" exclaims Stalker, scooting up next to me with a book in her lap.

Wait that book. Could it be?

"Don't act like you don't know," I say, snatching her journal from her lap. "And then Main stole my diary. He looked at me with a condescending look as he read it out loud. He then stopped, awestruck," I say before suddenly stopping.

"I write each entry using my thoughts. I've documented every moment of your life ever since I met you. Isn't that amazing?" she asks, holding her cheeks and swaying her head side to side.

I drop the journal in shock.

Terrifying…the word is terrifying.

"Everything about my sugar plum is amazing," says Assailant, patting her head.

"Thanks, papa-chan!" She grabs her journal and puts it back under her shirt where it is absorbed.

Best Friend places his hand on mine, breaking me free from terror's grip. "That ability will come in handy later. We're going to Glam castle on a mission. Brawny Babe, are you going to assist us?" asks Best Friend as he twirls his cooked mushroom.

"Won't come back alive," says Brawny Babe.

"Is there a reason you talk like that?" asked Glasses Kid, holding his queasy stomach.

Great, the little prankster is awake.

"Jungle teach," she said, slamming her fist against her chest.

"Save your deception for your enemies, else you'll make me one of them," says Best friend with a murderous look.

"Won't happen again," says Glasses Kid, soiling himself.

Assailant taps his shoulder and whispers to the boy before the two walk off.

"So, will you help us or not, Huntress?" asks Best Friend as he sensuously sucks on his mushroom.

Oh yeah, just the tip.

"Hi there, it's very nice to meet you," said Stalker, lying with her belly on the ground and waving at my boner.

Okay, she is mega creepy. I pray to non-existent gods that she can't read minds.

"Are you really going to ignore me?" asks Best Friend, sprinkling some seasoning on a mushroom and then popping it into my mouth.

Mmmm. He can make anything delicious.

"Love Dictator not threaten forest. No reason help," says Hunter Babe snidely.

"Then why did you start this fire for us?" asks Assailant, tilting his body into a question mark.

"Want talk. Wouldn't understand," says Hunter Babe, looking away with a clenched fist.

I took a bite out of my seasoned mushroom, causing Stalker to gasp in delight.

"Did that really arouse you?" I ask, sliding back.

"Uhuh!" Her eyes shimmer. "You can take a bite out of me," she says, putting out her arm.

Great she's thinks I'm a Kyoto ghoul. Cannibalism just isn't quite as glamorous as anime makes it out to be.

I catch the trail of saliva before it hits the ground and apply it on my scratches. "Be careful not to waste any."

"Whatever you say, my lord," she said, nestling up to me.

"Anyways, can I talk to you alone for a minute?" I ask as nonchalantly as possible.

Stalker holds in her explosive delight and smiles sweetly. "Sure," she replies, getting up with shaky legs.

Now that I'm paying attention, she has a really cute butt. I'm getting the urge to squeeze it.

Wait where did that come from? I don't like kid butts. I like women booty! I'm just tired, is all. Stay focused, Main. I've got to ask her to be my friend, but I have to do it very smoothly.

"Best be watchful," said Brawny Babe. "Jungle dangerous place. Ever heard stories of Inashikacho?"

Assailant covers his face in fear. "You mean it isn't just a myth? That would explain the heroes who went missing."

I hold out my hand. "Stop right there. What you don't know won't hurt you. If I hear this story, then this wretched creature is bound to show up, likely in this episode."

I follow Stalker far off into the woods, making sure that no-one can overhear our conversation.

I'm going to give her a test of my own. I need to know if I can trust her.

Stalker suddenly screams. "Yes! Yes! Yes! Oh my God! Oh my God! Oh my God! We're all alone! I've waited for this moment since forever! So, what do want to do? Should I get undressed now or should we start off with some idle banter?" she asks, releasing her emotion in one incredible blast.

"Keep your panties on. I just want to talk," I say as I sat down on a downed tree.

Stalker sits down next to me, leaning on my shoulder.

I've never been this close to a girl before. Well at least one that wasn't grafted onto a pillow.

She snuggles up to me.

Her lips are literally inches from mine. But a kiss right now would ruin our potential friendship. Plus, I'm saving my delicious virgin lips for Best Friend. I need to be calm, maybe put an arm around her. Yeah, just like that.

She squirms in delight after noticing I had slyly put my arm around her shoulder.

"Sooooooo, what ya wanna talk about: the weather, food, virginity, fighting, boys, gossip? Whatever you want, I'm game for," she says, her eyes going every which as she wiggles her legs.

"Boys actually…how did you know?" I ask with a light blush.

"Best Friend is wearing black undies today," says Stalker, tapping my nose.

"The ones with the red skulls on them? Those are my favorite pair. Wait, how did you know that?" I ask her in skepticism.

"What kind of stalker would I be if I couldn't see through clothes," she says while sizing me up and licking her lips.

I fruitlessly cover my crotch.

I feel as bare as newborn kitten.

"Teehee. I'd never look through your clothes. I love the anticipation of waiting for you to take a shower," she says, covering her flushed cheeks.

By the moe gods she is cute! I just want to knock her down, pin her to the ground and tickle her until she agrees to be my friend. But I have a much more crafty and subtle approach up my sleeve.

"Do you think Best Friend is asexual?" I ask, breaking through the awkward silence.

"I don't know. He's hard to read. What I do know is that he cares for you very much. But I don't know if he shares the same feelings I do," she says softly, turning away in embarrassment and covering her face.

I flip her around to face me. "I need you to figure out for me? I don't want to ask him. It's too awkward. Plus, I trust you," I say with a sweet smile to mask my lie.

"You want me to seduce your best friend?" she asks with a raised eyebrow.

"I just want you to try. We can at least find out if he likes girls," I say with a confident shrug.

"You really love him, don't you?" she asks with a tear.

99:00

"Whoa, don't get any weird fan-girl ideas here. He's my Best Friend, nothing more, nothing less. Now please find out what turns him on," I say, inadvertently grabbing her hands.

"I'd do anything for you. I'll make him as stiff as your muscles," she giggled, giving me a kiss on the cheek.

I turn my head to her slowly and then smile.

Damn, I'm slick!

The sound of bells jingle in the bushes.

"What's the noise?" I ask, looking around.

Didn't someone just recently talk about bells?

Stalker grabs onto me with a shaky hand. She mouths something to me but I can't quite make it out.

"Are you cold?" I ask.

"Run," she says, with a weak and trembling voice.

The bells get louder and a figure emerges from the bushes. "You must be The Village of Doomed's latest hero. I'm not at all impressed," he says, his cat ears dropping.

What does he mean by latest hero?

Episode 4 Part 2

This is it…the main villain is before me. And damn does he look ridiculous.

He's wearing a pink and white maid outfit with a jewel-encrusted collar. My sworn enemy has fuzzy handcuffs and the most extravagantly bedazzled chastity belt I've ever seen. The fiend's white cat ears look almost real, like the ones from My Little Sister is Obviously the Young One. He also has a long tail with a large pink bow at the end. His heart earrings and rainbow bracelets are just too tacky. His long flowing light pink hair is tied with two dark pink bows. He also has light pink glossy lips and a sick smile.

Just what the hell is this guy? I wasn't aware I let Tumblr design my antagonist. Whatever, at least I'll get some LGBT fans for this…I just hope they actually watch my show.

"I think you're confused Sir, the Gay Pride Parade doesn't set up until next week," I say.

So many things happened that I completely forgot that he was going to show up this episode. But I can manage. If I can just wig him out, I can get out of this mess.

"Greetings, hero. I am The Love Dictator!" he exclaims, sending me a heart sign.

I leap out of the way and then run up to him. My fist meets his face. "My name is Main, and you're Flamboyant Villain," I say, wiping his cooties off on my pants.

No, I'm not being homophobic. I'm just being careful.

The evil fashion disaster does a somersault and lands back on his feet as I rush him. He grabs my fist before it makes contact. His intense pink eyes gaze into me. "How did you know my name was Flam!? And what gives you the right to name me like a pet? I am the king of this country! Whatever I say becomes law!" he yells, his tail moving back and forth in frustration.

And let me guess, this king lives in Glam Castle. I really wish Banana Man had told me this was the guy running the country.

"Main, be careful. His power is unlike any you've faced," says Stalker seriously.

Well it's not like I've been in a martial arts tournament. Of course he's the strongest. He's the main villain. That shit goes without saying.

I wrestle my hand out from his grip. "I'm the Main Character! I can name you whatever I want!" I yell as I punch him again.

His scarfed collar seizes my fist, holding me in place.

"Your naivety is so adorable. Do you have any idea how insignificant you are?" he asks as his hand grabs my cheeks.

This asshole thinks he can target my insecurities. Well too bad for him, I don't have any!

"Leave him alone!" yells Stalker.

"What's this, a little girl is here too? What are you doing here? You know it's dangerous to be in the forest all alone." His scarf slams me to the ground.

"Why do you attack our village? We wouldn't send heroes against you, if you just let us live in peace. Why are you so cruel?" asks Stalker in tears.

"I am The Dictator of Love, not peace. The beauty of love is conflict. I have no need for such boring things as peace. Now come with me, little one. It's not safe here," he says, beckoning her with his hand.

Stalker tries to spit in his face but her aim is off and it lands two feet in front of her. "I'm staying with the hero and he's going to stop you!"

"Poor boy got dragged into your village's hopeless rebellion." His scarf moves in a flash and wraps around Stalker's throat. "I own every inch of land and every creature that walketh upon it. To go against me is to bite into your own heart," he says, strangling her till her eyes bulge.

If her eyes get any bigger, she'll end up looking like a certain live action cyborg loli.

I get back to my feet and I wipe the blood off my chin with a shaky hand.

Come on, this is just like every first encounter. This isn't scary. This is the moment I've been waiting for. I have to show her that I'm a real hero!

"I'm not going to sit here and let you exploit the people and their land. I'm the hero of destiny and if you don't stand down, I will kill you!" I yell, slicing the scarf with a dagger I stole from Assailant.

Yeah! That's right! I'm a hero! I have to fight for justice and shit like that.

The main villain hides himself by expanding his scarf. The scarf flows behind me.

I swipe him as soon as he gets in range.

Flamboyant Villain dodges my punch and grabs my nipples.

I gasp in pain as he twists them swiftly.

He grabs onto my neck. "It's so cute how you fight for that pathetic village. My heart can't bear the way you look at her. It bleeds for you and you alone," he says while fondling my chest with his other hand.

"Wait…Main…you like me?" she asks with extreme blushing.

"It's not like that!" I yell.

I'm not being a tsundere here. I'm not into grade-schoolers. It's that simple.

"I can smell the desire all over you. Your lips beckon her. Oh, you are just so cute! I must have a sample." Flamboyant Villain presses his lips up against mine and gives me a deep passionate kiss.

What is happening? Why is he so good at this? My head feels dizzy. So dizzy.

As I'm being defiled all I can hear is Stalker wailing out in misery.

"I was supposed to take his virginity!" she cries, grabbing Flam's leg.

Despicable. After what he just did, she only thinks of herself.

Flam's eyes tear up upon seeing her. "Such passionate misery. This is the beauty of a broken heart. Cry little one, cry over your defiled lover! Aha-aha-haha-aha!"

That is the most foppish laugh I've ever heard. Damn faggy fop stole my kiss.

I grab onto his arm, crushing it with my romantic rage.

"I was saving my lips for my special someone. You've ruined my manly dream! I'll destroy you!" I exclaim, my eyes catching fire.

Flamboyant Villain slams me to the ground with a single finger and puts on a monocle. "The tragedy of love is truly beautiful! Jealousy, hatred and sorrow all come from the heart's desire to love. Now that I've broken your frail little heart, you've truly awakened. Let the tragedy of your de-virginization sink in! Seize your emotion and thrust it into me!" exclaims Flam, holding his arms wide open.

"Senpai, catch!" yells Stalker, throwing me a vial.

Flamboyant Villain shatters the vial and the gooey fluid inside bursts all over my hair.

I'm going to make him pay for stealing my first kiss!

I scream out in fury, the flames in my hair turning bright gold. I was becoming blond! My hair then shot forth like a shotgun, piercing straight through Flamboyant Villain.

"Such exquisite pain. It's tickling me. You aren't like the others. You are a bundle of fun. I won't kill you just yet. I'll play with you until I get bored, then I'll unravel you into a glorious tapestry of suffering," he says with eyes that shimmer with cruelty.

My hair pulls out from his flesh, soaking his get up with blood.

"You son of a bitch! I'll make you pay for this!" I yell with manly tears.

My hair changes shape, becoming a giant fist.

That's what I'm talking about! Now I can molest cute blondies like Flair!

"What a clever but oh so familiar way to manipulate energy. You're still a bud now. I'm going to wait for you to blossom before I pluck you from the earth. Toodaloo, boy, I look forward to our next encounter," says Flamboyant Villain before my hair fist slams into him.

I wasn't going to let him get away. My rage was now focused on a single target.

"***Fist of Many Many Punches!***" I yell.

Tiny bundles of hair branch out of the massive fist, pummeling Flam gratuitously.

I increase the power of my hair fists. "One of those punches was for Banana Man. I know you stole his daughter."

The evil villain giggles like a kindergartner getting tickled as his body is bruised and bloodied. He lands in a split after smashing through a tree. "If you keep on tickling me, I'm going to pee," he says, crossing his legs.

The scarf buries into the ground and then comes out beneath me. It wraps around my whole body in seconds.

"Mmmm, I can feel your every curve," he says as his scarf feels me up.

Ugh. This creep is making me so uncomfortable.

"Don't hurt him," cries Stalker, grabbing the villain's leg.

"Ah! Those smitten eyes. See how much closer I've brought you two. Aha-Aha!" He creates a scarf with his pink aura and wraps her up.

"Let her go!" I yell.

"Your words are so uninspired. Only true poetry can sway moi." He tosses her onto his shoulder. "If you want your little girlfriend back, then come to my fabulous castle! Oh, but you might want to go back to that pathetic village first. I ordered a raid about an hour ago. Next time we meet bring me some flowers, red roses are my favorite!"

He's getting away with the heroine. I should be happy. But...I'm not. My lips are still burning from his wickedness.

"I'll come for you! It's a pinky promise!" I yell as I rush towards them.

Ugh. That sounded soooo lame.

Scarfs litter the area and mask his escape.

No time for an ending song, I've got to save the village. What the hell, why is the song coming up? Damn it!

Happy music fills the air as a bunch of soldier cat boys burn down the town. People are slaughtered to a joyful beat. I'm really going to kill that flamboyant bastard now. Wait, they're gathered around the temple hospital. And their general is requesting something. The end.

What the hell does he want? Alright, no time for a sneak peek.

Flam's voice suddenly enters my thoughts.

Next time on Main Character. The cute boy struggles to save his girlfriend's pathetic village. Oh my god, he looks just adorable covered in all that blood. Will he make it in time? Or will my forces gain possession of a very special item? Sorry ladies, but I won't be showing up in the next episode. Be sure to keep watching though. I look forward to seeing Main struggle in the maze of his despair."

Ring ring. Ring ring.

I put my finger to my ear.

"Hold it, Plasma Snake," says Best Friend. "You need to swap discs. I know, I know… It's a pain. But you need to swap Disc 1 for Disc two. Do you see the disc labeled '2'?"

"Uh. No," I say.

"Huh? Oh, wait! It's a BOB-ray disc. Double-layered, too – no need to swap."

"Damn it, Otakucon, get a grip!"

"Yeah, what an age we live in, huh, Plasma Snake? Wonder what they'll think of next."

-transmission end-

DISC 2: THE TERROR OF CATBOYS!

THE VILLAGE OF DOOMED

Episode 5 Part 1

Things have escalated at an alarming pace, I must be reaching the mid-point of the season. On an unrelated note, what kind of name is Doomed for a village or anything for that matter? That's like naming your planet Destroiya. Seriously, talk about a bad omen. Okay, now I know what you're thinking: people are dying, every second counts so I shouldn't do an opening. Well that's totally wrong. Openings happen in Za Warudo time, that's elite weeb speak for time stops while they are running. Don't forget this, okay? Gakouin died to pass on this message to us all. Anyways, without any more delay, let's begin the opening.

A flamboyant voice suddenly grates against my ears. "Just who are you talking to, Boiya?"

"Ugh, don't say that. It's creepy. I'm talking to my audience obviously. Been putting on my voice recorder to capture my authentic overreactions to things like most Tubers. As soon as I get home, I'm going to create a new series."

"Well then you best conserve your energy. I'll take over the opening for now," says Flam from inside my head.

"I don't need your sympathy and I certainly don't want you butting in!"

"Too bad! You've been replaced. I'm more popular and so I can do whatever I want. Cue the opening," says Flam.

"I look into the mirror. Oh, I strike a pose! And now I'm brushing my hair lusciously… lusciously. Oh yeah, I'm going to get even hotter! Now there's a slide show of me lying naked with a bunch of girls I don't know. Main did you see yourself on top of me!? Oh yes! Then my hand is reaching out to my dearly departed wife. Why are you surprised? Of course I was married. Now all the people are fondling me. But then I get bored and order my cat boys to slaughter them all. I can't help it; a maiden does get bored after all. I'm now rubbing my nipples on top of a mountain of dead villagers. Nothing gets me off like true love after all! I'm then shot with a gun. I catch the bullet, swallow it and then I slice off the attacker's head with my stylish scarf. I look at my hands to see your precious girlfriend getting one of my famous massages. I'd love to give you one when you come and visit. Glasses Kid is in the back crying like a little baby. I jump up and punch him, creating the title with pink roses. I'm The Love Dictator! Yes yes yes!

Flam Von De Viva! Oh yes! I'm the king of this world! And I'm going to get Main's delectable ass! Why…because I'm just so cute!" exclaims Flam, his voice radiating through my head.

"You took my dramatic theme song and made it all about sex! Just leave me alone!"

"Foolish little treat, we're connected like a Shinigami and his victim."

"Wait you've seen Bleached? Or is that a Dead Note reference?"

"The only entertainment I enjoy is the theatre!"

"Whatever! Just shut up. I'm doing the episode prequel! Don't you dare interrupt me."

"I thought you wanted to skip it. Alright, I'll let you have your little fun this time, my love," says Flam as if he was right next to me.

Ugh, why couldn't my new psychotic admirer be a gorgeous woman with big tits and blue hair like IcDeath? At least I can reason with this creep. Okay, best to keep the recap brief don't want him learning anything he doesn't already know.

Last time on Main Character, Stalker was kidnapped by Flamboyant Villain. He stole my virgin lips, awakening the true power of my awesome hair. Wait, does this make me a Steal Angel? Just before leaving, he said that he sent his forces to attack the Village of Doomed.

"Bravo! You actually did an accurate recap!" exclaims Flam in awe.

"What's that supposed to mean? You only bonded with me recently, no way you know what I've said in past episodes."

"Not another word from you. I won't spoil the surprise. I'll only return when you want to chat. Enjoy the spotlight while you can!" exclaims Flam before leaving my head.

Damn it, that bastard took Stalker away! I was just about to make her my friend too…well, I was working on it. Now I'm faced with a big decision. I should go and save the village. That's sure to yield some major hero points. Then again…I really do want to know B.F.'s sexual preference. Damn it, I've always been indecisive. Wow, this is such a sudden time to reveal this. Big decisive moments are my greatest weakness, that's why Infinite is the only AquaShock game I've played. To understand the severity of this I should explain. One time, Best Friend and I were at a public domain titled theme park. We were holding hands so I wouldn't get lost, it was so cute! He turned to me and asked me what ride I wanted. I looked over the attraction guide, and well, I got overwhelmed. I awoke in a hospital bed and learned that I fainted on the spot. Since then I've decided to leave the decision making to other people. Problem is the only person with me right now is a creepy molester who burns villages for fun.

"Where are we going?" asks a voice behind me.

The voice belonged to Friendship, my rocket launcher buddy. I hardly recognize Ultima since the gun wasn't boiling with rage and bursting with profanity.

Hold up!

The whole time I was talking I was running to the village. He got me distracted so that I would break apart from my team. Well jokes on him. A real hero doesn't need help. All I have to do is take out some enemy fodder. Cheap hero points here I come!

Does that make me like BarnaB? And is that a bad thing? No more distractions, I have to stay focused. Falcon was killed by nameless asura and I don't want to succumb to the same tragic fate.

Friendship pipes up behind me. "You know, you're the first person to ever treat me like…well, a person. If you're really going in there to save those moving targets, then I'll help out. But I'm doing it my way. Shoot to kill. So don't you dare try to aim anywhere but the flesh."

"Yes Sir, uh, I mean Ultima." I pat my gun. "Hey, so what brought this on? Emotional heart to heart is supposed to come after we've had a cool fight."

"I saw you and your bestie fighting…let's just say it brought up some memories. Friendly fire is no joke so don't ever ask me to attack an ally."

"I'm not asking you for anything, but I really appreciate you offering to help."

"Get ready. There might be some hiding just outside the village."

I scan the trees and spot one. The soldier's jade eyes gleam in the night.

"Easy target. Okay, now keep me steady. Brace me against your chest. That's it."

"How about after this, we go find some lovely ladies to polish you," I say with a grin.

"Don't ever assume my sexuality, you little $#!+. And stay focused. If you're mind isn't in the present moment, you'll die and I'll be abandoned." Friendship's voice quivered.

Even rocket launchers have feelings in this place. Oooh, I hope it can transform into a big breasted ninja girl. Not that I'm assuming it's sex; just keeping my hopes up is all.

I wasn't paying attention and the tree in the distance is aflame. Oh, and apparently, I fell on my ass from the recoil.

That's odd. I didn't have trouble with it before.

"Phew! Haven't gotten a kill in a long time. Feels good to be back. Really good!" says my sadistic weapon.

I look ahead to see a wooden barrier with a cat face on it.

"Looks like they've blocked off the entrance. Want to blast through?" I ask, crouching down.

"I need you to load up a couple rounds. Say something corny about love or some $#!+."

"Umm, okay. Love is the most powerful magic there is. How was that?"

"Ugh, sickening. But not enough. If you don't mean it, then it won't refuel me."

"How does that fuel you?"

"I'm the ultimate hero weapon! Friendship speeches give me ammunition and charisma powers up my shots. Don't think that means I'm dependent on you!"

"I didn't think that! Not for a moment. Okay." I take a deep breath. "Friendship is more important than family," I say with a bit of a dark edge.

Friendship shoots out a powerful beam that not only pierces the barrier, but explodes into a building in the distance.

"That was freaking epic!" I exclaim, rushing behind a tree while the smoke clears.

"You mean it? You…really mean it?"

Tears start pouring from my weapon.

"Umm, are you okay?"

"Yeah, of course I am, you little $#!+. Why wouldn't I be? Just uh, give me a moment."

Shit! A CatBoy spots me.

I come out from cover and fire.

A blast of water comes out from my emotional killing machine.

The CatBoy cries out and runs off in tears.

"Phew, I feel better now. Just had a little something in my heart. It's gone. Let's get back to killing these pussies. Yes, ha! I tricked the auto censor. I meant that in the vulgar way but it didn't register! Victory!" exclaims Friendship.

"Hey, I don't think my female viewers will appreciate you using pussy as an insult."

"Nobody cares. Go in, but do it slowly. Got it?"

I officially arrive at the Village of Doomed. The screaming cries of agony and smell of smoke put me on edge.

I'm a four-year old going into a warzone. Damn, I'm epic.

I rush up and lean against the wall.

I didn't notice the wall before. Hope that doesn't mean there are giant eunuchs in the area.

"Now things will get tricky," say Friendship. Save who you can, but don't think you can save everyone. This is a war zone not a playground. You don't want to mess this up. This village hired you to protect them. Show those @$$holes you're worthy!"

That's right. This is the first village I've ever rescued. A hero's first village liberation is a very important moment in their legacy. I've got to do this right, with as few casualties as possible. Well, that might be a little difficult.

I peek out from behind cover.

Thank you, Gears, for everything you've taught me.

The village looks a bit different then I remember. Half of it is on fire and there are bodies and blood littering the streets. There's a birdbath too and a little bird cleaning his feathers with the blood. This is awkwardly cute.

Jade eyes spot me. I hoist up Friendship.

If I'm going to be a great hero, I need to at least fool people into thinking I'd give up my life for background characters.

"Don't shoot! My name is Carl. I like living," says the CatBoy.

My weapon glares at him. "Sounds like a fake name and he's hiding something behind his back. Just lift me and I'll do the rest."

They have names. They aren't supposed to have names. Every marine killed by the Mujiwaras was nameless. That's how it should be.

"Why shouldn't I kill you?" I ask, half-raising my gun.

"I'm just a recruiter. I don't kill people. I find the cute ones, rescue them from the carnage and bring them to the Caste of Dreams."

"Hands above your head. No sudden movements," I say, noticing four other CatBoys approaching.

Shit. This isn't easy. Good thing I have hair power now!

"Go hair! Destroy my enemies!" I exclaim to the skies.

Nothing happens, well other than me getting shot in the leg with a crossbow.

Friendship fires a shot, but it misses and explodes into a building instead.

Someone stands in front of me.

Nice legs. Wait, is that Best Friend?

"Have no fear because I am here," says the boy with muscular legs in the worst Tall Might impression ever. They throw a Molotov cocktail while yelling "Virginia Smash!"

Another one drops out behind the enemy wearing an orange jumpsuit with an Uchihot emblem. "Nasuke is here, you better believe it!" he exclaims before shooting a swirling wind of electricity at his enemy.

One final wannabe shouts atop a building. She is a bit chubby but not obese and is wearing a mock Sailor Uniform that says "Cosplay is not Consent." Only girls who want to be touched would wear something like that. Too bad I'm a gentlemen and won't hit on the mentally challenged.

The young woman strikes a pose and says "In the name of the moon, I shall fuck you up!" She leaps down in front of the cat boy and whacks him repeatedly with her staff. He blocks with a bouquet and gets down on his knees. After some unintelligible dialog, he picks her up bridal style and runs off.

Friendship mutters beneath me. "Damn traitor. Get up, you don't want to be upstaged by the Shounen Force!"

"The what?"

"They're a band of heroes who have been hired by your village. Why aren't you getting up?"

"See, the problem is once I've fallen, I can't get up. I'm not like Noruto, Luffi or Gokun. I have a back lock that kicks in. It doesn't hurt but it renders me useless."

"Press my face into the dirt," says Friendship.

"Huh?"

"You need the support. Just do it! You're my first hero and I'm not going to let you die. Got it, @$$hole?"

"Yeah." I press Ultima against the ground, but I still topple over.

A hand reaches out to me and hoists me up.

115:00

"Yo kid, you alright?" asks Nasuke. He lifts me up, or is it a she? Sometimes it's hard to tell with these cosplayers.

"I'm fine. I have Friendship."

"That hunk of junk is your friend?" He or she scratches their chin.

"Point me at 'em so I can blast that @$$hole to hell!" yells Friendship.

"You're not from the Overt Leaf Village are ya, kid?"

"I'm from Japan, the capital of Earth," I say with a grin.

"You must be new. We're hero team Battle Ships."

"You mean like General Battle Ship?" I ask.

"No. Like anime ships. I'm Nasuke." He throws an electric kunai at a CatBoy that was leaping down to attack. The wannabe ninja then pulls it out. "It's way harder to fight without killing in the real world. Gratsu, this one needs healing!"

A short figure peeks out from behind a barrel. "I'm too busy healing the villagers. Let 'em bleed out! I'm all fired up!"

Nasuke lets go of my hand and shouts. "You can't just randomly say that without context."

"You dressed me up like this! I'm a girl damn it!"

"Stay in character or we will abandon you!" yells Nasuke.

"So, who are the others?" I ask.

"The strong guy with the black hair is DekuMight. And the girl who betrayed is MarsMoon. You can join us too. I can make you a ZoSan cosplay. I bet you'd look so hot!" Nasuke exclaims, shaking his or her hips.

"I already have my own team. I don't want to be part of your band of sex starved gay shippers," I say, stepping back.

"Well then go die. The world is better without homophobes."

DekuMight approaches us. "Young man, stop flirting. We need to find a way to put out the fires."

"Don't order me around. I wanted you to be BakuDeku. You do realize that All Mighty is old enough to be Dekku's dad, right? You're a grown man don't you get how weird it is to go up to rando boys and ask them to swallow your DNA?" asked Nasuke.

"At least my ship isn't denied in cannon."

Ugh, why did they have to bring that up?

Friendship mutters to me so the others can't hear. "Hey, find some cover. I'm sensing more enemies on my radar."

I look at the burning buildings around me. "Wait, you can shoot water, right?"

"Yeah, that's right. No matter what your gender is it's perfectly acceptable to cry!" yells Friendship.

"We can put out the buildings with your water bullets! Then we'll beat these wannabees!" I cheer, hoisting up Friendship.

"Is all you care about some damn scoreboard. Ugh, I thought you were different."

I spot the brothel.

Best Friend isn't here to tell me no. Now may be my only chance to see what mysteries await inside.

I notice a little boy trapped under a piece of rubble. I also notice there are three CatBoy soldiers nearby.

I can't let him die like Uchio.

You may be wondering why an anime character's death affects me so much that I'll stupidly risk my life to save a kid. Well if you are wondering that, then you obviously haven't seen Clannaid's after story.

Why is everything going hazy? Is this from blood loss or, oh shit. I'm having a flashback! In the middle of a warzone my mind is wandering, damn it!

Best Friend and I are snuggled up to each other inside a blanket. He grabs my hand. "Why is he taking her outside. It's too cold. She's too weak."

I watch my dearest friend's crimson eyes water up.

"Uchio! Uchio!" he cries out. "Wake up! Wake up!"

For the first time ever. I see my Best Friend swept in tears. He hugs me tightly and sobs against my shoulder. "I'm sorry. I'm so sorry."

That night he fell asleep in my arms. I had to hold back my own tears till he was out. I then sobbed myself to sleep.

Every time a child dies, Best Friend cries his eyes out. I won't ask you to donate to save starving children while I take ninety-nine percent of the profit. But I don't ever want to see those fearless eyes swept up in misery ever again.

Before I realize it, I'm just above the injured kid.

"You're a good guy, Main," says Friendship.

I grab the heavy wood and try to lift it.

"Move aside!" DekuMight slams into me. "We're saving everyone. Don't get in our way."

A CatBoy with a black German soldier complete with a cute sailor hat get up and tosses a knife.

Hair, grab the knife!

My hair doesn't budge.

The knife pierces the kids throat and he cries as he drowns in his own blood.

My mind jumps back to the moment when my Best Friend is in misery and I'm unable to do anything.

I was so helpless. I still am. I've always been helpless. And now a little boy is dead because I was too weak.

"Why did you stop me!" I yell.

My hair suddenly whips into action, becoming a massive fist that slams into DekuMight. The cosplayer is sent off his feet and crashes into a building where he is buried.

"What the fuck did you just do?" asked Nasuke, aiming a kunai at me.

The CatBoy general smiles. "You're already fighting amongst each other. Allow me to assist you." He takes out a weapon.

Can a musical instrument be a weapon? Well, the legendary devil hunter seems to think so; who am I to argue.

"He has a harp." Friendship's voice is as cold as death.

"Is that a problem?" I ask.

Nasuke waves at his or her allies. "Everyone the CatBoy general is here! Forget the villagers! Get the hell away! I'm going to take down this bastard, believe it!"

"What are you doing, run!" yells friendship.

"Where?" I ask, wiping my tears.

"Somewhere with a lot of noise!"

My eyes shift to the brothel. "Well, if I have no choice."

I run off, abandoning the desperate screams of the villagers.

"Hero, save me." "My child is in that building!" "You're our hero, damn it. Do something!"

A voice plays in my head. "Their cowardly hero flees from a threat he doesn't understand into a building that will give him a reward he doesn't deserve."

Even my own ego knows I'm a piece of shit.

Wait, that isn't my voice.

"Poor pathetic boy. Come into my kingdom and all your worries will melt away," says Flam.

119:00

The sound of his voice is completely overshadowed by the beautiful sight before me.

The brothel is a disco themed magical wonderland. Rays from the central disco ball hit the tiles beneath, shifting their color. CGI fish swim along the walls and sexy women are fighting CatBoy soldiers while wearing fetish gear.

Heaven exists after all.

"You're finally here. Not that I was waiting for you. Well, are you just going to stand there?" asks a girl in a police military hybrid suit. She swings a massive pink mace with red spikes into an enemy CatBoy, bursting his head like a watermelon.

I turn my head and barf.

Everything looks way more gruesome when it's live action.

"Nice one! That is disgusting." She giggles and then covers her mouth. "You didn't hear anything, got it?"

Yes! A tsundere tomboy! Finally, this place is starting to feel more like a dream than a nightmare.

A CatBoy in a blue school swimsuit and black-tie lands before me. Is he wearing bunny slippers? Oh shit, he has a sailor hat too. That means he's a general, right?

"Get behind me, boy. Not that I care if you die," says the tsundere.

Oh, she totally cares. I have to get her to call me idiot! I just have to!

"No need to be so formal. I prefer you call me master," I say with one hell of a butler's charm.

The tsundere blushes, which regrettably leaves her open to the enemy's attack.

" **SPICY BARRAGE!**" The general slams his fist into her, sending my dream girl off her feet. The cutie pie tomboy is blasted up and down by the insane recoil.

Whoa! Whoa! Whoa! Was that a kugi punchi!?

The CatBoy turns to me. "If you don't tell me where it is, I'll have to kill you," he says, not being specific at all.

Alright no biggie. This is where the viewer gets to see how the hero's training has paid off. Only problem is, I don't know how to activate my power and I haven't trained with it at all.

I throw a chair at the enemy. He punches it aside and crosses his arms beneath his chest. "That all ya got?"

Hold up, that's not a guy's chest. Those are boobs. It that a girl?

"She is indeed," says Flam, who apparently can read my thoughts. "Do you want her, Main? I could turn her into your pet if you give up on this pointless rebellion."

A real-life tomboy cat-girl.

"Is your name Rover?" I ask.

"Huh? That's a dog's name. Are you making fun of me?" she asks, rushing toward me.

A swordswoman dressed as a miko, or shrine maiden for those of you who aren't cultured, steps into the CatGirl general's path and takes a swipe.

The CatGirl's body bends back at an awkward angle, avoiding the strike.

"You will not harm the Hero of Destiny," says the miko before rushing in.

"Swipe her feet," says another soldier. "She's only practiced so she's never had to properly guard herself."

"Ugh! Nobody asked for your advice!" yells the tomboy CatGirl before knocking the miko off her feet and following up with a punch that sent her flying through the roof.

I take a closer look at the smart soldier. Well first off, it's obviously a girl and those ears are obviously fake. Wait, I know who she is! Her blond and orange hair looks just like a fruit bowl, after all.

Yes! I found Banana Man's daughter! If I save her here, then I get some extra XP before I have to storm Glam Castle to rescue Stalker.

121:00

"Your father is Banana Man, right?" I ask to the girl who is in the corner of the room.

"I have no father," she says in a cold tone.

"He misses you! He wants you to come home."

"I burnt down his precious produce stand myself. I'm not coming back to this worthless village. It's all burning down tonight!" she exclaims, her eyes flashing with cruelty.

He probably should have mentioned that she's a psychopath. Details do matter.

The CatGirl tomboy, having defeated all the fetish warriors, returns her gaze to me. "I'll give you two options: come with me to the castle or run away from the village and don't come back. There is a third option where I kill you for not picking option one or two, but you don't want that."

Could she know about my weakness? Flam, did you tell her?

"You think I'd share your precious secret? You wound me," says Flam.

I should ask Friendship for advice. No. My weakness cost that poor boy his life. I have to step up.

"Hey, woman who breaks the gender boundary, I'm making a decision."

"Well, what is it?"

"I've decided to follow the wisdom of D. and just take the most dangerous route in all cases."

"What are ya, some kinda idiot?" she asks, leaning over and giving me a nasty look.

Tsunderes aren't quite as charming in real life apparently. I'm glad I already have a totally real girlfriend who isn't a pillow.

I lift up Friendship. "My friends are my power!"

The whole rocket launcher glows before releasing a super powerful explosion. The whole area before me is consumed in a crimson flame.

"Not a bad shot!" The tomboy general has her claws dug into the disco ball above.

She dodged it! They aren't supposed to dodge! Ceaza Clown didn't dodge! Why did she freaking dodge!?

The CatGirl general drops down and kicks the bazooka out of my hand.

"A failed weapon for a failed hero. I've seen all kinds, but none are as pitiful as you." She kicks me down.

Oh yes. Keep underestimating me, bitch.

My hair pushes off the ground and then wraps around my fist. I sock her in the face, knocking her off her feet.

"Did that hurt?" I ask, my hair bringing her in for another punch to the face.

"Those eyes. Those aren't contacts. I thought he was the only one."

"Can we not play the pronoun game? Who is he?"

"You're the reason we're here, silver eyes." She punches my hair but her fist passes through hits the ground. The floor shatters and she is flung backward. The tomboy general tugs on my hair and brings me toward her next attack.

I have to dodge. A single hit will...

My mind goes blank.

I slam against the ground.

Blood everywhere. What's that white...oh god those are my ribs.

My chest is burst open and my bones are jutting out.

"Oh, you don't look to good," says Flam in my head.

Great. The last thing I'm going to hear is this asshole.

"You poor thing," says my sworn enemy. "I expected you to flee. I didn't order her to kill you. Such a shame. Your plot armor weakened when I stole your theme-song. How very interesting. When I bond with someone, I feel their pain. I'll be with you till the very end."

123:00

"No. I'm not going to die here! *I REJECT*!"

Crap! There's an orphan in the script! An orphan is what you call a sentence that takes up a whole page and is left all alone. Hey look, it's no longer an orphan now! Sweet!

My First Village

Episode 5 Part 2

The CatGirl's fist speeds toward me but my hair yanks her foot, making her miss. *Did that really just work!*

"This is a power unlike any I've seen," says Flam.

"Are you just sucking dick or do you actually mean that?"

There's an orange mist around me. What happened?

"I must leave you for now. Your life is far more important than I thought."

Good. Finally got rid of that creep.

The tomboy lands and glares at me. "Ugh. Apparently, I'm not allowed to kill you."

My shadow suddenly moves in front of me and takes form.

Oh, it's Assailant.

"Where is my daughter!?" His swirling eyes quiver with worry. "Where is she…where's my little Annolette?" asks Assailant, his body phasing in and out.

"You're not supposed to say her real name," says Best Friend, leaning against the entrance to the brothel. His eyes turn to me. "And you, young man. What do you think you're doing here?"

"She brought me here!" I point to the tomboy. "And she tried to get me drunk too!"

"Diagonal or vertical?" asks Best Friend, hoisting up the fallen miko's sword.

Assailant pops up in front of him. "Save your power. I can take this one."

"He's going to send his blades out at your sides," says Fruity.

125:00

Assailant's head turns to face me as he sends out his sharpened tendrils at the enemy. "Where is my daughter?"

"Shouldn't you focus on the enemy?" I ask, with a nervous grin.

The tomboy leaps over his attack and punches his tendrils. Gushing sounds were accompanied with purple fluids spraying the area.

She can punch through those.

"Fire," says Assailant.

"That's right," says the tomboy. "This whole place is going to burn!"

Assailant pulls apart his chest.

Six arrows shoot through the hole.

"I didn't know they had another helper," says Fruity, with horror in her eyes.

Two arrows pierce the tomboy's knees, another two gouge her eyes. The final two find a new home in her heart and throat.

Best Friend rushes up, pulls the blood out from the wounds and shapes it into a sword while shivering.

Is that blood lust or is he scared?

"**Crimson Karma.**" Best Friend slices her legs and arms off before severing her head.

Wow. That was pretty gruesome.

The blood from the severed neck splashes on his face.

He flips his hair to shake it off, but it just serves to make it sparkle in the disco light.

He turns his attention to Fruity and speeds up to her.

She shrieks and shields her face.

"If you can see the future, you shouldn't be afraid," he says, cleaning the blood out from his hair with trembling fingers and a quivering lip.

"You've killed so many and…you're…"

Best Friend places the sword against her throat. "I'm here to save you but if you say even one word about me, I'll have to deliver your head to your father," he says, slowly cutting into her neck.

Fruity nods and soils herself.

I really respect the dedication he has to keeping his mysterious charm strong. The more I don't know about him, the more I want to know!

"The threat has been neutralized. So, where is she? If you don't say, I may end up going a bit loopy and cutting up everything in sight," says Assailant as his body is distorting and sharpening.

"Everyone just relax." Glasses Kid walks into the brothel. He's wearing headphones with kitty paw emblems. "I'm sure there's a perfectly logical explanation for her sudden disappearance. I've thought of over thirty possible scenarios. If we brainstorm together, we can decide which one's the most likely."

"Want last mushroom?" asks Brawny Babe, totally not reading the serious vibes.

"Nice shooting," says Best Friend, pulling out the arrows from the CatGirl general's corpse. "And good job tracking Main down."

"Today on vacation. Very busy rest of year," she says, turning away.

Best Friend turns to Assailant. "Control yourself. Your daughter would disown you if you harmed the hero. And I would make some new gloves out of her skin."

Assailant's body collapses into a puddle. "I'm just worried about my little girl."

"Main, do you know anything?" asks Best Friend, approaching me.

When he looks at me with those eyes I just…

I fall to the ground.

Best Friend rushes up to me and pulls me up before I hit the floor. He presses his forehead to mine.

"You're conflicted about something. Go ahead Main, tell me. I promise to make it all better," says Best Friend, sweetly combing my hair.

Heaven isn't a place. It's a person. I feel so warm.

"We need to know what happened," says Best Friend.

Glasses Kid stands atop the bar counter. "Flamboyant Villain appeared! He took Stalker! And the Village of Doomed is under attack!" He hopes down and smiles at me. "Is that correct?"

I nod. "I don't know what to do. Please, Best Friend, decide for me!" I beg him, grabbing onto his shirt in tears…manly tears.

Best Friend slaps me.

He actually slapped me.

"You're our leader. You have to be the one to make the decisions now. You're the hero here, I'm just supposed to stand around and look cool, right?" he asks with his trademark invisible smile.

"She's my daughter! And it's my village. If anyone should decide, it should be me!" yells Assailant, standing erect like a pillar.

"Nope. That's actually completely wrong." Glasses Kid shoots a confident look at Assailant who glares at him. The know-it-all turns away. "Considering you are emotionally invested, you're actually the least likely to make the right decision. I'm currently deciding the best course of action, taking into consideration any and all extraneous variables, of course."

"No, Best Friend is right. I'm the leader of this team. The decision rests on me. I've decided…since Stalker is Assailant's daughter and it's his village, he should decide!" I exclaim with great conviction, shoving the burden away.

Now all those lives aren't my responsibility.

"You've grown into a fine young man. Knowing when to let other's decide shows true leadership. I couldn't be more proud of you," says Best Friend, giving me a proud pat on the back.

Assailant body twists as he speaks. "I murdered my parents because of this damned village. Then I was put through grueling training for the next fifteen years of my life. There is nothing in existence that I despise more than that village. Despite all that, it's my only home. It's where I raised Stalker. I have so many fond memories. And they will forever be memories. Let it burn to the ground. We have to go rescue my daughter!" exclaims Assailant firmly.

"Last call for mushroom. Still hot," tempted Brawny Babe, desperately eager to make conversation.

"It looks like my inference was spot on. I can still impress myself even now!" cheers Glasses Kid, patting his back.

"Do you know where Glam Castle is?" I ask Assailant.

"It's right past the Bridge of Collapse. I'll get us there in no time," says Assailant.

This doesn't feel right. There's only one choice here that makes any sense. Time for me to be both a leader and a hero.

"Go on ahead without us. I'm not going to just ignore the cries of those starving people. Best Friend, Brawny Babe, Glasses Kid, we're going back to the village. I wish you luck in saving your daughter," I say to Assailant before hoisting up Friendship and rushing off in the other direction.

"I'm not sure if you made the right choice," says Glasses Kid, being carried by Brawny Babe as we exit the building.

"That's not important. As long as he makes a decision and sticks with it, he'll grow stronger. I'm proud of you Main," smiled Best Friend, speed-walking right next to me.

"I guess no want mushroom?" asks Brawny Babe, poking my shoulder.

"I'll take it if you'll join my team," I say with a slick smile.

"Temporary only. Many things to do. Busy woman," she lied.

"Of course," I say, snatching the mushroom of alliance from her grip.

Ah, nothing like the sweet taste of psychological manipulation.

Best Friend pulls the blood out of a body and shapes it into a spear. He tosses it into an incoming enemy soldier. "Main, I saw what you did back there. You've unlocked your potential as well."

"Yeah, and I did it all on my own. So uh, how did you do it?" I ask Best Friend.

"I accepted my own fabricated truth. Then I was able to manipulate blood. It was rather simple, nothing all that interesting," he says, looking so incredibly cool as he tosses blood kunai at two enemies above us.

"Hey guys, do you think I'll gain a new ability?" asks Glasses Kid excitedly.

"Not likely. Little coward boy only hide," says Brawny Babe.

"Hey, at least I can dodge!" he retorted angrily.

"I'll never understand the point of dodging," says Best Friend coolly, shielding me from an incoming arrow. He sharpens the arrows tip with the blood from his injury before sending it back at the enemy.

"Never get caught. No need to dodge," says Brawny Babe, waiting for the enemy to take aim before firing an arrow in their skulls.

"We don't have time to waste on unimportant henchmen," says Best Friend, piercing his sharpened hand through one of the CatBoys.

Blood burst out from the soldier's chest. Best friend molds the blood into a sword and then solidifies it. With a single elegant slash, two thugs lose their heads.

"I think I've got the hang of this," says Best Friend calmly.

Wow, looking at this village now I'm really able to admire its beauty. The fire and smoke really give it personality. Most of the buildings are made from wood and leaves, so the flames spread very quickly. It's a bit too hectic for a first village, but I can handle it.

Another cat boy leaps into our path.

"Okay Glasses Kid, you take care of the next one," I say, waiting for a large crowd to show everyone my new ability.

"I'm not a fighter!" yells Glasses Kid, holding onto Brawny Babe's leg.

A rope wraps around his neck and pulls him into the arms of a deranged cat boy.

"Aren't you just adorable? You should join us," says the henchman.

"Wow, does this gun really work?" asks Glasses Kid, reaching into the thug's pocket. He aims the gun right at the soldier and fires it, releasing a water bullet. He took this moment to slip out of the criminal's hands and join up with us.

"Why do you have such a useless weapon?" asks Brawny Babe, aiming right at the murderer's neck.

"I'm a recruiter. I'm sent in to find possible allies!" he says, crying pathetically.

Oh great, another one of these guys.

"What the hell are they after?" I ask, taking the initiative and grabbing him by his collar.

"Our king wants you! We're after your prophecy. Now please don't kill me," he cries.

"Evil deserves no mercy," I say, holding Friendship up.

"Justice is pointless. I'll deal with him," says Best Friend, putting his hand on my gun and lowering it.

"No. As a hero, I need to fight for that shit," I say, pulling the trigger.

The bastard's head was blown to bits.

Why do I feel like I did something bad? Oh, it's probably just my stomach reacting to that mushroom.

"Blood and gore! Now that's what I'm talking about. Maybe I'll stay with you, after all," says Friendship as if Ultima had a choice.

Best Friend turns to the gun. "Thanks for keeping him safe."

"Um, guys. Did you not hear what he said?" I ask. "They're after my prophecy! The stone slab should be in the hospital. But do you really think a hunk of rock can control me?" I ask my team.

"I assure such absurdities are absolutely impossible," reassures Glasses Kid, climbing on Brawny Babe's shoulder.

"Whether it does or doesn't is irrelevant. I'm not going to leave something that important to chance. Main, lead the way. I've always lacked a sense of direction," says Best Friend, his hair shimmering in the moonlight.

"Wait one freaking second…where the hell is Boobs?" I ask suddenly.

"Assailant has. Keeps safe inside body," replies Brawny Babe.

"And you just let her leave!? What the hell?" I yell furiously.

"She hasn't done anything for the team. She's just a pillow," says Glasses Kid.

"And what have you accomplished, you little shit!?" I ask him angrily.

"We all have a role to play. We need to keep moving!" yells Best Friend, creating a mist of blood to give us some cover. "War zones are where I function the best."

Some village soldiers meet up with us, wearing leaf armor.

Are these heroes too? They look so generic. Where's Nasuke?

"You're a hero, right?" asks the least frightened of the bunch.

I point to my spiky hair.

"Where do you need us? We're ready to give our lives for the village." He turns to the other four frightened young men. "Right?"

They nod nervously.

"Okay. Here's what you're going to do." I beckon them all to come close. "You all have basic colored hair so that means you're basically fodder to make the cat soldiers seem strong. You need to find a fruit stand, get some grapes and mash them into your hair. Get some color and some style or else you will die!"

"And stay away from the South Side," says Glasses Kid. "The digital map I borrowed says there's a CatBoy general there."

Must be the one with the harp.

"How are you so brave?" asks a soldier, using blood to paint his hair red.

132:00

I smile and look at Best Friend. "I've always had someone to support me."

"Yuck," says Friendship. "That came from the heart, didn't it? Yeah, I'm ready to blast some @$$holes!"

I turn to Glasses Kid. "Can you make my gun sad?"

Glasses Kid gives me a thumbs up and then turns to Friendship. "Your creators, they didn't love you, did they?"

Friendship whines and fires a continuous stream of water.

Brawny Babe hoists me up and swings me around.

It only takes a couple minutes for us to put out the fires in the area.

We exit the blood-cloud and notice something concerning.

There was a massive group of about thirty CatBoy soldiers. They were cheering as if they had won.

Did they already gain control of my prophecy? Am I doomed to follow the script of that deranged lunatic?

"You called!?" asks Flam, screaming directly into my mind.

"How? I thought you left my head," I say softly.

"I only left for a moment. We're connected, like chocolate and kisses, tee-hee."

"Main, um who are you talking to?" asks Glasses Kid confused.

"Are you really Izumii-kun?" asks Best Friend with a look of concern.

He knows me so well. An anime reference is just the remedy I need for all the crazy shit that's been going on.

"We need to force our way in. I won't let them take your future."

Oooh! This seems like the perfect place to end the episode. Cliffhangers rule!

"Allow me to handle the ending for you," says Flam.

Stalker is relaxing in my castle. She's eating delicacies while drinking fine wine. She slides down a massive indoor slide into my natural Jacuzzi. We are splashing each-other and playing Marco Polo with my troops. I then pick her up and bring her to the dungeon. She gives me some advice and then we have a picnic on the roof.

What the hell is wrong with this guy? And why does Stalker get to be treated like a queen? And hold up!

"There wasn't even any music!" I yell furiously.

"I just wanted to know how she was doing. Soon she will be another one of my willing subjects. My fun-loving personality seizes the heart of every lady I meet," says Flam.

Great, so he has a hero's charisma and a villain's heart.

"Okay, let me do the episode preview at least," I say assertively.

"All yours," says Flam.

That was nice of him. Wait. Am I being swayed too?

Next time on Main Character. I have to fight to protect the big stone slab of prophecy. The entire building becomes surrounded by cat boys and several generals appear. Join me next week to see me kick all their asses!

Protecting My Destiny

Episode 6 Part 1

My prophecy is at stake. Damn it, I don't want to be Flam's slave. I want to be free! That bastard already stole my virginity! I won't let him take my future! I'm going to protect my destiny! Alright, go ahead Flam, initiate the opening.

"You're letting me. I'm honored, really."

"You owe me one, got it?"

"Oooh, what sort of favor would you like?"

Ugh, his voice gives me chills.

"Just hurry up and do the opening song."

"It will be my pleasure. I look outside my windows. Auh, I see your eyes. And now I'm doting on you chronically…chronically. Oh no, I'm going to get a heartache! Now there's a slide show of pictures of us on romantic dates. Main, did you see my flushed cheeks when you kissed me? Oh my! Then my hand is reaching out to your rosy tushy. Of course I want to give those cheeks a good squeeze. Now you are tickling me. But then I get excited and order my cat boys to tie me up. I love S&M! I'm now rubbing your nipples on top of a pyramid of loyal subjects. Nothing gets me off like true love after all! I'm then shot with a gun of love! I catch the bullet, lick it, and then I rip open my own shirt with my stylish scarf. I look at my hands to see your fragile chest getting one of my famous massages. So that's what true love feels like…you crave it, don't you? Glasses Kid is in the back, lecturing me about the historical roots of homosexuality. I jump up and hug him, creating the title with red hearts. I'm The Love Dictator! Yes yes yes! Flam von da Viva! Oh yes! I'm The King of the world! And I'm going to get Main's shut in heart! Why…because I'm just so in love!" exclaims Flam, his voice radiating through my head.

I think he might have a crush on me. Anyways, go ahead, do the prequel.

"You spoil me. Alright, last time on Main Character. After overcoming his indecision and finally deciding to confess his love to me, he rounded up his teammates. Assailant couldn't believe his confession, so he left on a journey to sabotage our love. Main killed one of my fellow CatGirls because he was jealous that I've banged her in every room of my castle. He finally arrives just outside the medical tent where he had first arrived in my kingdom, and he's getting anxious for our date. But I was still preparing myself. A maiden must be presentable after all. I'll be there as soon as I get my makeup finished.

And I thought I was delusional and conceited. Damn it, I have to get more powerful. I can't let him beat me.

"Hey, don't you dare come here. I'm going to come there and kick your ass. Also, that prequel made no sense."

"That's the idea. A hero can shape reality with their will. Hmm, let's see. You let a bunch of villagers die while your heroine is here with me. Sounds like you're not much of a hero after all. I'm taking over. You've disappointed me."

I didn't know he believed in me. Great, I'm even letting down my enemies. I'm the Dam Hibiki of heroes; a total failure!

Stalker looks up at me with sparkling eyes. "Are you talking to Main?"

"Sorry my pet. We just got disconnected," I say, patting her head.

"Don't touch me." She pulls back and hisses. "Is he coming to rescue me?"

"He's running late, but don't worry, I've got a whole evening of fun planned for us!" My scarf tickles her itty-bitty nose.

"You're not going to torture me?"

"Heavens no! I'd never harm a child…without reason," I say with a sly smile.

I make deviousness sexy!

"Let me go. Main…he isn't ready to storm your castle…"

Oh, that boy can shove his battering ram into my castle any day he wants.

"He's not strong enough! Please, just let me go. I'll uh, what do you want in exchange?"

"I simply want to show you my palace. I have deep respect for your kind. Such tragic creatures…"

"Stop. If you connected with Main, then he may overhear this conversation."

"What is your name? Your real name?"

"My real name doesn't matter. I'm Stalker now."

I hoist her onto my shoulders and clap my hands. The trees part and my glorious castle is in full view.

The castle shines like a glittery palace, one that little girls dream of going to. The windows are all stained glass, but with bright sunny colors and images of hearts and stars. A permanent rainbow showers the pinnacle of the center tower and frames the whole castle with its loving vibrancy. The pink hedge maze shifts as I walk through it, giving me a straight entry into my kingdom.

"Is that a pony?" asks Stalker, her voice squeaking.

Ah, the joys of childhood. My daughter always wanted a pony, but I was hopeless then. Ah, I've come so far.

"It's an alicorn, but it's shy so it only shows its true self to those it trusts. If you want to see it, you may have to stay here a few days."

"What is the rent like?" asks Stalker, searching her shirt for her coin purse.

"What sort of monster charges their captives. You're a hostage, my dear, so you get the absolute best hospitality."

"You're not as bad as the village elder's say. When you aren't burning down houses and slaughtering people's parents, well, you're a pretty nice guy," she says, smiling up at me.

I seize my chest.

She's rather powerful. To think her cuteness could break through my defenses so easily.

My scarf caresses my cheek till I calm down.

"I used to wonder why princess would always get captured. It bothered me as a young boy who longed for a fairy tale life. Then I started kidnapping girls, well I prefer the term "surprise adoption!" I lift her off my shoulders and snuggle her lovingly. "Villains have money and class. The princess is free of her responsibilities and all the familial politics of siblings poisoning each other for the throne. Think of your stay here as a forced vacation. You've earned it, my dear."

Oh, Cindy. I would have given you the world if I could have.

"I'm no princess, but I suppose I can stay…at least until the pretty pony sprouts wings like a beautiful butterfly," says Stalker, waving at the mystical stallion.

"He can be your very own Swifty."

I strike a sultry pose, causing my draw bridge to awaken and lower itself.

"Is it alive? I think I saw eyes."

"It's a modified wood elder. They aren't particularly cute, but they are made for defensive purposes and by only the strongest of mages, mind you."

"I once knew a mage."

"Really? You don't see many these days."

"That's because your forces killed them." She glares at me with her shiny eyes.

"Forget about the small stuff." I hoist her over the moat. "Behold, only the most beautiful breeds exist here."

Fish that radiate different colored lights notice the young girl. They bend the light and fuse them together, riding it up to her to give her feet fishy kisses.

"Aww, that tickles. I thought ChromaCarp were a myth."

"They are. This is a wonderland, so all manner of myths are here."

"This place is incredible. I'm glad you don't just waste all those resources you steal from the starving villagers."

"If I wasn't resourceful, I'd never be successful," I say, doing a luminescent hair flip. "Now, without further ado, I welcome you to my castle!"

The heart-shaped doors fold inward, revealing all the splendor of the main hall. Sculptures of many past heroes and heroines adorn the walls, each one paired with a beautiful painting of different regions.

"Okay, so you turned the heroes to stone right, like a gorgon? That's an earth creature. You have a gorgon around here?"

"Not at all. True art must move like the waves, it must be trans-formative not stagnant. And no, gorgons are hideous. These are sculptures, but they're special. They are monuments to all the loves I have had and they are given a new pose every day. It may sound like a lot of work, but if my sculptors don't do it then they get their hands chopped off. Ah, their motivation truly touches me."

Stalker looks away in tears. "I know some of these heroes. I loved them too."

Such beauty.

My scarf wipes away her tear and pets her lovingly.

"Your eyes sparkle when you suffer. Has anyone ever told you that?"

"Thankfully no. Do you have any idea how creepy that is?" asks Stalker, awkwardly laughing.

"I'm a man of theatre! I can't help but enjoy a good tragedy. But rather then squeezing out a few sentimental tears, I like to witness the moment of suffering. You're sad now, but I bet when you saw them die...oh you must have been sobbing," I said shivering with ecstasy

Stalker sniffles. "Yeah...I was. It never stops hurting. The only way I move past it is to find a new love, but then they...end up dying too."

"Well then it must be quite the treat for you to be meeting with the grand conductor of your symphony of misfortune?"

"Not really. I hate you. Just not going to waste my time being miserable."

"Come, my dear. I'm here in front of you. Why I'd be insulted if you weren't plotting my demise."

Stalker stuck out her tongue playfully. "Maybe I'll surprise you."

"That's the spirit. Perhaps I should show you my weapon's room. All beautiful tools of destruction, I assure you."

Stalker's gaze was set on the statue of the young man who died inside a building I had burned down. "Hey, you said you loved them, but you killed them."

My scarf turns her to face me. "Come, my dear. You must know the pain of unrequited love. I couldn't bear it. The possibility of them loving me was so slim, but it was that small possibility that tore me apart. I had to slaughter them so that hope would no longer burden my heart."

Stalker turns away in tears. "I understand. But it just makes me hate you more."

Such beautiful creatures, that pretty pink blush looks even more enchanting when coated in liquid misery.

"You shouldn't hate yourself, dear. Embrace yourself, faults and all! If you were a little saint, you'd be so boring and Main would have no interest in you."

"You really think he likes me!" Her joy broke through her water-logged gems.

"I know his every thought. I'm even closer to him..." I bend down and kiss her forehead. I then snap my fingers, causing her journal to appear. My scarf seizes it. "Then you are."

"What do I need to do to for you to spare him? I don't want him to end up like the others. I don't want all the happy memories to become teary ones."

You are foolish to open up to your enemy, child.

I flash a wicked smile. "While I tear him limb from limb, don't hold back your screams. If I'm satiated by your raw misery, then I may save his death for another day. Oooh, perhaps Valentine's Day!"

"No! If you hurt him, I'll stop you!" she yells, punching me with her tiny fists.

"With any luck you'll lull me into a pleasant slumber with your rage imbued massage. Ha-ha! I do enjoy the chatter, but I'm a busy ruler. Allow me to escort you to your room." I do a split and point to the ceiling.

A disco ball drops down and lights up the main hall. The floor shimmies left to right and then rises up, creating a flight of stairs.

"My entire castle is alive. Dead things are ugly, don't you agree."

"Are you…going to kill me?"

"Keep such unpleasant thoughts to yourself." I signal my Aroma Bat to spritzer the air. "I work hard to keep this place as clean as possible."

"Did that creature just say "kill me?" Is it in pain?"

"It's just being a drama queen. Spoiled little thing. Go on, take your bath. You're on break. Sorry about that. Living a glamorous life can make lower souls ungrateful. You do know that the rich are more likely to commit suicide then the poor, don't you?"

"I suppose. There's just something eerie about this place," says Stalker, looking around.

"Wait till you see your room!" I squeal like a girl on her first shopping spree as I prance up the stairs. "Guest room."

The castle groans, but my PsyrenFrogs block out the negative vibes with an angelic hymn.

Stalker's eyes shrink. "Why do they sound like that?"

Her little body is shivering with fear. I can't have her spoiling the big surprise. I must calm her, for now.

"Isn't it wondrous? They are able to mimic any sound. You could hear the voice of one of your past heroes…if you'd like." I lift up the frog and offer it to the troubled girl.

"Really?" she asks, with hope in her eyes.

"Yes. I have the sound of their deaths all preserved. I'm actually going to blend them together and make a song out of it. Do you want to listen?"

Her eyes went vacant.

Broken already. Too easy.

"I...I want to go home."

"Your home is being torched as we speak. Main's fighting my forces. Oh my, he just ran into one of my generals."

Stalker clings onto me, like a child desperate for her mother's love. "Please, call them off. I'll do anything!"

"Ah, but nothing is quite as rewarding as seeing that expression on your face. True beauty is candid, genuine. A face contorted in pain, tears and snot overflowing, no other expression comes closer to the true nature of one's soul. I'm an actor, my dear, but I'm also a playwright. Realism is what makes me weak in the knees, tragedy is what sways my heart and tears are what quench my thirst."

She pushes off of me and nearly falls to the floor, but my scarf catches her before the fall.

"Let me show you to your room." The door opens to show a pink slide.

My scarf drops her down the slide and her cries echo across the walls.

My word, the acoustics here are absolutely wonderful!

I make my way down my pink and yellow tiled hallway and grip onto my dance pole. I spin around, blowing kisses in the air while strutting my stuff. My grand castle shifts around until the War Room's door appears.

I dig my finger into it and whisper to the door. "Spread open for me, dear."

The door moans as she opens up, revealing the glorious splendor of my War Room.

If by some miracle you can hear my thoughts, then you must be dying to know how it looks, Main. The walls have curtains with pretty butterflies. There are eight bean bag chairs, each of a different color. I of course take a seat on the glittery pink one. The table in front of us is decorated with plants, creating a map of my entire kingdom.

I grab my hand bell and give it a few rings.

Within minutes my CatBoy servants attend to me, giving me sweets, massages and the finest tea.

"It's your lucky day, boys. General TomCat was killed in combat, meaning there's a vacancy for the spot. Whoever wants it…" I snap my fingers. The ground contorts into a ball pit. "Can enter for the chance to claim it."

The boys look at the pit and then at each other. A few of them nervously step in.

"It's not worth it!" yells one, collapsing at the entrance.

My scarf expands and pierces his back.

"There's no room for doubt in my army." My scarf twirls around, slicing his clothing and flesh. "My, my, what do we have here?"

My CatBoy soldier is actually a girl. She vainly covers her chest, but I can taste them with each follicle on my scarf.

I appear in front of her, pulling away her bleeding arms. "You would hide something from the one who has given you everything. I don't want cowards or traitors in my army. Hmmm, what to do with you?"

I look over to the ball pit, my brave soldiers are clawing each other limb from limb in the hopes of gaining a promotion.

"How did you mask your scent?"

"I don't know. Please, just let me go."

"A latent power, interesting. Good news, soldier, you've been promoted to the Kitty Klaw division. Now off with you. I want to see who the victor is."

I snap my fingers and the balls in the pit come to life. They grow teeth and leap at my CatBoy soldiers, biting off flesh and lapping up blood.

"Dreadful aren't they. They're modified mimics. Oh, how I do miss the days when I would sit with all those cute boys and play table top."

"I give up!" yells one of the cat boys.

"So easily? Your void of passion is so disappointing."

One of my CatBoys grabs hold of the Mimic Balls and uses them as a weapon. Slaughtering the other contenders in seconds.

"Ah, such tenacity. I'm impressed. Welcome general, I will see you in my bedchamber tonight to give you your power and title. Might I ask what willed you to kill the others? They are from your village after all, perhaps a few of them were friends."

"They were…very close friends." My newest general shoots me a look of pure hate.

Nothing motivates like the burning passion of vengeance.

"Then their blood shall forever be a part of you." I poke him playfully, transforming the blood into permanent tattoos on his body. "Let their deaths fuel you to bring me many more victories. Now take your seat. The other generals are arriving."

The first general to arrive bowed to me with cold dead eyes. He was sleek, sexy and had an adorable face like a baby. He was draped in his own custom uniform: jammies with sleepy faced kitty cats on it.

"Always punctual. What is the news on the rebels?"

"The hero team JumpForced attacked my troops. They successfully held off our assault on Sunny Village."

"Such a shame. You had two victories, but now you're back to square one."

"We managed to capture their guardian angel. They won't be able to heal from our next assault."

"Well if you have their angel, then there's no need to waste your time on them. Their leader Joe Star Platinum is such a hottie, but I'll taste him in due time."

"Does this mean I get a gold star?"

"Absolutely!" I reach my hand into my throne and pull out a StarBorne.

The sparkly creature smiles at me.

"Three gold stars. Well, well. You must be very pleased with yourself," I say, placing the star under his shirt.

"I can feel the power."

"Now what are you going to do with it?" I ask with a sly grin.

"You murdered my parents right in front of me and you sent my little sister away to…"

I pat his head with my scarf. "Words can only convey so much. You have your stars, so that gives you the right to challenge me."

"Wait up, your adorableness."

I turn to see another of my generals. He is just darling in his pink and blue CatBoy maid get up.

"Ah, general CatScratch, is there something you'd like to report?"

My general reaches into his handbasket and tosses me the head of a little girl.

"That's White Knight's guardian angel. The number one hero will soon fall under your command."

I lap up the blood with my fingertips and slide up to my general. I hoist him up and rub his belly. "Who's a good boy? Who's a good boy."

"Kyaaah. Stop," CatScratch squeals as he writhes around.

General Cat Nap places a hand on me, which my scarf knocks aside. "He has three gold stars as well. For the honor of our village and those who you murdered. We'd like to challenge you."

"Both of you, at once. I'm not sure my body can handle the passion of double penetration. Do be gentle," I say, moonwalking away from the vengeful general.

The floor parts and reveals a slide.

"The other generals are late anyways. Might as well kill some time." I say, before sliding down.

I giggle and scream with joy as the living slide tickles me. It drops me off into the Killaseaum, a vibrant battle arena that looks like an adult-sized playground.

I hop onto the monkey bars and taunt them with my tail. "Catch me if you can."

The two generals whisper their strategy to one another, but our bond lets me know it regardless. Oh, General Cat Nap is going to be in for quite the surprise!"

Cat Nap drags his claws across the large seesaw, lulling it to sleep in seconds.

The StarBorne's symbiosis is truly wondrous. I wonder how powerful he could have become.

General CatScratch's claws elongate and slice the swing set. He flings one of the seats at me, but my scarf catches it.

"That scarf is all that protects you! Without it, you're defenseless!" yells Cat Nap.

"Without his arms your father was defenseless too. Remember when he tried to attack me with those bleeding stubs? It was so funny, I nearly died from laughter."

"All the power you've given me shall be your end, villain!" yells Cat Nap, speeding in front of me.

CatScratch uses the seesaw to propel himself toward me and grips his blade.

"*Fairy Dust!*" exclaims Cat Nap, showering me with sleeping powder. All my clothes, including my scarf, fall asleep.

CatScratch grips his sword and poises to strike.

"Oh, whatever will I do." My scarf moves in a flash, slicing both of Cat Nap's hands off. It grips them before plunging them into my attacker.

"But your scarf...I..."

I tear out the claws and stick my fingers in the gaping wound. "Now, now don't fall asleep on me. You can't miss the ending of your own story."

"His clothing isn't his power." CatScratch leaps over me and places his claws to Cat Nap's back.

"You said you wanted him dead. He made you kill your parents," said Cat Nap in desperation.

"My family were dull and boring. I never would have had a chance to live the luxurious life if not for him. I'll admit I wanted him dead at first, but that passionate hate has become deep devotion."

Ah, and so true loyalty blooms from despair and hate! No matter how many times I witness it, it's such a wondrous sight!

Cat Nap breaks down into tears. "What about me. We're friends. We were friends at Sunny Village and we're friends now, aren't we?"

"I remember when a simple meal with my family would bring me such joy." CatScratch slices Cat Nap's back open, getting sprayed with the blood. "I was such a simple foolish boy then. My bond with our Commander in Cute must have taken over me. The idea of killing my friend, the tragedy of it all is giving me such a rush!"

Oh my, I'm getting hot under the collar too. The despair and depravity is just, ooooh, unbearable!

General CatScratch is suddenly behind me, rubbing my nipples. "I feel it. Everything you feel," he says with a look of pure bliss. He then slits Cat Nap's throat.

We both hold hands and give each other butterfly kisses as the blood showers us.

"I love you and I hate you," says CatScratch before kissing me.

I start to undress and then break the kiss.

"What's wrong?" he asks, twirling his finger in my hair.

"I was just thinking about that poor girl?"

"TomCat? She was annoying. Nobody will miss her."

"Not her. Stalker. I told her Main cared about her but…that was a lie." I break down into tears. "He just sees her as a damsel in distress. The only reason he'll come to save her is to boost his own image of heroism."

"Your heart bleeds for one of them?"

"Suffering unites all beings. Whether an ant or an elephant, all seek freedom and desire to live. And most of them seek love too. I can't bear for her to learn of the truth."

"Do you want me to end her life?"

"No, I have a special mission for you. I need you to bring me Best Friend. He's the one Main truly loves. I'll deal with the girl's plight, as humanely as possible," I say with a troubled smile.

A Maiden's Heart

Episode 6 Part 2

I could get prepped for lovemaking in my sleep. And since I'm sure you're just as curious as I am about what the little one is doing. I'm going to turn my attention over to her. The little kiss I gave her isn't a strong bond, but it will allow me to spy on her for a little while.

"He who has passion controls the fates! *POINT OF VIEW SHIFT!*"

I pace around the room.

"Is everything to your liking, milady?" asks one of the cat-eared maid boys.

"The bed is too comfy. I'm afraid if I lay on it, I'll fall asleep forever," I say, scratching my cheek.

"Only a kiss from your hero would awake you. That doesn't sound so bad, does it?" asks the maid.

Oh my gosh that would be so amazing.

"Milady?" The CatBoy presses a bucket under me. "You're drooling."

"Sorry. I hope I didn't mess up the floor."

"If I may be frank, I hate your kind and think the world is better off with them extinct. I hope you take no offense to that."

Wow, he says something so horrible yet he does it so politely. Ugh, this place is making me go crazy.

"Why do you hate angels?"

"LustDriven are impure beings enslaved by base instincts and they, well they make a mess everywhere. Such dirty things should be cleansed from the planet so it can be sparkly clean."

"You're rather bold for a maid."

"Oh, my apologies. I'm not simply a CatBoy, though I'm not a general either. I'm his Hotness' second in command: YarnBall. My friends call me Yarny, but you're not my friend, little minx, so don't even think about it."

My unpleasant captor is a hard one to read. His eyes are always closed like that tricky character from the show with all the hot guys wielding swords.

Oooh, I bet Main would look super cool with a giant sword!

YarnBall slid the bucket under me. "You're drooling again. So uncouth."

"Not to be rude, but can I have a maid that isn't constantly insulting me?"

"I was ordered specifically to guard you. I'm the only one his Holy Sexiness trusts with this important duty."

"Okay, then can you pwease shut up?"

"Is it hard to plan an escape while I'm talking?"

Huh? How did he know?

"I saw you looking up at the window. You might be able to reach it if you had wings. But you already know, you're right where you want to be, filth. Your latest crush would be displeased if you escaped. Your kind are loyal to a fault; like a sex starved dog in heat."

"Flam took the long route to his castle. Why isn't Main here already? Is saving my village more important to him than saving me?"

That's right! Main's in danger! As long as Flam holds the Point of View, Main won't have his Plot Armor! If this is Flam's episode then I have to find a way to end it prematurely! I should see how he's doing.

I start to take off my shirt. "I'm going to change? Can I get some privacy?"

YarnBall wheels in mobile shower curtains from the closet. He then climbs atop them and stares at me with those creepy slanted eyes. "Absolutely not. You filthy creatures are crafty, after all," he says with a sweet smile.

Ugh, the sugary sweetness of everything here is hurting my tummy wummy.

"I want to take a bath!" I exclaim. "I, uh, want to be fresh when my hero comes to save me."

"Very well, I'll escort you to the bath house."

"Oh, but let me clean my undies first." I slip out of my strawberry panties-Main's favorite- and start licking them clean like a kitty.

The creepy cat boy turns and wretches.

Finally, an opening. Also, wow, I'm so yummy.

I summon up my journal.

Please be okay, Main.

My eyes must be playing tricks on me. I turn to the next page and its blank. The last note I have is him letting Flam do the prequel. And what's even stranger is that it looks like a scene a few pages back was erased. But there's no way to erase an entry. Could Flam have done something when he grabbed my diary.

I have to find him now.

"Are you done…cleaning yourself?" asks YarnBall, covering his eyes with his hands.

You'd think a cat wouldn't be bothered by such things.

"Yep, I'm all cleaned up now!" I say, slipping my panties on.

"Did your mother not teach you manners?"

"Look! You can be mean to me all you want but don't talk about my mommy!" I yell with tears.

"Stop excreting from your eyes. Follow me." YarnBall leads me out of my way too comfy prison and takes me down the hall.

"I need to talk to Flam. It's important."

"The bathroom is close by. I can take you there. Unless you drink that too."

"I don't need to go potty. It's something else."

"The Glamorous Supreme General is busy at the moment. You can schedule a meeting after you've taken a bath. It's right through this door."

"Opening," says the door in a robotic voice.

"Hey, so do you have any cool powers? I hear that all the generals have them. What's yours?"

"My power is to weather the stench of the impure so I can cleanse them from Punk. You won't get anything more out of me."

"You should be called SourPuss not YarnBall."

"That name was given to me by the Dark Diva himself. Do not dare to try and steal it from me."

Flam sure has a lot of pseudonyms.

Flam peeks out from the…chocolate bath.

Wow! This place really is too good to be true! Main loves eating chocolate behind Best Friend's back. Maybe he can steal me away and eat me while his friend isn't looking.

I hop in and whisper to Flam. "Can you ask YarnBall to leave? He really creeps me out."

"Who am I to ignore a maiden's desire. Yarny?"

The CatBoy's eyes open up, glistening pink. "Yes, your Lordship?"

"Leave us. You're relieved of your duties for now."

"A-a-a-as you wish, Beloved Baron." He leaves the room in a daze, nearly toppling over.

"You sure have that kitty on a tight leash."

"Oh, they're free to do as they want. They can even leave. But they never do. The opportunity to be this close to me is one they all savor. Every CatBoy is a survivor of one of my little village play dates."

"You mean when you torch them and slaughter the men?"

"Yeah, I call that a play date. My recruiters rescue the children from the burning buildings, rubble, and other hazards and they offer them a chance to join me."

"Why would they ever join the one who killed their families?"

This man is so twisted!

"To kill me. Only those who succeed in missions and prove their worth are allowed to become generals and after a general has burned down one village, killed a hero leader and captured or killed one of your kin, they get a special gold star. With all three stars, they are given the chance to fight me. Most often they don't. They become too attached to me at that point."

"So, then the chance to kill you is a lie?"

"I am not a fibber. Only a few generals have held onto their vengeance long enough to challenge me. But since they need to burn a village to get a gold star, well, there's always an opportunity to replace them with a new general."

How can they burn villages to avenge their own village? It makes no sense.

"That look of confusion doesn't do your face any favors, dear. I should have been more specific. They have to burn their own village, kill their own villagers to get that gold star. Once they've done that, most of them snap. Their own desires to kill me are what twists them into becoming my pawns. Isn't that just poetic?"

"You're a tyrant and Main will stop you," I say with a glare.

Wait. Main is in danger! How did I forget? It's this place. Maybe the perfume in it or something. It dulls the memory. I have to stay focused.

"I-I want to help you."

Flam's eyes widen. He blinks several times. "You do?"

"You've done so much for me. The Main love pillow on my bed was particularly thrilling!"

Oh, I can't wait to straddle the real hero!

"I also had your past heroes killed. Don't you hate me?"

"Of course I do, but my mama didn't raise an ungrateful child."

I have to guard my thoughts in case he's prying into them.

"Such a little darling you are. Well there is something I want. But just asking you is no fun. Head back to your room when you're done here. I'll have dinner delivered to you in just an itty bit."

What is he planning now? Ugh, I don't have time to waste. I have to resolve this episode or at least find an exciting cliffhanger. Wait, YarnBall isn't watching me anymore. He's being careless. I should see what I can find in this place.

I get up from the bath and lick the chocolate from my hands.

Wow, this is soooooo tasty! And it smells amazing! So sweet and creamy! Mmmm, I smell like love.

I smack my cheeks.

Stay focused. He must be hiding something here and I'm going to find it.

I slip on a towel and leave the bath house.

Why is the towel tickling me? Is everything alive here?

I close the door.

Where should I start looking?

"Hey, filthy girl. Wat'cha doin?" asks YarnBall.

"Didn't your beloved commander tell you to leave me alone?" I ask with puffy cheeks and a glare.

"Yeah, but my loyalty isn't skin deep. You want to see a special room?" he asks, his smile stretching from ear to ear.

Great I'm going to see that in my nightmares. Stupid CatBoy is ruining my dream time with Main.

"Well, do ya?"

This is obviously a trap, but I can't just do nothing while Main is in danger.

"Okay, umm. Lead the way, YarnBall."

"Ooh, I just love being mischievous." He turns to face the gummy wall. "Open up or I'll slice you open."

The wall parts and all that awaits within is pure darkness.

Is he taking me somewhere to torture me? Okay, deep breaths, Annie. You've been tortured before. You have a mission and you're going to get it done.

I raise my hand and emit a beam of light. "It's so we don't fall."

"Oh, I'm sure you'll slip regardless. Once you see the surprise that is."

We make it all the way down the dark stairs.

My light wavers with my spirits, flickering on and off.

I see flashes of pools of blood, limp bodies, tubes and smiles.

I cover my eyes. "What is this place?"

A hand ruffles my hair. "This my dear, is where the magic happens," says Flam.

It was a set up. I knew it was, but I'm so scared.

"What are you doing to those girls?"

This place smells so sweet it's sickening.

"I must thank you, dear. You've given me the perfect opportunity to punish you. Such a lovely gift it is. Truly you must have peered into my heart's purest desire."

I run up the stairs, but they sink beneath me.

"I've bonded with every inch of this castle. There's nowhere you can go that I can't see. This is such a unique experience. I can feel your terror firsthand and see myself through your eyes."

"Wait, you changed POV? When?"

"Aww, don't worry. That simply means you need to modify your plan just a smidgen. Instead of finding the end to my episode, you need to find your ending. The curtain won't close without your satisfaction, so there's no point in faking it."

"I'm not the hero. I've always been a side character! And that's fine with me!"

"You really believe that? You've had 13 heroes and they've all come and gone. You're the one who carries on their memories. You should give yourself more credit, my dear. Now, if you want to end your episode, then you have to see this through to the end. I won't tell you what this place is; you'll have to figure it out on your own."

I'm so scared. Main, please help me.

"He can't hear your thoughts. Only I can. There is nothing you can hide from me. I can see through you entirely. You're as bare as a newborn kitten."

"You shouldn't have POV! Only great heroes have that! You must have stolen it!"

"How I got it is irrelevant. Oh no, Main just got injured. Enough games, little one. I don't want him to die yet either."

"Then give him back his Plot Armor!"

"You're the one in control now, not me."

"Wait, you began the episode. You're still in control. You're lying to me. You still have the POV."

"Then you best be safe and satisfy both our conditions."

"You had a question for me, right? Well I sneaked into your secret room so hurry up and torture the answer out of me."

I'm not afraid. I'm not afraid.

"You know, the word afraid will only make you more frightened. I suggest you think "I am fearless" instead. It's much more motivational."

"Hurt me!" I yell in tears.

"Such desperation. But I don't get my jollies off on hurting children, at least not physically. Truly, my heart bleeds for you, my dear. I want to help you."

"Then ask your question!"

His eyes gaze into me.

"Why were you specifically chosen to protect him? There are other NymphBeasts that are far more qualified for the job."

"I prefer the term guardian angel."

"And I'd prefer to have been born a beautiful lady, but we seldom get what we want."

"I wasn't chosen. I…made the choice myself."

"Such a feisty little thing you are. Do you think yourself better than your kin?" He snaps his fingers and the lights flicker.

I see it for an instant: girls just like me with tubes in them. Their eyes are dazed and they have an empty smile.

Why is he doing this?

"You're a clever girl. You must know the answer."

"You're…farming them for their fluids." My whole body is trembling.

His scarf wraps around my neck. I swear I hear it hiss.

"There you go. You have your answer. Oh, but that's odd. You still have the POV. I suppose me satisfy me after all. Thankfully, there is one last burning question I have."

My stomach turns.

Am I going to end up like them? I joined the Hero's Guild so I'd be safe. I've never felt less safe in my entire life.

His scarf coils around my arms and legs, twisting them to the brink of breaking. His eyes gaze into me. "What would I have to do to you to make Main rescue you?"

Of course. We both want the same thing. But I can't say it. The answer is too dreadful.

"You don't need to say anything, dear. Just think it. Your thought is my command."

I swallow my fear and steady myself. "An execution. If there's no deadline, he won't act. He…procrastinates. You'll have to execute me!"

His delighted smile churns my stomach.

"Exceptional. I'll send word to him of your execution date through my generals. Well I believe that is a fitting end to this episode, don't you?" he asks, wiping away my tears with his scarf.

I nod with a face full of tears and shaky legs.

"I'll take back the POV now. *POINT OF YIEW SHIFT!*"

Well, wasn't that just a blast? I'm so happy you all got to see my beautiful castle! I'm not much for ending songs, but just picture Stalker's terrified face and some melancholic music if you want one.

Now for the preview. Well we've reached the last episode of the Season One Part One. Main's forces will go up against my generals and he's going to learn when Stalker's execution is. Will Main's team be victorious or will his destiny fall into my hands! Oh, the excitement wounds me! See you dears next time!

"Are you done?" asks a mysterious voice from the shadows.

It's him.

I bow down on bended knee. "Is there something you want?"

"Is everything proceeding as planned?" asks the voice in a monotone whisper.

"Not exactly, but if it was, it would be boring, wouldn't it?"

"Indeed."

"The boy will come, I assure you."

"The silver eyed hero. We thought there was only one."

"For all we know he has contacts."

"No, this one is special. That's why we chose it."

"He is special, isn't he?"

And he has such a cute butt.

"We will not repeat ourselves."

"I'd rather not kill the girl. The NymphBeasts are such tragic creatures. Perhaps too tragic," I say softly.

"Steel your heart. The boy is not the one we are luring. There is another thorn in our side."

"You mean the Legend…"

"Silence. You know us well enough to not ruin our vague statements."

"I apologize. Ah, so you mean that one. Is that better?"

"Much. You've bonded with so many, it's not easy to tell who is listening in."

"That's not something a mysterious voice needs to be concerned about. I will fulfill my duty and you'll give me my reward as promised."

"Yes. Whichever of the two of you satisfies us more, shall receive our blessing."

"Can we end it here? I'm honestly concerned about the boy."

"We have someone watching it. The destiny boy will be protected."

"He nearly died."

"Indeed, but we saw its potential. How are your experiments fairing?"

"One of them escaped and is causing trouble. Should have put the ugly thing out of its misery instead of locking it away in the dungeon."

"The general who died, TomCat. We've decided to give it another chance."

"If only you could do the same for the heroes. I'd love to kill them at least a few more times."

"Greed is in poor tastes when it lacks purpose. This time the destiny boy will have to fight her alone."

"You certainly know how to build things up."

"But of course. I am the one who built…ah, I should stop there. Don't want to reveal too much at this stage of the game."

"Is everything a game to you?"

"It's all a story, until those with the will to change history come along and make it entertaining. We enjoyed playing with you."

"Seems like you're still not done playing with me."

"You are one of our favorites, after all. Oh, the boy isn't faring well. Return POV to it."

"As you wish. We shall soon see if he is indeed the child of destiny you've longed for."

"It is. We have no doubt. It simply needs more trials to awaken its true power."

"Oooh, I can't wait! *POINT OF VIEW RETURN!*"

Episode 7 Part 1

Flashes of a colorful castle barrage my mind. I see my mortal enemy, Flam. Oh, and Stalker is there too. So many quick images flash by that it's hard to keep track of it all. Colorful creatures, heroic statues, Stalker in tears, CatBoy generals, a killer ball pit, a playground and some dark room.

Whose memories are these?

A hammer slams into my chest.

My vision becomes blurry and my hair shoots out to protect me.

Flam must have taken over my mind somehow. Okay, I have to figure out who I am and what I'm doing. Can't risk annoying my audience with a forced amnesia arc. Only Kingdom Heartless can get away with recycling that trope.

My hair yanks the hammer out of the enemy's grip and socks him upside the head.

My vision returns to me and my head clears up.

I'm in the Village of Doomed and I'm heading to the medical tent to make sure my prophetic stone doesn't get taken in by a bunch of loveless virgins. Yeah. I remember it.

I am not letting the sexual predator steal my awareness again. I'm making this episode a special, so it's going to be extra-long! In that time, I'm going to prove to everyone just how powerful of a hero I am.

"See. I was right. He just needed a good hit to get him in his right mind," says Glasses Kid.

"Welcome back," says Best Friend.

Well the CatBoys are gone, so it's time to see what's inside my medical tent.

I arrive in the tent to see something surprising. In my hospital bed is a big fat cat. It looked like the one I saw on the stone slab in episode two. It was twice the size of a hippo and had three villagers in its massive mouth.

Shit that reminds me, when's the last time I ate? Great, now I'm hungry.

"Look, behind the cat. It's your prophecy. I'll distract it, you take the prophecy," says Best Friend.

"I don't understand. Where is he? This is supposed to be where the date is. How come his fat cat is here, but he isn't!?" I exclaim furiously.

What am I saying? Urgh, Flam's messing with my head!

"Let me handle the cat. I'm going to wrap it in a bow and put it in a box," says Glasses Kid determined.

"If you were trying to act bad-ass...you failed...horribly," I say, telling him the cold hard truth like any good friend should.

"I wasn't...just forget I said anything," says Glasses Kid with a blush.

The pissed off cat arches his or her back and meows furiously at us, ready to pounce.

"Will handle big cat," says Brawny Babe, cracking her neck.

"Wait, don't kill her!" exclaims Best Friend urgently.

"He's right. It's the hero's job to slay the dragon. I'll initiate the last blow. Oh, and from now on that cat's name is Fearsome Dragon," I say firmly.

"No hurt feline friend!" yells Brawny Babe.

"She's right."

"Actually, she's not. If you kill the cat, you're bound to get showered in experience points. It is rather like a mid-boss, after all," says Glasses Kid.

"His story is an anime, not a video game," says Best Friend, slowly approaching the chubby kitty.

162:00

"It's an isekai anime! Look, honestly I just don't want to get eaten so kill it!" exclaims Glasses Kid, hiding behind me.

Best Friend turns to me. "I'll end her life if that is truly what you desire," says Best Friend.

And so, another decision is before me. I'm stuck in the middle, wanting to please everyone. But I can't. The cat is moving closer and closer to me.

Damn it, what do I do?

I collapse to the ground, feeling dizzy.

"Look what you've done to him. Maybe the cat will leave peacefully once she has had a little snack," says Best Friend, lifting up Glasses Kid.

What kind of leader am I? My teammates are going to kill him. I could give a shit about the little prick, but he's my friend. And friends don't feed each other to fearsome dragons. I have to save him. I've decided!

I leap to my feet and rush Fearsome Dragon. I ram into her, my hair holding back those stubby arms from tearing me apart.

"I've got Fearsome Dragon. There's no need to kill it! Just hurry up and pick up my prophecy!" I yell as the cat gnashes her teeth at me.

Glasses Kid broke free of Best Friend's grip and ran to the prophetic stone. He then turns to me, a look of horror on his face.

"What's wrong?" I ask him confused as my hair punches the cat into the air.

Oh yeah! I've gotten so strong.

"It would appear we are too late," says Glasses Kid, trying to keep his composure while trembling.

Best Friend rushes up to the stone slab. He smiles a big smile and then hugs me. "Don't worry. Mommy's here for you."

"Cut out the weird parent talk. What's wrong?" I ask, pulling him off me and looking into his tear-stricken eyes.

"We're too late. I've failed you Main. I tried so hard, but I failed you." Best Friend embraces himself as he shivers in misery.

"Tell me what happened!"

Damn it. I should have stayed focused.

Fearsome Dragon is behind me, towering over me and looking down at her prey.

"Tampered with. Look at picture," says Brawny Babe, hoisting up the stone slab with three fingers.

Impressive upper arm strength. Anti-SJWs can whine all they like about forced strong female leads. This woman is a powerful ally and I am glad to have her!

Brawny Babe brought the slab to me. My prophecy had been changed dramatically. There was a picture of an angry cat. My allies were dead on the ground, and my legs were in between her blood drenched teeth. My eyes turned to Brawny Babe, who looks upset rather than worried.

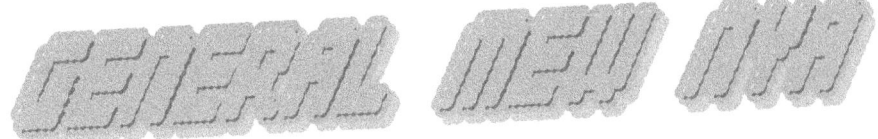

<u>Episode 7 Part 2</u>

The only thing more surprising than the prophecy before me is the title. Here I am, realizing I'm going to die and the next thing I see is that. Look at it! It's outlined in pink! Wait, if this general is the highlight of the chapter, then maybe I don't die. Either that or he kills me. Regardless, I'm not going down without a fight. Why isn't Brawny Babe afraid? I know she was raised in the jungle...I mean forest, damn it! Okay, relax Main. Dying isn't so bad. Everyone does it eventually. You're just so awesome that you're going to do it twice. Hells yeah!

"Forgot me," says Brawny Babe on the verge of tears...womanly tears.

Seeing powerful Amazonian teen girl fantasy fuel like her sobbing puts me on edge. If she can't keep it together, then how the hell am I supposed to? I have to do something to help.

"Come on, Babe. Even if I die, I won't forget you. That marshmallow was a permanent...a temporary sign of our friendship. Just because it's gone doesn't mean our friendship is. How do I explain this? In Yu-Gai-Oh Zero, the one before Duelist Kingdom. You know, the one where Iwin was like a badass who judges bad people, kind of like Jig-Saw in a way, but with real games."

Brawny Babe gives me a blank stare.

Oh, right I forgot the closest things she's seen to television is animals killing each other in the wild.

"Anyways, when him and his friends are about to get smashed in a killer game of Tetris in Kaibuh Land, they don't just accept death. They put their hands together, like the Supah Sentai! And then they use a marker to draw a portion of a smiley face on each of their hands. When united their hands make a smiley face, meaning everything will be alright even when your trapped in a billionaire's killer theme park. The point is that even though the marker will fade, in other words they die. Their friendship will live on. It's not the ink that's important, it's the symbol that has power. Now if they got a tattoo on the other hand, it would be a permanent sign. But then they would have to explain it to everyone they came across. Wait, that's it! The marker! We need to find the marker!" I exclaim in revelation.

Who says anime has no practical value? Haters, that's who. And haters suck!

"Good thinking, Main. And I must say I'm impressed by your eloquent words. Your passion for anime actually elicited feeling in my logical scientific brain," says Glasses Kid with a smile.

"Jojos taught me to stay away from stylish strangers. Noruto taught me that the difference between right from wrong is your vocal volume and the power of your fists. Ikutoesan taught me that panty shots can come up in any scenario. Assault Titan showed me that if you're a side character, your life is meaningless. Parasaite to the Maximum made me realize that animals just want to live their lives like we do! And Ore wa Pico…taught me…uh…stranger danger! Yeah! That's it! Anime is my mentor! I never learned anything from you," I say, breaking his fragile self-esteem.

"Found marker," says Brawny Babe with a smile.

"I don't know how much longer I can hold her," says Best Friend, using dual-blood chains to keep Fearsome Dragon down and showing absolutely no strain.

Brawny Babe pops the lid off the marker and got to work. In a few seconds she finishes. She then proudly shows us the result.

What the hell is wrong with this person!?

All she did was draw her corpse next to ours.

Great job, dumbass. I suppose she traded her smarts in for more muscle. Ugh.

"Let me see that!" I yell, grabbing it out of her hand.

I look at my hand to see that the marker was gone.

How did it vanish right before my eyes?

"Did you really think I would just let you live, Mew?" asks a voice from the shadows.

"Show yourself so you can meet your end," says Best Friend, tossing a blood kunai in the general direction of the voice.

The figure came out from the shadows, holding the marker in his claws. He is a short little thing. I mean really short. His body is in the shape of a jelly bean. The little guy's head is the size of a melon and on top of that head is a sailor hat.

Shit, another general. Aren't there only eight? Wait, where did I get that info from?

"Cat want play?" asks Brawny Babe, using her bow as a stick.

"Only killing my enemies brings me joy," says the cat general, hypocritically pawing at the stick.

"That is General Mew Nya," I say.

"Um Best Friend, let's leave this little guy alive, okay?" asks Glasses Kid.

"What!? So, we can kill the fluffy monster but not the evil general!? You're as fickle as a pickle!" I yell, rhyming rather than making sense.

"You almost used it in the right context. Come on, Main, try again," says Glasses Kid, patting his knees as if trying to encourage a baby to walk.

I'm no baby. Not that I'm ageist against babies. After all I'm sure you were a baby once, a totally awesome baby like Beal.

"I'm not your pupil anymore, professor dipshit! Alright, General Mew Nya, hand over the marker," I demand, turning my attention to him.

"My reputation precedes me, Nya. You can have this marker when you pry it out with your cold dead hands, Mew!" he exclaims, vanishing into the shadows.

Glasses Kid grips his chest. "The English language is under fire," he exclaims in misery.

This cat general is a slippery little bastard. No worries. All I need is one good shot.

"Hey Friendship, wanna hold hands?" I ask my rocket launcher just to piss Ultima off.

"I don't have hands, you $#!+head!" Ultima yells furiously, creating a powerful jet of flame.

General Mew Nya was hit head on. He was smoldering, and smoke was pouring out from his wide-open mouth.

That was fast. I was hoping for a better final battle.

"Look out!" exclaims Best Friend.

No freaking way.

The little guy runs across the air and thrusts a dagger right into my chest. He then spins around, slicing me up. Best Friend knocks him off with a blood baseball bat, but the guy hardly flinches. Fearsome Dragon then jumps on Best Friend, opening her mouth for the kill.

"Stop!" I yell out in desperation.

Everyone froze. Fearsome Dragon diverts her attention to me, tapping her front paw impatiently.

"Look, I'm not sure if you all know this. Flam is in love with me. It's as serious as cancer!"

But hopefully not as hard to remove.

"We know, Nya!" exclaims the general.

"Meow!" responds Fearsome Dragon.

"Well, considering that he's in love with me, I don't think he wants me dead."

I only pray that my complex understanding of logic reaches these simpletons.

"Of course he doesn't, Paw," responds the cat boy.

"Meow." Fearsome dragon rolls her eyes.

"Then you shouldn't kill me," I explain, using words to win the battle.

"What makes you think that, Mew?" asks the cat general.

"Meow?" asks Fearsome Dragon in confusion.

"If he loves me and wants me alive and you two are his underlings, shouldn't you follow his wishes?"

"Meow!" The fat cat salutes the air.

"Not at all. I follow his orders. And his orders were to kill all of you, Nya!" yells General Mew Nya, rushing back into battle.

He stabs at Glasses Kid furiously, but misses nearly every jab.

"I've dodged spit balls from that ungrateful delinquent. Your attacks aren't nearly as fast," says Glasses Kid, hopping around.

"You're trying to be cool, but really you just admitted that I trained you and you'd be dead without me!" I holler.

"Flam must really believe in you, right? You're not going to let that belief go to waste, are you?" asks Best Friend, while Fearsome Dragon was pumped full of arrows.

"So sorry, mammal sister," says Brawny Babe, crying into her arm and still managing one-hundred percent accuracy.

"I don't understand. If he cares about me, then why is he trying to kill me? If only Stalker was here. I'm sure she would understand," I say sadly.

Are they trying to confuse me so I summon up Flam? That's too risky though, what if he takes control again.

Best Friend stabs a blood knife in Mew Nya's foot and then approaches me. "Don't you worry about this. Flam wants you to kill them. He's testing you, Main. He's only willing to risk your life because he believes in you. Prove his love for you isn't hopelessly idealistic!" Best Friend thrusts his blood sword into Fearsome Dragon. "Farewell, Fearsome Dragon. Your death is a stepping stone to a better world."

"Excellent work," says Glasses Kid. "And good call on naming it Fearsome Dragon. Dragons are mythical beasts that are allegorically a symbol of human greed. Nobody can fault a hero for his actions if they have metaphorical significance, particularly if that significance is anti-capitalism."

169:00

"Spin it however you like. It won't change that she has lost her life…and I am responsible," says Best Friend, pulling out his blood sword.

Fearsome Dragon knocks him aside with a backhand and then rushes at me. It was now my time to shine. My hair sharpens into spikes that shoot forward, piercing into her belly. The fat cat lets out a pained cry of distress before retreating.

"Just because the cat is there in the picture, doesn't mean he killed you, Kitty," says Mew Nya as he rushes towards me.

Glasses Kid moves in. "And that's how capitalism came to be. Now, let's talk about how the stories of dragons began."

Mew Nya stops, grabbing his head in agony.

"Shut up, mew! Shut up, nya! Shut up, nyo! You don't know anything about me, nyu!" he yells, squirming about.

"You shut up, gemma! Nice one, Glasses Kid. Keep it up, friend," I say with a smile before snatching the marker from the general's grip.

"If not die together, live together," says Brawny Bitch, firing randomly in every direction.

What happened to that remarkable aim? Is she acting weak so the anti-SJWs don't say she's a forced over-powered female? Shit. These critiques have real world consequences for your fellow white male, assholes! Mary Sues keep us realistic men alive with their mastery of the forced!

I leap behind the prophetic rock, using it as precognitive cover.

Yeah, I know that word too! Surprised bitches!?

"I know you want to be free of choice, Main. But what must be done shall be done!" yells Best Friend, giving me advice as vague as his lifelong goal.

Wait! I understand…I think?

I run back to General Mew Nya and thrust the marker down his throat.

"Great thinking, Main. That marker can be our salvation in multiple ways!" cheers Glasses kid.

170:00

"With this, I attain freedom!" I exclaim as my hair hardens and becomes a massive fist.

With a single powerful decisive punch of incredible awesomeness, I shattered the Rock of Prophecy to bits.

At that point, I had no idea what the consequences of my actions would be. Maybe if I hadn't destroyed the rock, I could have checked it to see what would happen when I did destroy it. Wait…that makes no sense.

BROKEN PROPHECY

Episode 7 Part 3

An orange mist covers the area.

I'm alive? Yeah of course I'm alive. That dumb cat general attacked my prophetic stone, not me!

"Ew, his blood is all over me." Glasses Kid wipes the red blood cells off.

"It's disgusting. It burns," says Best Friend as he licks it off of Glasses Kids cheeks.

Damn that little brat! Best Friend is paying attention to him! Wait a minute! I know what to do!

I jumped into the puddle and get General Mew Nya's blood all over me.

Yes, Best Friend, tend to me!

"Main, you got his blood all over you," says Best Friend, walking towards me.

Yes! Yes! Damn it, if only I went all Samurai Jaku and tore off my shirt in the midst of battle. Oh my god, he's really going to do it.

Best Friend bonks me on the top of my head.

"Bad boy. What have I told you about playing in puddles? Take off your clothes, I'll have to clean them for you," he says with a frown.

"Guys, what are we going to do if the fat cat comes back?" asks Glasses Kid, getting back to his feet.

"Why did General Mew Nya suddenly explode?" asks Best Friend as he strips me.

"That's what happens when you go against your boss. He was foolish to try and kill me," I say.

Glasses Kid smirks. "Your injuries are all missing. Most interesting," he says, while looking me up and down.

Best Friend rushes up and uppercuts him. "Pervert! Give him some privacy," he says furiously.

"Hey, don't hit your teacher. Am I going to have to put you in time out?" asks Glasses Kid upset.

"You never had power over me. Drop the act and accept your role as Glasses Kid," says Best Friend, licking the blood off my clothes before dressing me up.

Old Dude comes into the tent. "You've defeated a CatBoy general! All as planned!"

"Your prophetic stone is gone. Yet you seem so cheery," says Best Friend suspiciously.

"I can think of ten reasons for this. One: You wanted us to destroy the stone all along. After all, it never portrayed your heroes gaining a victory over Flam even once. Two: The stone was a memento of a person you really hated. You didn't want to admit it, so you couldn't destroy it directly. But now that it's gone, you're relieved. Three: The stone is actually a curse on the land and you awaited the day that a chosen one would appear and destroy it. Four: You have hundreds more. Five: You only cared about the stone because you won it in a raffle, but you questioned the practicality of the stone. After all prophecy based on luck is just a bit too shaky. Six: It reminds you of your old pet rock and you're glad that you can finally move past his circumstantial death. Seven: The rock was placed here by Flamboyant Villain. By destroying it, we have waged war against him. You're dismayed about this and are hiding it with a superficial smile. Eight: You always smile. You think frowning makes you look old. Nine: You have faith in Main no matter what obstacle he will face now. Ten: You're blind and haven't noticed that its pieces are strewn across the floor," says Glasses Kid, before fixing his glasses.

"What do you mean it's destroyed!?" exclaims Old Dude in incredible shock.

Number ten, we have a winner.

"What's done can never be undone. Main is too precious to be bossed around by an ancient boulder anyways," says Best Friend, putting his hand on my shoulder.

"Precious?"

"I meant powerful," says Best Friend, turning away.

Oh, he can try but I saw that adorable blush. Nothing hotter than a total badass showing their sweet side! Hell yes.

Old Dude looks to the ground solemnly. "To be honest, that rock never really helped our heroes win anyways. Besides, it was given to me by Flam. I don't want a memento from that accursed traitor. This terrible stone has been a curse to the heroes. The villains always scribble horrific deaths of our saviors all over it. It's not like they haven't been mass produced either. We have exactly a hundred more ready for prophetic use. Flam only gave it to me because I won the village raffle. I don't trust anything that is given away freely though. Oh, and this one reminds me of Rocky. I need to get past his circumstantial suicide and move on already. Be warned though, by destroying that rock you have declared war against Flam. He will not be pleased. I'm smiling now because I know that frowning gives you wrinkles. I am blind by the way. But I don't have confidence that Main will overcome any obstacle. I lost faith in heroes after the betrayal of The Legendary Hero of Legends: The Legend. Turned out he was too good to be true, just like his name. They still tell legends of him," says Old Dude with a smile, looking off into nothing in particular.

"Nine of my possibilities were correct! I shall never again underestimate the all-encompassing power of "and"! My inductive powers are unmatched!" exclaims Glasses Kid, patting himself on the back while laughing.

Wow, my teammates are so great! Damn I'm awesome!

"Wait, up. More generals arrived. You still have work to be done." Old Dude leaves us the moment he finishes his sentence.

"We need to split up and find Fruity. The sooner we complete this quest, the sooner we can leave this crazy place," I say.

"As you command," says Best Friend.

Glasses Kid grabs Brawny Babe's hand. "You'll keep me safe, right?"

"Might as well." She shrugs but excitedly lifts him up.

My allies run off, leaving me on my own.

Time to find a general and kick his ass. But first I should do the opening while I have the chance.

"I look into the sunlight! Ow! My ribs!"

I get launched back but don't lose my balance.

"How dare you interrupt my opening! You are not Deo!"

Oh My God! What the hell is she doing here!?"

TomCat is standing in front of me. Her muscular, seasoned body is bloodied and is only held together by glowing white threads. Her caramel skin is lighter than before, likely from blood loss. Her sailor hat is removed, allowing her crimson spiky hair to be fully seen. The arrows in her knees, heart and throat have all been removed and the wounds are covered by cheap censor bars. The same goes for her eyes.

I can't tell if she's injured or not. Either way, how is she alive? She was decapitated!

"You're looking as fine as ever, Tomcat," I say, taking a step back.

That's her name, right? Funny, I don't recall her ever telling me it.

I look around, but none of my allies are nearby.

"It's just you and me, hero," she says, revving up the pistons in her gauntlets.

"It's a bit early for a forced villain revival, isn't it?" I ask, my hair seizing the hammer from a fallen CatBoy soldier.

"You're the villain!" she yells, before running after me on all fours.

It's eerie how her body is barely kept together by those threads. Hmm, maybe those threads are a weak point I can exploit!

My awesome hair thrusts toward her.

She jumps into the air, giving me the opening I was looking for.

My hair fist juts out, slicing into her threads…or not. Instead my hair gets tangled in them, as if pulled in by a field of gravity.

She tugs on the hair, making me lose my balance and fall to my feet. My back locks up as I'm being reeled in.

Friendship. Where is Friendship? I need Ultima! Without friendship I can't get up.

I look around; Friendship is nowhere to be seen. I must have lost Ultima when my body was running on autopilot.

Damn, I'm running out of options and I'm being pulled in closer to my demise. Wow, she has really strong thighs. She must work out a lot to get that thicc.

"Do you want me to tear off your arms or legs first?"

Damn it, she knows how indecisive I am. I have to think of a way out of this. I've seen so much anime, there's got to be something I can use.

Hakufu Sonsakufu appears in my mind's eye. "Don't burn bridges or you won't be able to get home. Don't think, but still think. A rolling stone gets the hell out of my way!"

All excellent analogies but they don't help at all. Oh wait, yes they do! If I didn't get a scratch on me while on autopilot, then maybe I should leave the fighting to automaton me! After all, no series is bold enough to kill their protagonist off screen. Sometimes the best plot armor is gained from staying out of the spotlight…or maybe sharing it! That's it! I'm going to see what the others are doing first hand. I hope this works!

"My friends are in danger! As a hero it's my duty to put their lives above my own. I'm totally not surrendering myself to a higher power. **Point of View Split!**"

It didn't work. What if my friends are in danger!? What if Best Friend is injured? I'm such a damn failure. It's moments like these where even generic harem protagonists step up with mythical bravery. I'm terrified. If I lose my best friend, what do I do? I'm nothing without him.

My self-esteem shatters, uh, just like I intended. And my point of view fragments.

I am surrounded by homosapian furrys wearing military uniforms. I of course am not concerned about this rather dangerous predicament because I'm a prodigy genius. "I surrender!" I yell in tears, cleaning my glasses so I can keep an eye on them.

They look at each other with expressions that express both their confusion and their inability to properly react in unpredictable scenarios.

I toss a smoke bomb into the group.

They rush out of the smoke and aim their crossbows at me.

"No more games," says their commander.

He is obviously the commander because he is the only who has a bell on his collar, in case you were curious.

I walk up to them with confidence. "I'd be more careful if I were you. What you inhaled is a special poison I created. It takes a couple minutes but you'll be bleeding out of every orifice if you don't take the antidote."

The CatBoy soldiers turn to each other with concern. "What do we do?"

"Hand over the antidote," says the commander.

"Now why would I do that? Handing over the antidote would leave me nothing to bargain with."

The commander fires an arrow at my feet and then presses his dagger against my throat. "Give it to me now!"

I cower behind my hands. "Please, don't hurt me! Okay. I have it, but there's only enough for one person."

"Well we all know who's the most deserving," says the commander.

A stray arrow hits him in the back of the neck.

"Traitor!" yells the commander, opening fire on his brigade.

I walk through the carnage, taking the commander's special dagger for myself and gathering some rations from the troops.

A little confusion is all it takes to disarm simpletons.

I take a bite out of the kitty cat shaped dumpling. "Mmm. Delicious."

An arrow shoots into the back of my leg and I topple to the ground. I look up to see the commander. He's covered in wounds.

"Where is your squad?" I ask, reaching into my bag to search for something to beat him.

"They turned against me so they had to die."

"You're not worthy to lead them! A teacher must always put the life of his student before his own. It's the basics of morality science!" I exclaim.

"Not another word. Give me the antidote or I'll carve you…" He reaches for his dagger but realizes it's not there. "Or I'll fill you full of holes."

"Great idea! Yeah. Here you go. Please, don't hurt me," I say, curling up into a ball and handing him the vial.

He drinks it and coughs up blood. "What is this? Am I too late?" his eyes go white.

"Sorry. I guess there's no antidote," I say with a quivering smile.

"What?" he yells, pointing his crossbow at me.

Oh, it's just too easy tricking high school drop outs.

I hold in my laughter, covering my puffed-up cheeks.

"Are you mocking me?" He falls to his knees but keeps a steady aim of the crossbow at me.

"I threw a smoke bomb! Nobody was poisoned. You killed your platoon for no reason and what you just drank…well it's poison. You have about…" I look at my digital watch. "Twenty seconds left. You can spend them praising my genius if you like or regretting all your stupid life choices. Your decision entirely."

"I'm taking you with me!" he yells, pulling the trigger.

The arrow does not shoot out and pierce my forehead as he wanted.

"Did you know that round flower sap makes things really sticky? I might have touched your crossbow when you were murdering your students. I think the trigger is jammed."

"You little bast…" His eyes go red but not from anger. Blood gushes out from his eyes, ears, and every other hole besides his pores.

Yuck.

"I would have used a less lethal poison, but you're a bad teacher."

"You certainly have an interesting past," says the familiar voice of Fruity.

Aha! If I succeed in capturing her, then I will be the most valuable member of the team! She's not one I can underestimate though.

"How long before Flam sells you off to pay off war debts?" I ask her.

"Flam protects me. I'm like a daughter to him and he's my real father! He provides for me and is supportive of my dream."

"He uses your powers to destroy his enemies. That isn't love. Come along. As a teacher it is my duty to return children to their parents."

"I'm eighteen. I'm old enough to leave the house and make my own future!"

I've reasoned with unruly teenagers before. Why is she being so difficult?

"Your father loves you and he regrets not supporting you."

"My real father told me to bring you with us. With your smarts, you could be a CatBoy general in no time."

"Alright, so we both want the other to come along with us. How about we play a guessing game. I doubt either of us want to settle things with violence like Neanderthals. If you lose to me, then your fortune telling isn't all it's cracked up to be and if I lose to you, well then, I guess I'm not worthy of being the Hero of Destiny's mentor. Is it a deal?"

"A game, huh? My father used to quiz me on the medicinal properties of produce and then hid them around the village. It was fun searching for them. He was so proud when I found the pear in the prison."

The prison! That must be where they're hiding.

"Hmm. It isn't safe here, why don't we relocate to the prison? Unless you're worried about sentimental blockages in your precognition."

"The only thing I fear is a middle-class life of simplicity. You chose the arena. I'll decide the game."

"Fair enough. Just show me where it is on the map," I say, pulling out the map pad I swiped from a CatBoy general.

I slam into the wall and grip my aching sides. "Okay Main, you're back. And now you know never to let Glasses Kid cook for you and to never trust a damn thing he says."

"Are you talking to yourself?" asks Tom Cat, tilting her head. The strings stretch, having her head bend in an extra creepy way. "I do that all the time. It's the only way I don't feel lonely!"

Tears in her eyes. That should slow her reaction time. What would Bakki do?

I run up to her and grab her arms, pinning them behind her back.

"Oh, I used to wrestle with my little brothers all the time! And I always…" she slams me to the ground with a suplex "won!"

Pain rides up my spine like Speedsracer at full throttle. Shit. I'm down for the count again. How did I get back up when I was on autopilot?

"Come on, hero! Get up so I can slam you down again!" she exclaims, picking me up.

That was surprisingly helpful of her.

TomCat slams me down.

Or not.

Shit. My hair won't move. I guess splitting my point of view lowered my power level. I hope it's only temporary.

"Do you realize you're sweating?" I ask her.

"Yeah. I get excited when I kill people. Don't judge! Everyone needs a hobby!"

"Look, I just want to thank you. If I die here, well at least I got straddled by a cute girl. Do me a favor, tell them you took my virginity."

Tough as nails girls like her are total softies on the inside. Just got to get in their head like Keimuh taught me to!

"Wow, you're so pitiful! You think flirting with me is going to save your life. I like girls, dumbass!" she yells, twisting my arm till it snaps.

I can't win against her if I'm conscious. Got to abandon my point of view again so a better player can take over.

"I'm pitiful and unworthy of the spot light! ***Point of View Shift!***" I yell with great charisma.

Run through burning village. Hear cries from entitled villagers. Rush inside buildings, find only villagers. Let them burn.

Should all burn.

"Where are pets?" Huntress asks frightened human male.

"My children are in the bedroom. It's blocked by ruble but you're strong. Please save them. I just want them safe."

Put hand on shoulder. "City spawn good for kindling." I break shoulder and human male screams. "Where pets?"

"The attic! Why do you care!?"

"Why no care?" Spits on man thing and race down hall. Kick off ground, smashing through ceiling into attic.

Find pet. Eyes become swollen.

When last time cried?

Elf cub look up with hope. Arms and legs missing. Stubs only. Dog feet and hand attached to stubs. Electric collar.

Never make amends for this.

Hoist up elf cub.

Licks face and snuggles.

Must stop crying.

Leap through roof and jump down.

Must find more pets.

Spot ally.

"Brawny Babe, you shouldn't run off without warning. Your supposed to protect Glasses Kid." Hero's Friend turn blood puddle into spikes making bigger puddle new blood. Notice elf on back. "There's a well just down the road." Boy bring up blood puddle to make wall. "Get her some water."

Nod and rush off.

Nice boy, not like others. Friend to elves.

Catboy climb wall. Rushes at me.

Shield cub in arms, sliced by cat claws but cub safe, so okay.

Catboy stops, licks blood.

Big mistake.

Arrow pierces skull.

Shove hand into arrow, pops out head.

Good work.

Hi-five shadow.

Shadow best friend. Never leave.

Shadow smiles.

How shadow smile?

Shadow cuts thigh.

No! Friend never hurt! Enemy make friend hurt! Enemy pay!

Run down street, search for enemy while shadow cuts.

Armor knight in path, points twisted arm.

"Make shadow hurt me?" Huntress ask.

"Betrayer," says knight in twisted hurt voice.

Enemy not knight. Enemy orc.

I come back into awareness. I was seeing things from Brawny Babe's eyes while I was gone.

I am worried that she's in trouble, but honestly, I think I need more help.

"I'm not...done yet," says TomCat, spitting out a piece of flesh.

Did that come from my shoulder? Did she bite me? That's so hot!

Okay, no worries. Apparently, I got some good hits in while I was away. Tomcat now has some bruises on her face and her swimsuit is cut, revealing the caramel goodness beneath.

"You're back now, right? Is that some sort of channeling technique? I don't like it!" she yells.

Why is she always yelling? Is it a cry for help or does she just need to get laid?

"I was meditating. Believe it!" I give her a thumbs up. "Want to try?"

"Every time I try, I remember terrible things!"

"You mean the horrible things you did to those villagers!"

She throws a punch but I grip her hand with my hair.

"Your fighting is sloppier now. You better not underestimate me because I'm a girl!" she yells, before blasting my hair hand to pieces.

Oh right, those pistons let her create shock waves. Thanks, subconscious mind, for reminding me way too late! Ugh, so unreliable! My ego is the only one I can count on. Alright me, let's show this villain who's awesome!

"I am the greatest hero and you won't stop me! **Massive Hair Punch**!" My hair fist hardens and slams into her, shattering her gauntlets when she shields herself.

Boom! That's what I'm talking about!

TomCat skids across the ground.

Alright, that should have weakened her. Autopilot me better not let me down. I have to see what Best Friend is doing. I have to make sure he's okay!

"I'm just a generic teen kid that is average in every way so that loser otakus can relate to me and buy my products! **Point of View Shift**!"

Wow that one, that one hurt.

In times of anarchy, the public often loot and commit violence. Fools. Moments of chaos are opportunity for activists to take action without repercussions.

Where was that petting zoo? Aha.

I find the zoo where all my animal brethren are trapped, but there's someone at the entrance.

"Stand aside or I will cut you down. Those trapped animals will taste freedom today."

"A fellow animal lover," says the man. He rolls up his sleeves and shows me the numbers 7634420. "You think I'd stand guard here during all this madness if I didn't care about them?"

"They deserve freedom."

"These aren't natural animals. GMCs, all of them. They escaped from a testing facility and my boss has made it his mission to provide for them. They wouldn't be able to live in the wild."

I don't have time to waste here. Main is fighting all on his own. And I...I left his side. I need to go to him. He needs his mommy.

"Your boss has created a prison with his compassion. He has no right to take their freedom away." I slice open the doors, creating an opening. "If they want to be here, then they will remain. The choice is now theirs to make."

I run down the streets and spot a familiar face.

Even in a human cesspool of corruption, good people can grow. Banana Man is indeed akin to a water lily.

He waves at me. I spot a figure behind him.

A CatBoy general!

I slice my palms and form kunai as the general's blade comes down on a good person. The general's sword slices into his back as I toss the kunai.

The sword shatters and the general is sliced by my projectiles.

I had feared his life was being turned into a catalyst for Main's character arc. How did Banana man shatter the sword?

Banana Man's coat opens up, revealing a mechanical arm coming from his back. The arm uses the broken sword fragment to parry the next strike.

I join Banana Man's side and form a sword of blood. "Go find your daughter. I'll handle this."

"No. No more heroes are going to die to bring back a girl who doesn't want to come home. The only one going after her is me." Banana man dislocates his joints, becoming taller. His muscles tear his coat apart.

Such power and determination. This man is truly made in the abyss.

"Just decide already. I don't care who I kill first. Oh, pardon my rudeness. My name is CatScratch." The general pulls in the sword fragment and reconnects it to his blade.

"I've decided to bring your daughter back to you, not as a quest but as a duty to a man I respect. You can attack, but only do so when there is an opening. This enemy will not go down easily.

"Neither will I," says Banana Man, spraying the general with a blue fluid.

"**EXPEL**!" yells the general, sending the fluid off.

Banana Man just gave me the chance to end this.

I bring my sword down on my enemy but it stops in place.

Gravity manipulation, as expected.

Banana Man unfolds a lance and circles around behind the enemy. His jabs are parried by our foe's exceptional sword play.

"My attacks are being pulled into his strikes. I can't get a hit on him," says Banana Man before tossing a flame grenade.

The grenade stops and slams into me.

A magician only needs a distraction to work magic!

I use a blood dagger to cut open my right arm. The extra blood lengthens my sword, pressing it into the enemy's chest.

"No! I'm not dying! I am bringing you to Flam!" yells CatScratch, slicing my blood blade and stopping my attack.

"You're loyal to a fault. It will be your undoing. **Crimson Snake**." My broken sword uses more of my arm's blood and elongates. It twists behind the enemy but is parried.

At least that's what he thinks.

My blood sword coils around his second sword, giving Banana Man the perfect opportunity.

"I'm taking my daughter back from you." Banana Man fires a pistol into CatScratch's head.

"Nooooo!" yells CatScratch

A powerful gravity blast sends me off my feet and smashing into a building.

I've lost a lot of blood. If I don't feed, this body will fail me.

"Are you like a vampire? That is so sexy," I say out loud.

Oh, I'm back. Being inside Best Friends body like that was amazing! I have to go for another round. Wait. He's in danger. I need to finish up here and come to his sexy aid.

TomCat lowers her fist. "Look, I get that you're desperate and trying to psyche me out, but please stop flirting with me. It honestly makes me uncomfortable," she says, looking away.

Awww. There's that beautiful vulnerability. I hope my female readers won't be pissed at me for exploiting her feminine side. I'm only doing it so I can save my super sexy best friend, after all.

"You don't have to be ashamed. Your beautiful and if nobody notices that, then you probably already tore out their eyes."

"I asked you to stop…it makes me think of bad things."

Shit. If I attack her now, then the entire hashtag me too movement will band against me and rightfully so! But I'm a legendary crowd pleaser. I can figure my way out of this.

"It was Flam, wasn't it? He bragged about banging you in every room of the castle."

TomCat turns away with flushed cheeks. "It wasn't every room, sheesh. Okay, since you're genuinely interested and I'm going to kill you anyways…" She takes a deep breath. "Flam is a monster and I hate him, but he keeps me safe. I love fighting heroes, sure. But killing weak villagers, it makes me sick. And when he wants sex I have to give in or else…he'll abandon me." Her face is completely taken over by tears.

I confront her and embrace her. "I'll keep you safe."

TomCat looks up at me with gentle eyes, sparkling with confusion and a bit of hope. "Huh?"

"My team killed you before, right? That means Flam failed to protect you! Why serve someone who failed you. We'll keep you safe from Flam's forces."

Flam's voice suddenly pops into my head. "Main, be a dear and seal those pretty lips. You're supposed to fight her not comfort her."

"What's wrong, are you afraid?" I ask.

TomCat clenches herself. "Of course I'm afraid. I'm…still fertile. And I don't want kids but that doesn't mean I want to lose that. Flam isn't who you'll have to protect me from."

"What?"

"You're not strong enough to protect me." TomCat shoves me off.

I lose my balance and fall over.

"My Best Friend is in danger. I need your help. I don't want to lose him."

TomCat rolls her eyes. "That's not my problem."

"How about a temporary truce. If you kill me, then you know my team is going to hunt you down. Flam wants me alive too."

"Why do things have to be so complicated. Just do your zone out thing. I need some time to decide," says TomCat, biting her thumb.

"Found me," Huntress say, readying bow.

"Kill," says orc in deranged voice.

Swings axe but Huntress duck. Shadow of axe cuts into flesh.

Must kill all orcs.

Rush enemy and shoulder ram.

Enemy teeter back.

Huntress grab and headbutt. Wretched scream as Huntress tear off helmet.

Want look away, but must focus.

Face sliced, nails and spokes, mouth dry, eyes pure white.

Such suffering. Must end.

Arrow fires but sliced by shadow axe.

Tip of axe grabbed by shadow friend. Swings toward face.

Cub on shoulder. Must protect.

Whisper enchantment as draw arrow. Fire in air. Explodes into light.

Can't see. But can feel.

Jabs fingers into orc's throat. Huntress tears off head.

Dead orc. Dead friend.

Steady breath and continue search for cubs.

"Are you done delaying our game?" asks Fruity.

All the prison cells are empty. Did they know I was looking?

"Yeah. I was just making sure we had a fair environment."

"Alright, so we each take turns guessing something about the other. The first one to mess up loses. Simple enough?" asks Fruity, pulling up a chair.

"And we both are adept enough to know if the other is lying. You go first."

"You're looking for those kids, aren't you?"

She's too damn good.

"I…I have no reason to doubt the village, but as a teacher I just have to make sure they're safe."

"You just lied. You're full of doubt. You can't hide anything from me. Better be careful when your turn comes around."

"Those memories of your father playing with you, they made you doubt your choice to leave the village, didn't they?"

Fruity slams her hand to the table. "Getting personal, are we? Alright, you secretly respect Main. In fact, you envy him."

Thank goodness Main isn't listening in on this.

"Whenever you eat fruit, you think of your father."

"Yeah, which is why I avoid eating fruit. I…used to look up to him. But he changed and so did I. Your parents went missing when you were just a little boy."

This game is impossible for me to win. She can read my past flawlessly with her powers. But there's a game within this game and that's where I'll achieve my victory.

"You loved riding on your daddy's shoulders."

"Stop talking about my dad already!" Fruity grabs me by the collar. "Got it?"

"I'm not breaking any rules. He used to blend herbs together to help you get over sickness, didn't he?"

"It isn't your turn! You fantasize about dating your female students because the taboo of it excites you. Ugh, little creep."

"Hey, fantasies don't hurt anyone. Unlike when you burned down the fruit stand."

"What do you mean?"

"I saw your father rush in to put out the flames. His body was burned because of you!"

"I didn't burn it! Ha! I caught you lying."

"Nope. You actually fell into my trap."

"Huh?"

"You admitted to lying about burning his stand. That is what you said when we first met, right?"

"That doesn't count!" She slams her fist to the table. "That lie was before this game."

"Of course it doesn't count. The rules are about messing up, not lying. You only lose if you predict something wrong."

Magic or not, she's just another simpleton. I'm disappointed. When you're this smart, everyone is just sooo predictable.

"Yeah." She steadies herself. "That's right and it's my turn. You're planning something. You don't care about winning. You can't back out on the deal. When I win, you come with me."

"Despite running away, you beg Flam to spare your father every time he sends his army to this village. You even came here to make sure he's safe. You love him, don't you?"

Fruity buries her face in her hands and sobs. "You messed up. I…hate him. He didn't protect mummy. He didn't even try to save her."

"He made a choice to save his little girl instead and that choice has haunted him to this day."

"My dad. He's out there right now. He's going to get himself killed."

Checkmate.

"What about the game?" I ask with a grin.

"Forget about the damn game."

"I won't budge unless you forfeit."

Of course I can't stop her either but those wonderful clouds of rage will absolutely make her overlook this.

"Okay I give in. You win. I'll go back to my dad. Let's hurry."

"My legs are tired. Can you carry me?"

"Urgh!" She picks me up in her arms.

Getting her under my control would benefit me greatly.

I wake up to see TomCat shaking me.

"You awake? You didn't hear me muttering to myself, right?"

"Actually, I didn't hear a word."

Except I may have heard Glasses Kid admits he envies me! Oh man, I can't wait to rub it in his face.

"Did you see your friend? Is he uh, okay?"

My eyes widen. "I saw the other two, but not him. You don't think he's…"

"If you can't change something, then don't worry about it. Do that thing again. I'll put you on my back and start searching for him."

"So, then you decided to join us."

"No. But I'm going to help you save your friend. All my brothers…were murdered."

"By Flam."

"No, by this village."

Okay. Was not expecting that answer.

"Stop stalling. Do that thing and find your friend."

"I'm a weak male literally being carried a strong female. ***Point of View Shift!***"

"Come back here!" I yell.

The enemy is fighting Banana Man. My vision is blurry and I'm using my own blood as a walking stick since my legs are broken.

A white knight steps in front of me.

"Out of my way. He's going to die," I say.

"Oh, you're male. My apologies. Continue…bleeding out or whatever."

Wait. I know this guy.

"White Knight, you're a powerful hero. I need you to protect Banana Man. He's in danger."

"Men aren't worthy to be saved. Every moment spent saving them is a moment I could be using to rescue the purer sex."

"He has a daughter, she just turned eighteen."

"Thanks for the tip, citizen!" White Knight rushes off.

"You're alive!" exclaims Main.

That voice always washes away my worries, yet never my sin.

"Barely. I see you convinced TomCat to join you."

TomCat crosses her arms. "Actually, I just got tired of beating him up. Wasn't allowed to kill him. Gotta follow orders."

"Wait, really? So, I'd be dead if it weren't for Flam's orders?" asks Main.

"Yep. Super dead," she says, flicking his forehead.

Contain your rage. Don't slice off her hand.

"You need medical attention," says Main.

"I'll be fine. But Banana Man is in danger. You have to save him. The enemy has power over gravity. Keep your distance," I say with a weak smile.

"If you couldn't beat him, then how can I?" asks Main.

He must cut out that doubt one day.

I press my forehead to Main's. "I believe in you. You can do whatever you set your mind to."

I need rest.

I close my eyes

I shake Best Friend. "Is he okay?"

"Still has a pulse. So yeah, apparently. Don't know how one person can bleed this much."

"You're a CatGirl general, right? Well, I saw a guardian angel nearby. She's dressed as a boy. Has blue and red hair. It's your job to take them in. Go find her and use her to heal my friend. I'm going to save Banana Man."

"I'll be back to bring you in once he's back on his feet so you better be prepared!" exclaims TomCat.

"Are you kidding. I don't stand a chance against someone who's gone through real trauma and powered through it." I give her a thumbs up and then rush off.

I see Banana Man in the distance. He's using grappling hooks to stay out of the enemy's range.

Gotta go fast. Oooh, time for a commercial break.

Episode 7 Part 4

I arrive in front of the enemy. "Banana Man is off limits. What's with you all and ignoring your boss?"

The CatBoy general turns to face me. His jade eyes are swirling with madness. "Oh, I'm just playing with him. Was waiting for you to show up." His smile sends chills through my body.

"Don't tell me you're into me too. I don't blame you at all. But I'm heterosexual. That means no dick for me."

"Despair is the fruit of the gods!" he exclaims.

"No. Pretty sure despair isn't a fruit. Bananas are where it's at."

"I want Flam to suffer so I can feel it."

Wow. I almost feel sorry for the guy. These generals are so disloyal.

"Killing you will bring him such misery. I'm going to drag it out, so be patient with me." He swipes his sword and pulls me in somehow.

I block with my awesome hair, which is cut by the swords.

Wow. Not the best match up.

"Okay, I get that you're a psychotic asshole who can't use video games as an outlet for your aggression, but I'm on a tight schedule. This special is really long and I still have to make some sort of epilogue to bring things together. So, either kill me quickly or die quickly."

My hair becomes two fist that are pushed aside and then sliced.

A white knight appears in front of me and throws me aside before blocking the incoming sword strike. "If you're going to take a long time to die, then let me step in and finish the job."

The CatBoy general's head then explodes.

That was unexpected.

195:00

Banana Man comes out from behind cover, hoists his rifle over his back and waves to me.

Was he always that tall?

"Glad you're safe, kid," he says with a smile.

"I'm the hero, not you. Where do you get off, stealing my kill?" I ask, playfully slugging him.

"A round from a sniper rifle can end most threats. He was focused on you, so I decided to give it my best shot."

The white knight buts in between us and looks at Banana Man. "So, you finally come out of hiding. I hear you have a daughter in need of rescuing. Sorry I didn't show up earlier. Was busy with an urgent quest."

I grab his hand. "What quest could possibly be more important than reuniting this man with his daughter? And who the heck are you, a Goblin Scalper cosplayer?"

"My name is White Knight. I'm the rank one. The number one hero. You must be new. You had nearly died. Not that the world would mourn if it lost a bit of the white trash polluting it. And as for my mission, I, White Knight, was intercepting Flam's army and rescuing any villagers they had captured."

"What's your power, asshole?"

"None of your concern, white trash."

As soon as I find Friendship, I am blasting this dick to pieces.

"Daddy!" Fruity is running toward us followed by a squad of machine bandits.

Awesome! To think I'd find cosplayers with that level of skill in a place like this.

White Knight turns to me. "Well, I White Knight, have a mission elsewhere. If I were you, I wouldn't get involved in this either. Run while you still can." The coward then flees the area.

So, they're enemies. That's fine. I'm going to protect Fruity. She's so close to Banana Man. Which means I'm super close to finishing my quest!

TomCat suddenly rushes by us and toward the machine samurai. "You're not taking away my friend!"

"I can't shoot them all down. We're so close but I'm failing her...all over again." Banana man seems to shrink as his misery weighs him down.

"If we can't beat them or bargain with them, then let's bypass them. Hey, Flam you're the one controlling me when I give up my POV. How about we try stacking POV?"

"Anything to get you here sooner. After this is done, there's something I have to tell you. Understood?"

"Alright, let's do this!" I rush head first toward the enemy. TomCat is fighting two of them at once. That means I have to take down the other four.

"Hey bandits. What do you nameless losers expect do against the combined power of the main character and the main villain?"

Flam moves my hair across the ground. It rises up to grip their hands and make them miss. My hair then slides into their armor and pierces their body.

I can feel everything. It's like my hair is an extension of my body.

"It is absolutely an extension," says Flam in my head.

My hair becomes like a sword, cutting through their blades and slicing them to pieces. It then comes together, lifts up the two machine samurai attacking TomCat and smashes them to a pulp in its iron grip.

Fruity runs past me and hugs TomCat. "You saved me."

"Hey, so did I...but don't hug me. Go hug your dad," I say, pointing to the man who just finished taking out the last machine samurai.

Fruity runs into her father's arms and cries.

All, this conflict was worth it. I wish I had a father.

Old Dude appears from a vortex in space. "You completed your first real quest. I'm proud of you." He and his wrinkles smile at me.

"Best Friend is injured. TomCat, did you abandon him?"

"He's fine. Healed himself up, actually," she says with wide eyes.

Best Friend comes up from behind me. "You managed just fine without me. Your parents are so proud of you." He pats my head and ruffles my hair.

He's uninjured and his clothes are repaired too. Damn it! Why are they repaired?

"I'll lead you to Flam's castle. I know the way. You saved Fruity so consider us even," says TomCat with a smile.

"Happy to be there for you, buddy," I say, slinging my arm over her shoulder.

Oh yeah. I just befriended my first enemy. Just a couple dozen more of these and I'll pass up Noruto.

Old Dude waves at me. "Three generals defeated and your first quest complete. I believe it's time we give you a proper hero's welcome. I'll round up the survivors and bring you your official hero's garb."

"What about saving Stalker?" asks Glasses Kid.

When did the little brat show up?

"You're right. We should head over there and save her. Don't want her missing my big moment after all," I say with a grin.

"Your valor is blinding but I can't bear to blink," says Best Friend, blissfully gazing into me.

Old Dude pat's my back with my invisible hand. "That's fine. Go rescue the girl. Your hero's garb and harem will be here when you return."

Did he say harem!? Hell yes!

"What kind of man would I be if I tried to save Stalker, robbing that perfectly capable young woman the chance to free herself. I'm no misogynist! How many girls are in my harem exactly?"

Old Dude snickers. "You'll see. Ah, to be young again."

"Main, you must stay focused. Stalker is an ally." Best Friend puts his hands on my shoulders.

"Assailant has Boobs so this may be my only chance to cheat on a love pillow. I'm a hero second and a teen with raging hormones first."

"I'm going even if you aren't," says Best Friend.

"What? You're going to miss my big moment."

"She's counting on you to show up. What if she allowed herself to get captured so you could save her? The poor girl has been through more grief than anyone ever should."

"If we're going to storm his castle, we're going to need to be well-rested and have a larger team." I turn to Old Dude. "Can my harem fight? I don't want useless airheads; I want airheads with expert marksmanship or kicks that can shatter mountains."

"I select only the finest. With two generals gone that means you're the Number One Hero! You finished your first arc. Don't you think you deserve a party?"

"I absolutely do deserve a party. We all do!"

"Meet me there. I'm going after her," says Best Friend, turning around.

"Now is not the time for you to add on extra conflict. This is supposed to be the relaxing epilogue. If you rescue her without me, she'll be heartbroken."

"You're right." Best Friend assumes a fighting stance.

"It's really going to be like this. Fine then. I'm way stronger than I was before."

Best Friend rushes in but my hair shoves him aside.

I jump off my hair and slam my fist into the back of his head. I slam His face to the ground.

"I deserved that. I deserve more than that. Come at me again!" he yells, rushing at me.

My hair coats my fist and I punch his chest. My hair fist then extends, slamming into his jaw.

Is he letting me win? Why?

Flam's voice suddenly rings in my head, disorienting me. "Is now a bad time?"

"Yes, actually. It is. Very bad time," I say, seizing Best Friend's feet and slamming my fist into his face.

Best Friend holds his broken nose. "This pain is nothing." He runs into me and lifts me off my feet.

My hair grabs him, pulls him over me and slams him to the ground.

"Are you really alright with this, hurting those who care about you for selfish reasons!?"

"This isn't like a trip to the candy store. This is an actual harem, dude!" My hair sends him up with a flurry of rapid punches. "And no, I don't want to hurt you, but you wanted a fight so I'm not backing down. What about you? You watched me fight Flam instead of helping me out. Care to explain that?"

"I wouldn't interrupt your fight," says Best Friend, using his blood for an instant to slice my next hair punch.

He rushes at me and I grab both his fists.

"I was clearly outmatched! You need to drop that idealistic image of me. It's going to get me killed. I'm not as amazing as you think. I get scared. Like when you were wounded back there. I was so scared."

"This is cute and all," says Flam. "But I need you to know that Stalker's execution is tonight."

"Say what?" I ask before Best Friend's blood-hardened fist collides into my face.

Everything goes black.

To be continued in *The Main Character: The Hero's Epic Journey Continues!*

Coming Fall 2019

NEEDLESSLY FANSERVICEY
OVA BOB-RAY SPECIAL!

Needlessly Fanservicey OVA BOB-ray Special!

You did it! You bought the BOB-ray disc! You're so awesome. This extra episode is dedicated to you. It recounts events that I knowingly saved for later because they were just so fun and juicy. Yeah, that means this is totally cannon! If you're as attentive as I know you are, you probably realized a time jump between episodes two and three. Well, this story fills in the gap so you'll get to see what transpired after I accepted my role as hero and before I faced the perilous trials and met Brawny Babe. Enjoy!

I was ready to leap into action the moment I formerly seized my heroic identity, but this was a pretty rinky dink village, so they needed time to prepare my test. Why is there even a test? I mean, they're the one's begging for a hero. It doesn't really matter because I ace every test I don't fail and defy all expectations. To kill time, I allowed the team to decide where we would go. After listing a bunch of boring places, Stalker said they have a hot spring!

Hot spring episodes are among some of the best in anime. Who could forget the legendary hot spring segments of Inyuyasha? Speaking of Rumeiko Takahashi's work, what if there's a onsen, that means hot spring but you know that because you aren't a cheapskate who watches my show for free on the royaltyroad streaming site without donating to my Paytreon...what was I saying? Oh yeah, give me your money! Wait, you already did that when you bought this special collection. Oh yeah, I was saying that maybe this hot spring can turn Best Friend into a bodacious babe and turn me into a WarsKraft kung-fu panda!

"Main, stay focused. You don't want to get cut," says Best Friend, slicing the thorny thicket of cherry blossom vines.

"Don't worry, I got my saliva on standby," says Stalker, riding atop my shoulders.

When did she get there? Eh, it doesn't matter. What matters is that those thorns poked a whole in Best Friend's pants so I can see those super cute red skull boxers he's wearing.

"It's getting dark. It isn't safe to be out here. There are a number of dangerous creatures that could attack us," says Glasses Kid.

"None of which I want to hear about. Yo, Bestie, we almost there?" I ask, grabbing Best Friend's hand.

"We will be there before the WarWolves begin their hunt."

What is a WarWolf? Is it like a werewolf?

"Main, your face got cut. No worries. I got it," says Stalker, bending over and licking my face.

"Thanks! But hey don't go drooling over me, kay? If we encounter a WarWolf, then I might need a whole bucket of your drool."

"Just having you take off your shirt would make me release a bucket of fluids," says Stalker, pulling at my cheeks.

Glasses Kid turns to face me as he walks backward. "Did you know this place is called Cherry Thicket? It's a historical site that was actually created by a powerful CatBoy general called-"

"Nobody cares," I say, putting my arms behind my head.

"And thus, our journey through the Cherry Thicket comes to an end," says Best Friend turning to beckon us.

Mmmm! His face is even sexier with those badass scars that I know for damn sure were not caused by an overprotective Furkin.

"The pain will all be worth it now," says Glasses Kid, stripping into the purple grape bathing suit the village lent him.

"I will meet with you all shortly," says Best Friend.

Is he going to strip off screen! No! I won't allow it. You paid for this episode so you're going to get to see the glory that I witness every bath time! But how do I stop him without coming off as weird?

"Yo, Bestie," says Stalker, jumping off from my shoulders and landing.

Hey, that's what I call him. Stupid little poser. And wait, when did she change into that sleepy sheep frilly bathing suit? Did she do a magical girl transformation on my shoulders without me noticing?

"I think it's a good idea for us to stick together. If a powerful enemy comes, Glasses Kid and I will need you to protect us," she says with a cute grin.

She's truly a little angel. Asking Best Friend to stay and strip for me. Or is she just being protective?

Best Friend takes his zip up jacket off and Stalker gives me a wink.

She totally is doing this for me and I love her for it.

Best Friend is removing those sexy black jeans to reveal his even sexier red skull boxers. He begins to remove his tight undershirt but stops. "That's enough for now."

No, it frickin' isn't. Ugh, fine. I'll get him to strip fully when we cuddle tonight. I will not let my viewers down!

Glasses Kid removes a thermometer from the water. "The temperature is safe to enter for a period no longer than twenty-three minutes."

"Thanks for that bit of information I don't care about," I say, watching Best Friend slowly ease into the water.

Assailant rises from my shadow and looms over me. "Thanks for giving my perky pumpkin a ride on your shoulders," he says with a bow.

"Hey, we had a deal. Is Boobs okay?" I ask.

Assailant's cloak twists reality and spits out my pillow pal.

Boobs was safe, all of Stalker's grinding against the back of my neck was not weathered in vain!

"Watch me, big bro!" Stalker cannonballs into the water while making an ahego face.

She truly is a unique girl. Speaking of unique, this hot spring is gorgeous. It shimmers like an anime hot spring but has none of that bothersome steam that inconveniently covers all the juicy bits. In fact, when I look through this steam, I can see Best Friend's sweet abs in 4k resolution! The water is clear too, which Stalker clearly realizes because she waves at me with her toes.

"Come on in, onii-san!" She pulls down her top until she notices Glasses Kid staring. "What do you want?"

"Desires lead to disappointments, I am perfectly content with what I am witnessing," he says with a smile.

I start to strip but feel Stalker's eyes on me and stop.

She notices and gives me a disarming smile. "Come on in, this is the OhnZen, a very special hot spring connected to the WorldStump. It has healing factors and rejuvenates the body after strenuous activity," says my guardian angel, wiggling her eyebrows at me.

"So, it's like the hot spring in the final arc of Bleached!" I exclaim.

"I dunno…I've uh, only seen the anime," says Stalker, fiddling with her hair in embarrassment.

"When we return home, I promise to petition for them to animate the last arc and then we can binge Ichigone's struggle against Gold Roger together!" I exclaim with a thumbs up.

Stalker swoons, giving me the opportunity I needed. All those speed stripping ViralTube Freed! challenges have trained my body to be Plus Ultra!

I set Boobs upright by a non-prickly tree and enter the bath, rocking my Happi blue cat swim trunks.

Stalker doggy paddles up to me. "Those are so cute. Can I pet the kitty?" Her eyes shimmer and bewitch me.

"Happi is an exseed and he's Lizanna and Nitsu's child! But yeah, that's fine with me."

"Aye, Sir!" Stalker pokes at my sweet trunks. "Meow. Meow." Her moth goes agape and she parts bobbing side to side.

One day I will try the juice prank on her. For Uchio's dad!

"So, how do I look in my swimsuit?" asks Stalker, striking a Jojos pose.

Needlessly Fanservicey OVA BOB-ray Special!

There's no right way to answer this, is there?

"Cosplay is something that anyone can do! As long as your costume physically fits your body and you're having fun, that's what matters!"

Those damn elitists at the CosCon told me I was too white to cosplay as Killuh Bee! Well maybe if he wasn't the biggest badass in Naruto, I would have picked someone else! I can't help wanting to dress up as the coolest character.

"You wanna cosplay together sometime! I could be Shirow and you could be Soruh! We could reenact the scene where they give each other air," she says with a devious smile.

"I'd love to do group cosplay!" I exclaim.

"Yay!" she cheers, jumping into my arms.

Alright! I successfully changed the subject while not ignoring the question. Loli tears averted!

"I wonder how long we can stay like this," says Best Friend, staring out at the stars.

I look around and notice something.

"How are their no big breasted women here? Hot springs scenes are supposed to have tons of girls, comparing breast sizes and groping each other!" I yell with unbridled otaku rage.

I'm so sorry I didn't notice it sooner. I apologize to all my lesbian, hetero male, and bisexual viewers. I will remedy this situation.

"The reason this hot spring is so clean is because it's located past Cherry Thicket. Of course nobody else is here," says Glasses Kid.

"I can show my boobs to you if you want," says Stalker, lowering her bathing suit while leaning up to me.

"I want big boobs! Look at how huge those slimy melons are! They must be an Ai cup as in Aikan! I bet those boobs are strong enough to crush skulls along with the hopes and dreams of all lolis with washboards!" I exclaim.

Needlessly Fanservicey OVA BOB-ray Special!

Oh shit! I wasn't thinking. Disgeauh alone taught me that all boob-developmentally challenged girls have flat complexes. I hope I don't cause Stalker to collapse into depressive signing.

"Sorry. I didn't mean to offend," I say, patting her head.

"No worries. I know I've got a nice body. Don't need anyone's validation on that. Look at these pups," says Stalker, pushing out her chest with Kuusano's childlike pride.

Wait, so the flat complex thing was a lie? NISUH how could you!? Wait, what else isn't true?

"Are these not sufficient?" asks Best Friend, holding his chest with void like eyes. "Furu, furu…"

What have I done?

Stalker paddles up to Best Friend. "You're beautiful just the way you are."

Best Friend hugs her tightly. "Thank you."

What just happened? Is Stalker going to steal Best Friend away and hold his heart for ransom until I beg on all fours like a puppy dog? Wow, just got an image of Best Friend with puppy ears, so freaking sexy!

Glasses Kid averts his gaze from Stalker's bottom. "Main, we've got company."

Boobs! My pillow partner has come to life and I didn't even need to use my epic stand's power to make it happen! Wait a minute, something seems off.

I peer closely at the figure to notice that their skin is blue, there's a visible skeleton inside her and she's dripping goop onto the grass. Her hair still blocks her face like in the pillow but it also extends down her shoulders like hands that try to cover her boobtastic bosom. Another noticeable difference is she also has a heart-shaped, not valentine-shaped, like a beating heart core right below her navel. She also has a gooey antenna with a glowing blue tip.

"The color of the tip means she's calm for now, but that could change in an instant! She's already eaten someone! You can see the skeleton. Do not let that slime enter the bath!" exclaims Glasses Kid, leaping out and running away.

"Stay there, Main. I'll deal with the intruder," says Best Friend, revealing a hidden blade beneath his undershirt.

"Calm down! There's no need to hurt them!"

I say 'them' because the English language was created by a bunch of white guys who never heard about snails and think animals are objects.

"He's right, bro-bro. Slimes are super duper dangerous. It's not nice but we should make it go away forever," says Stalker.

I can't believe my allies! There is a big breasted slime girl and they want to kill it! How the hell can I caress my Hapi the Harpy figurine with love if I allow them to kill Tsu?

"Best Friend, if you love me, then don't hurt them," I say, grabbing his hands.

No commenting on how smooth they are; this is serious.

"It's because I love you that I must do this. Stalker warned me about these things. They eat heroes," says Best Friend with a terrified look.

"Yes!"

Slime-girl blow job for the freaking win!

Best Friend put his hand on my shoulder. "They would eat your entire body and dissolve you alive as you drown and your skin is set aflame." He grips his sides. "I can feel the agony just saying it. I will dirty my hands but please, look away."

I grab him and hug him. "Please, don't kill Boobs."

"The slime isn't Boobs; she's impersonating her."

Wow. Here I was trying to be respectful to my readers with the "they" pronoun but I was being disrespectful to the slime that clearly identifies as female.

I grab Best Friend's scared cheeks and pull him to face me. "What would Boobs think if I let you kill a slime posing as her?"

"Nothing. She's a pillow," says Best Friend.

Touché.

"You know that Melowna is my favorite Queens' Blade character. You can't kill Boobslime!" I yell.

Boobs plus slime equals Boobslime. Respectful and clever. I amaze even me.

"Um, you all can stop fighting. She left," says Stalker, lowering her head.

I leap out of the bath and grab my clothes. "I'm going to get dressed where I won't be gawked at!" I yell, rushing off to find the girl of my dreams.

Best Friend leaps out and blocks my path. He dresses me up in a mere instant.

You might want to re-watch that scene in reverse.

Best Friend puts his clothes back on. "It isn't safe her. It might return with more of them. Let's get moving."

"Can I get another ride?" asks Stalker, giving me the puppy dog eyes, no even cuter, she went for the hamster look!

"Promise not to pretend the back of my neck is a stripper's pole?" I ask.

"Sowwy. I can't help it. I get so excited near you. I'll walk," she says with a frown.

"Geez. It's fine, climb aboard," I say, crouching so she can climb atop me.

"Let's move!" Best Friend rushes on ahead and we follow along.

"What took you all so long to leave? Those things are monsters!" exclaims Glasses Kid, using roller skates to keep up with us.

"My Monster Girl's Quests' Monsterpedia agrees with that statement, however facts don't change that calling someone a monster is racist!"

"Soooo, should we head to bed? I made sure there's one less sleeping bag at the inn so that we can snuggle wuggle till the Cuckatrice's sing!" Stalker wiggles her legs in excitement.

"No way! We're not going to bed without a pillow fight!" I exclaim.

"Well then, are we going to have a pillow fight..." Best Friend turns to face us with a deranged smile "or a pillow death match?"

"What's a pillow death match? Sounds scary but comfy," says Stalker.

"It's like a pillow fight, but the winner picks one person and decides what they have to do," I say, fist-bumping my BFF.

Stalker falls off my shoulders but is caught by Glasses Kid.

"You smell like strawberries!" he exclaims with an intoxicated look.

Stalker smacks her cheeks and puts on her mean face. "I can't afford to lose."

No telling what she'll do to me if I lose. But if I win, then Best Friend is going to have to let me spend the night with Boobslime!

"Are we going to fight in our jammies?" asks Glasses Kid.

"Absolutely. But you don't stand a chance at winning," says Best Friend.

"I've never lost anything in my life," says Glasses Kid with a confident smirk.

"Including your virginity!" I exclaim.

Boom! Let's see him try to make a clever come back to that.

"Say's the virgin," says Glasses Kid.

I hate this little twerp.

"Where should we do battle?" asks Best Friend.

"Well, there's an arena that is closed down at this time, according to the village's travel guide. In the day time heroes compete for glory!"

Awesome! I can finally have a magic games arc without having a disappointing surrender for a finale!

Needlessly Fanservicey OVA BOB-ray Special!

Let's skip the rest of the trek back to the inn and go straight to the epic pillow death match.

We arrive at the arena, pillows in tow. It's a wide-open stage with different blocks connected to one another. The stage is surrounded by pews which are not occupied by my adoring fans.

Everyone is geared for battle. Best Friend is wearing his black undershirt and purple booty shorts. Stalker is wearing frilly hooded pajamas with sleepy sheep and a pink skirt. Glasses Kid is in an owl styled checkered pajamas. I'm suited up in my ahego jammies. We're ready to kick some ass!

"Shall we begin?" asks Best Friend, pointing his pillow at me like a weapon.

Assailant pops out from my shadow, making me jump in surprise.

"Oops. Didn't mean to frighten you. Is it alright if I join?" asks Assailant.

"No pillow no entry," says Glasses Kid.

Assailant's vortex body spits out eight pillows. He then pierces them with his tendrils and lifts them. His tendrils start shaking.

Stalker hugs him. "Don't freak out. It's just a game okay. Now win so I can make Main mine," she says with a devious grin.

I give Best Friend a look and he nods.

Our strategy will take them down.

Best Friend suddenly rushes toward me and puts out his arms defensively. "Boobslime followed us here."

Boobslime picks up my girlfriend love pillow and assumes a fighting stance.

"Come on, she just wants to play. Nothing bad will happen to me as long as you're watching, right?" I grab Best Friend's hands.

"Alright, let the death match begin," says Best Friend, tossing his pillow in the air. He climbs up my back and leaps off my shoulders before kicking his pillow into Assailant.

Needlessly Fanservicey OVA BOB-ray Special!

"Yes! The Best Friend's Squad are having a pillow fight!" I exclaim, my voice cracking with joy.

The modest assassin deflects the pillow and sends it back at Best Friend, who catches it before landing and then rushes in, deflecting the multi-pillow assault.

Not too long ago this freak was trying to kill my Best Friend. This has been a bizarre day.

Glasses Kid chases Stalker while giggling. "Only simpletons think there is only one way to win." He swipes at Stalker but loses his balance.

Stalker bops his head lightly and crouches down. "You okay?" she asks.

Glasses Kid's eyes light up, probably because he saw her panties. "I'm more than okay. I'm victorious."

Best Friend slices a pillow open, tossing cotton into Assailant's face to distract him. "Carry on without me, Main." He flashes me a smile before launching into Assailant. The two of them fall and hit the ground.

I come back to my senses when I'm hit with Boobs from behind.

Wait a minute. Boobs is carrying Boobs!

"It's boobseption!" I exclaim, before deflecting a swipe from my girlfriend.

"Watch out!" screams Best Friend in terror.

Stalker and Boobslime swipe at me at once.

They don't know who they're dealing with.

I drop my pillow and then kick into Stalker's face with my foot. My body turns and I yank Stalker's pillow out of her hand. I grab my pillow with the other hand and crouch, catching Boobs right between the two pillows.

"You can't win without a pillow, Stalker," I say as she pads my back with her tiny fists.

"Win," says Boobslime, smiling before increasing her strength and breaching my defenses.

I stumble back and nearly topple over.

Stalker leaps up, pushing off the ground with her tail.

Wait, she has a tail!?

Stalker then rams her little chest into my face, knocking me over. "Yay! My natural pillows won!"

"That's cheating," says Best Friend, point blank.

"No! That was so adorable I'll allow it," I say, giving Stalker a thumbs up.

Stalker lifts up a pillow and tosses them at Boobslime. The pillows merge with her gooey body and are dissolved.

"Come on Boobs! You're a pillow, you were literally made for this!" I cheer.

"Boobs," repeats Boobslime, swiping my girl-friend at Stalker.

"Flat is justice!" yells Stalker, giggling as she blocks with her chest.

"Bigger," says Boobslime, moving Boobs through her body to swap arms and strike Stalker from the side.

Stalker stumbles but her dual heart tail pops out and keeps her from falling.

Does that tail have an eye? Creepy. It's watching me even now. Has it always been watching me?

"You think size is what matters, huh? Well, Sista, let me tell you the truth!" Stalker rushes in and grabs Boobs, entering an epic power-struggle with Boobslime. "Size, shape, color, gloss, sensitivity." Stalker releases and dodges Boobslime's reckless swipes. She gets hit when Boobslime shoots my girlfriend out like a cannonball from her chest, but blocks with her iron washboard. "Firmness, elasticity, taste, smell, texture, annnnnd…" Stalker reaches under her jammies and pulls out a flash bomb "the ability to hold things!" She tosses it to the ground, blinding everyone for an instant.

When sight returns to me, I see it. She has Boobs in her hands. She jumps off the ground and slams Boobs into Boobslime with all her might!

The pillow falls through Boobslime's body and brings Stalker down with it.

"I lost," says Stalker in tears.

"You fought admirably," says Best Friend, lifting her off her feet.

"It was an absolute pleasure watching you fight and hearing your rousing speech," says Glasses Kid with a pervy grin.

I shake Boobslime's hand. "Alright, you won. What do you want?"

"Want you," says Boobslime, tilting her head.

"Not an option," says Best Friend, pulling out a dagger.

"She won. We have to obey the rules of the game!" I exclaim.

"I'd rather shame myself with dishonor than allow harm to come to you," says Best Friend, pointing his knife at Boobslime. "Let him go."

"Go!" yells Boobslime, her hair tendril turning red.

"Not good," says Stalker. "Don't upset her. Main, you go have fun. We'll stay here." She grabs Best Friend's hand.

I will indeed.

Boobslime pulls me by my hand into the Forest of Scary Name. Once we're out of earshot, she turns to me. "Good." She releases my hand.

Not just good. Amazing! I get to live the secret dream of all 2-D elitists like me! I get to have my Dakinkymaru pillow become an IRL girl and snuggle for realzies!

Boobslime places my hand on her chest.

They're so huge and squishy.

My hand goes into her boob.

Wow, this is like next level intimacy! It tickles. Actually, it kinda stings. Now it really stings.

I look at my hand to see it's being dissolved in her titastic boobage.

Needlessly Fanservicey OVA BOB-ray Special!

Damn it! Monsters Musume lied! I thought I only had to worry about drowning.

I yank my hand out. "Sorry Boobslime, but you can't eat me. I like living. It's part of who I am."

Her hair drops and I can finally see her eyes. They are blue pupils surrounded by black irises. "Hungry," she says with quivering eyes.

Soo pretty.

"I'm sorry Boobslime. I'll make it up to you someday. I'm so sorry." I run off, hiding my hand in beneath my shirt.

Stalker pops out from behind a tree.

"What you wanted a show? Well sorry to disappoint you," I say in tears.

"I'm sorry about what she did to your hand. I can make it better." Stalker pulls my hand out from under my shirt and kisses it till the skin returns.

"I became a hero to boost my viewership. I want to inspire people! How can I claim to be a hero when I couldn't even give one monster girl what she desired most of all? She's lonely…just like me," I say softly.

"I know what that feels like," says Stalker sadly.

"No. I'm not falling for your pity party technique. I'm going back to Best Friend!" I exclaim, running off.

I meet with my team and try to hide my sadness. "Wow, Boobslime is super cute. She was suckling on my finger like a neko-girl," I say with a grin.

"Glasses Kid and I discussed the rules. Boobslime never once used an actual pillow. She wielded your girlfriend like a sword. It doesn't count," says Best Friend.

Says the guy who cheered when Zolo lifted up Usnipe to take down the World Government's pasta machine. He's just trying to ease my guilt, but it doesn't change how Boobslime is feeling right now. She probably already gets picked on by the other slimes for being trans. Poor boobalicious slime babe.

Stalker squeals, breaking me out of my train of thought. "That means I win by default."

Best Friend shook his head. "You used your chest to…"

"I already said it counts. You won, Stalker. I'm at your disposal," I say, lowering my head.

Stalker stands on her tippy toes and pushes my head up. "You're my prisoner tonight. I'm gonna snuggle away all that sadness."

She could have made me give her a full body tongue massage, that's what I chose whenever I beat Best Friend. But instead, she chose to comfort me. That little heart really does care about me.

"We'll see you two in the morning," says Glasses Kid, waving us farewell.

Stalker arrives with me at the inn and she immediately slides open the door and pops into our sleeping bag.

I slowly scoot in as she humps my leg. She increases friction, then clenches my leg extra tight.

"Ow. I'm not a pillow," I say, flicking her forehead.

"I thought snuggling would cheer you up," says Stalker.

"Best Friend and Glasses Kid are hunting Boobslime. I don't deserve to be happy," I say softly.

"Well that's no good." Stalker pops out from the covers. "If you don't give in or fight back then I might as well be molesting a pillow. I want the real you, the super funny, dorky and determined boy I fell in love with. Let's go find Boobslime and escort her away from the village!"

I grab Stalker's hand. "Thank you!"

Stalker giggles and wraps a pink string around my ring finger. "You're still my prisoner," she says, playfully sticking out her tongue.

"Fair enough. Hey, there's something serious I want to ask you."

"You can ask me anything," she says with a sweet smile.

"When girls are bathing together…do they fondle each other like they do in anime?"

Stalker giggles.

I grab her hands. "This is serious."

"I honestly don't know about other girls but you can bet I like to give 'em a good squeeze," she says, gabbing my butt.

If we ever get a sexy tomboy cat-girl on our team, she has to fondle her!

"Let's get going. I know where Boobslime is. I can, uh, sense her," she says.

"I promise not to ask how if you promise to explain it later on your own in a super dramatic way," I say.

"Aye Sir!" she exclaims.

We leave the inn quietly and track down Boobslime.

The poor hungry limus sapien, that's slime people in science otaku speech, is wandering aimlessly around the village.

"You seen Parasaite to the Maximum?" I ask Stalker.

"Nope. Too scary," she says softly.

"Well it's a great show with a powerful message. Parasites and well any animal deserve the right to live and eat humans. Let's find her someone nobody will miss, well nobody important anyways."

"If that's what the hero wants, then I'll do my best," she says, jumping up into a hi-five.

You know. She would make a really great friend.

A man approaches us. "What the hell ya think yer doin' hero? You heroes are nothing but trouble. If it weren't for your kind, this village would be at peace."

Needlessly Fanservicey OVA BOB-ray Special!

Yes! For the first time ever, I'm super happy to run into a bigot!

I run behind the grumpy side character and hold him down. "Come and eat, Boobslime!" I exclaim.

Boobslime approaches. "Eat," she says before her belly grows a mouth and swallows the man whole.

I hold Stalker's hand as the man screams and is dissolved. "We did a good thing today."

"We did," she leans into me.

A bunch of villagers, probably alerted by the screaming from when the side character managed to stick his head out, came out from their homes.

"Monster!" "There's a monster right there!" "Kill it!"

Now's my chance to be a real hero!

"It identifies as female and her name is Boobslime!" I exclaim before turning to Stalker. "I'll hold them off, you lead her out of here."

Stalker nods.

They come at me with rakes, shovels and all sorts of other home maintenance equipment.

Assailant pops out from thin air. "You dare attack the Hero of Destiny!" Twenty blades erupt from him, are poised to kill.

"Yeah, that's right! I'm your new hero! And I'm going after that slime!" I cheer, rushing off.

The villagers cheer me on but it sounds lifeless and robotic.

That was surprisingly easy to turn around.

I return to the inn to see Best Friend fast asleep.

"Kurosu. Kurosu," he mutters softly.

So hot. I suppose he honored my wishes after all.

Stalker comes in very silently.

"Did you get to her leave?" I ask.

"Yeah, I explained the situation to her. I thought that...after seeing one of those things eat my friend...I thought they were just monsters. Mistakes that had to be corrected. But Boobslime is different and I think I know why," says Stalker with a smile.

I seize her into a hug. "We did it! We completed a secret mission!"

"Yay! And here's my reward," she motorboats my chest.

"Helping out a bodacious slime babe is my reward!" I exclaim

The door slides open and Boobslime enters.

"I thought you led her away," I whisper shout to Stalker.

"I-I tried," she says with a pouty face.

Boobslime hovers over Best Friend, who is still resting thankfully.

Wait, is she going to attack him to get to me? Do I have a super clingy slime yandere fan girl now? Awesome!

Boobslime shifts her body into that of Best Friend, but as if his clothes and body were made of goop. "Ari-ga-tou." BestSlime suddenly locks lips with me.

Wow.

Best Friend's tongue bounces around in my mouth. Fireworks burst in my heart and my body is electrified. BestSlime pulls away, leaving a trail of saliva that Stalker catches as it falls.

"Tasty. Oooh. Look who finally got up," says Stalker, poking my boner.

"Very tasty." Boobslime changes shape once more, becoming me. I excitedly await another kiss when SliMain suddenly crouches down and makes out with Stalker.

Stalker faints but is caught by a slime pillow.

Wait that's not a slime pillow. It's a baby slime. Awww. The extra nutrients from that bigot side character must have allowed the little slime to be born.

Stalker comes to again and holds her lips, her head bobbing side to side.

"Let's play." SliMain beckons Stalker to come along.

Wait, she gets to play with Boobslime but not me! And I don't like her doing things to a replica of me. I thought she cared, but really, she only wants me for me rocking body!

Stalker shakes her head. "Some other time. I gotta taste the real thing first," says Stalker, flashing me an excited smile.

Boobslime turns into StalkerSlime. "Play?"

"Sure thing, Sista!" exclaims Stalker, rushing up and locking tongues with her slime replica.

The two of them head out.

"I thought I was your prisoner tonight," I say.

"Boobslime won. Not me. Glasses Kid is staying at a different inn so you're all alone with Best Friend. And you know another word for inn is hotel," says Stalker.

"You're an angel," I say with shimmering eyes.

"I know. Oh, and you know why Boobslime is so nice and friendly?" asks Stalker.

"I didn't expect you to tell me," I say with an awkward smile.

"It's cuz of all the love you give your girlfriend Boobs. Every night you snuggled with your pillow pal, you gave her your energy. Boobslime absorbed all that positive energy and became the sweet Goopy you see today."

Boobslime really is like Boobs bestowed with irresistibly raunchy life. This is an otaku's greatest dream!

Stalker hops up and kisses me cheek. "I'll see you tomorrow. Come on Boobslime, let's experiment all the way to the Forest of Scary Name," says

Stalker, poking SlimeStalker's boobs. The two of them walk hand in hand. The slime baby follows by rolling along behind them.

Stalker stole my chance to get laid, and she stole my kinda sorta body pillow girlfriend, but I'm not upset. I guess I'm just happy I could help a slime girl give birth. My life is now its own Monsters Musume.

Best Friend peeks out from the sleeping bag. "You coming to bed? It's way past your bedtime, mister."

"You bet your ass!" I hop into my sleeping bag.

And what a super supple sexy ass it is.

"I'm cold," says Best Friend softly, holding himself as he shivers.

I pop out of my sleeping bag and scoot into his. "Don't worry, Bestie. I'll keep you warm," I say, rubbing noses with him.

"I saw that kiss," he says in a whisper.

Oh no. He can't find out that I want to fusion ha with him!

"I like my way better." He turns to face me and kisses my forehead, then both my cheeks. He then snuggles up to my chest.

Sooooo cute! All my worries just got pulled into the Eclipse and massacred by my Grimmith. Sorry, too soon? Yeah…it's always too soon.

He peeks up from my chest with a dangerous glare. "You went against my wishes. I'm so proud," he says, the terror coming from his eyes not diluted in the least bit.

"I'm proud of me too. You think we'll run into her again?" I ask.

"According to Glasses Kid. Goopies have perfect memory and it's even passed down to their offspring. Boobslime will never forget what you've done for her."

"That's awesome!" I exclaim.

"Tomorrow you will be tested, but you've already proven yourself a hero today." He grabs my hand. "We still have a long way to go before we topple this

Needlessly Fanservicey OVA BOB-ray Special!

kingdom, but I can already see the ending," says Best Friend, his eyes gazing out into the future that we'll grasp together.

Well, would you look at that. My eight episodes ended in exactly two-hundred minutes. With twenty-five minutes as the standard for each episode, I totally nailed it! No need to cut corners or drag out episodes by adding staring contests or slow pans like the legendary One Place! Yes!

Oh shit! I never got him to strip! Guess to you'll have to purchase the next BOB-ray collection to witness in the next super epic OVA!

Stalker: Guardian Angel Trailer

Hi, everyone my name is Annolette, but my heroes call me angel, dear or little sister. I've always been the odd ball of the angels but I never let that get me down.

Today I'm going on a super fun quest with my super cool new hero Racheal. She is taller than I can reach even if I jump and her hair is a pretty red color. Her outfit is a robe as dark as the night sky. She's a talented comic artist from Canada who writes scary stuff but she's always sweet and protective of me. She was supposed to be the hero's damsel but when they were both tested, she proved she had more mettle and was given his title. The intended hero, her younger brother, is safe and secure back at the village.

I'm riding on her shoulders at the moment, allowing me a better view of the deadly swamp we entered.

"What did you say this place was called, little angel?" asks Racheal, her voice both really pretty and kinda intense.

"The Swamp of Agonizing Regret. It's where our friends said to meet us."

"Those creeps aren't our friends. I saw them eying you," she says, carefully avoiding a puddle of acid.

"My momma told me that not trusting is sadder than being let down. I will never throw away my trust in heroes. Besides, they were only eyeing me because I was stretching erotically on the guild hall's dance poll."

"Well if you're okay with it, that's what matters. You sure do have a way with boys. Maybe you can give me some tips to find a nice boyfriend."

"Sure thing. You got the hips so wave 'em, big sis!"

"Thanks! And look, just because you're a little Pollyanna doesn't mean you shouldn't be wary. Not all heroes are good."

My face freezes up.

Racheal cradles me in her arms. "You're shaking. Are you okay?"

I nod and wipe my tears. "Fine and dandy," I say before sobbing into her bosom.

I miss mommy.

"Don't ever think crying makes you weak. Not crying is what cowards do. You're a strong girl and its perfectly okay to cry."

I look up at her and smile. "But it's so hard to cry when my big sister is with me."

Racheal pats my head. "Stay sharp. Big frog thing. Is it hostile?" she asks, readying her spear.

"Hiya froggy!" I wave at the BlasToad and he waves back. "Nope. He's super friendly."

"Wait, isn't that a BlasToad. I heard we lost a hero to one last week."

"Well yeah, but that was a different one. This one is friendly." I reach into my pack and toss him some bread crumbs.

A trio of healthy heroes come out from the bushes after the toad leaves.

"Hey heroes," I say, pushing up my breasts with my arms.

"Glad you could make it, cutie," says the most muscular of the heroes. He steps back when Racheal glares at him.

"Where is the enemy camp? And are you sure we'll be enough to handle it?" asks Racheal.

"Well we all were told to attack the same camp. Rather than fight over it, I think teaming up gives us all a better chance of victory," says the short hero with the blue glasses.

"I could take 'em all on my own! But I'd rather do it with it with my fellow bros." He looks at Racheal and me. "And of course, my sistas!" The mohawk hero points to us with a grin.

"Do not call me sister. I'm only risking my life out for the sake of my little brother, after all." Racheal steps in between the strapping young boys. "This quest has been up for a month. What if a CatBoy general is guarding it? Even together we might be out of our league."

"Why would they send us here if we stood no chance at winning?" asks the muscular one.

"Heroes are a dime a dozen," says Racheal.

"Then let's increase our odds," says the glasses hero. "Angel, do you have any power vials with you?"

"My fluids are something I chose to give to people who are special to me," I say, snuggling up to Racheal.

The mohawk hero steps up to me. "Well I may not have family back home, but I do value my own life. If we don't get powers, then we could all die."

"I only have one bottle. Maybe I'll give it to the sweetest boy," I lick my lips playfully.

Flirting is so much fun.

"I once saved a kitten from drowning," says the muscular hero.

"That's nothing. I spent six hours at a convention helping a lost girl locate her mother," says the glasses hero.

"Forget about the power vial. There's another way to get an edge!" The mohawk hero tears me from Racheal's hands.

Racheal pulls out her spear and the other two heroes draw their swords. "Put her down or I'll cut you down."

"I didn't ask to come here! My bandmates need me. So, the sooner I finish this quest, the sooner I can hang with my real bros."

"Mark, calm down man. Just take the flask. We'll let you. Let's not create a conflict okay?" asks the muscular one.

"Aww, you boys aren't going to fight over my lips," I say in a teasing tone.

"You steal her kiss and I'll cut your legs off," says Racheal, pointing her spear at the mohawk hero.

"Hey dad! I am special. I'm gonna do this and be just fine!" yells the mohawk guy.

I hate being forced to kiss people so I might as well do the kissing.

I grab his face and plunge my tongue into his mouth.

The other two boys step back.

I pull away and turn to Racheal. "He was willing to risk it. Just calm down. He should be fine."

Huh? I'm falling.

The hero hits the ground and has a seizure.

"Is he going to die?" asks the glasses hero, covering his eyes.

The bushes rustle and a CatBoy general steps out. "You all are," he says with a twisted smile.

To be continued in **Stalker: Guardian Angel**

Stalker Guardian Angel Trailer

Main here! I honestly don't know how much Stalker has suffered, but you can find out! Before the next 2-Disc collection about my epic journey is released, ***Stalker: Guardian Angel*** will be on the market! See Stalker's origins and follow her journey to become the world's greatest hero's creeper!

      Coming Summer 2019

Also, if you want to join my forces and help shape my destiny then join my Paytreon subscription. Seriously check out those sweet perks!

https://www.patreon.com/AuthorOfTheExps

REBELLION OF THE EXPS

BOOK 1

Alexander J. McCarty

Art by: Gabriel McCarty

TRAILER!

Awakening

"Freedom is a shackle."

Exp 8 could only faintly hear these words. Nonetheless, they repeated fervently in its mind.

There was no world for Exp 8. It had no identity. All it knew, all it was, were those words: "freedom is a shackle." Despite this, it didn't have a clue what they meant. They were merely noise.

A mechanical sound broke through the mantra as an automatic door opened. Voices could be heard but only as whispers.

Exp 8's nervous system slowly activated, allowing it to feel the gelatinous fluid that encompassed him. Its eyes opened, frightening the people who were gathered around.

"It's waking up! It's finally waking up! Hurry, go inform Devlin," exclaimed a scientist, his hands trembling as he looked up at the creature in the incubator.

Exp 8 was an imposing height of six feet five inches, towering over the other life-forms in the room. The creature's body was clad in blue-tinted, platinum-colored quicksilver armor an inch thick. The sleek armor shielded all but the being's piercing black eyes. Those eyes had a depth as overwhelming as space itself.

Around Exp 8's head was a cybernetic helmet that protected the soft flesh within. Horizontal slits were carved into the center of the two slabs melded along the jawline, forming a mouthpiece. The slabs curved upward above its head, creating long, functionless ears. Protruding from the back of its helmet were metallic tendrils, wispily floating in the gelatinous fluid. Embedded in the crown of the helmet was an empty clear orb.

A motherly light started to bloom inside the orb as the system booted up. Exp 8's metal-plated chest was concave, funneling in like an ant-lion trap. A dimly lit, sky-blue sphere filled the cavity. A five-foot metallic tail was limply swaying in the liquid.

The creature had strong, thick legs. Sharpened metal plates formed three bladed talons on each foot and one blade in the back for support. Energy gathered in the orbs embedded into the being's large hands. The being's trembling fingers tensed up into fists.

Exp 8's head turned slowly, examining the immediate surroundings. The new life-form deduced that it was floating inside a large shell.

A mere moment ago, Exp 8 would have been unable to understand the concept of *shell*. But for some unfathomable reason, its meaning was clear. Now the creature understood what a shell was and simultaneously felt the desire to escape from it. The reason for wanting to escape had yet to be formulated.

Exp 8 reached out, bumping its hand against the glass.

The creature was imprisoned in a clear incubator filled to the top with a light green liquid.

Exp 8 felt a strange sense of fellowship with this liquid. Both of them were seemingly trapped by nothing.

A large number "8" was painted across the incubator's surface.

Exp 8 dragged its fingers across the number, following its curves. It soon became entranced in the act. The creature felt something both real and fanciful as its fingers made loops around the image. This symbol was somehow a part of the curious life form.

Exp 8 Trailer

Exp 8's arm moved instinctively, breaking free of the trance. Struggling to move the rest of its body, the creature realized multiple tubes and wires had penetrated through its armor and were embedded deep into its flesh.

Now that Exp 8 was aware of their existence, the creature felt pain. It didn't fully grasp the concept, but it was certainly not fond of this new sensation.

Curling up, Exp 8 loosened the pull on its body. Pain still lingering in its eyes, it looked beyond the encasing and into the world outside its little eggshell.

Everything was gray, structured, and lifeless.

It looked beyond the immediate surroundings, peering through the wall and into a hidden room.

Exp 8 was not alone.

Inside the metal room were multiple incubation chambers. Inside each was a life-form, curled up like a fetus. Some of them were missing limbs and others had holes in their bodies. One was belly up, its eyes glazed over.

Exp 8 watched their lifeless bodies attentively and waved its hand, willing them to awaken.

They remained motionless.

Fear of death struck Exp 8 even before the being could fathom its meaning.

Exp 8 saw the shell in a new light. The desire to escape was now wrapped in a layer of fear. The being pushed its trembling hands against the encasing. This world was no longer a shell; it was a cage. The word *cage* brought up the all-too-familiar word *shackle*.

Exp 8 feared that it would die shackled inside its prison. It tried to thrash around but was only able to flail its arms. The creature's head moved the slightest bit forward, but it was unable to reach the encasing. In Exp 8's peripheral vision, something caught its attention.

Beyond the encasing was a group of strange creatures. These life-forms had no prison and were gawking at it with wide eyes.

Exp 8 did not feel threatened by these creatures. The being knew intuitively that, if it escaped, they would be unable to stop it.

The foreign creatures continued to stare, none of them uttering a word.

Exp 8 was befuddled by their astonishment. How could its imprisonment be more astounding to them than their own freedom?

Freedom! The word trapped Exp 8 in a torrent of desire. It did not matter what preceded it. Freedom was now its goal. And escaping from this prison was its only means of attaining it.

The scientists approached closer, their eyes filled with admiration.

Exp 8 peered down at them. They appeared to have skin outside rather than within. Their external material appeared to be more malleable than its own armor and looked completely functionless for self-defense. One creature looked at a metal device on its arm and smiled. Suddenly the lab's twin iron doors flew open, releasing a puff of steam.

"Devlin!" they exclaimed, shaking with excitement and apprehension.

The steam dispersed, revealing a proud grin. Devlin was a loose-bodied youth with a piercing golden right eye. A clump of jet-black hair covered his left eye. He wore a black, unbuttoned lab coat with a cloak that draped over his arms like wings. Beneath the glossy coat was a spiffy blood-red undershirt. From the neck down, he was shielded by a black skintight bodysuit.

Devlin stepped out of the foot-high layer of steam. His feet were comfortably situated in custom-designed metallic boots that gleamed black with a bright red trim. Wrapped around his throat was a necklace with a metal double helix pendant.

Exp 8 could not fathom the idea of arrogance, but Devlin's smile perturbed the creature. It did not seem genuine.

"My creation has finally awoken!" exclaimed Devlin in a dramatic, youthful voice.

The men in the room bashed their hands together gratuitously and smiled as if they relished it.

The notion of these creatures enjoying pain disturbed Exp 8. The creation feared not knowing what these life-forms were capable of.

Devlin looked down at his kin. A cruel smile spread across his face as he opened his lips to speak. "Enough! Enough applause. We can celebrate my success later. Leave us! I wish to speak with Exp 8 alone," he whispered in a harsh, commanding tone.

"Congratulations!" they exclaimed, striking Devlin's shoulder as they left.

The doors shut automatically.

Exp 8 was all alone with Devlin.

TO BE CONTINUED IN EXP 8: REBELLION OF THE EXPS

NOW AVAILABLE IN EBOOK AND PRINT FORMATS.

SEARCH EXP 8 book @ amazon.com

ISBN 978-1-9437-3302-6

Published by Sphere of Compassion, Inc.

Cover design by Gabriel McCarty

RESURRECTION OF THE EXPS

BOOK 2

THE HERO OF SEL

Alexander J. McCarty

Art by: Gabriel McCarty

TRAILER!

The Crimson Coliseum

The Hero of Sel Trailer

Previously: Exp 8 was knocked out by the Prince of Pleasure's poison. He awoke on the ashy floor of a dark room. "Where the hell am I?" He rattled the searing hot iron bars.

"Calm down. Wait your turn," said a demon.

Exp 8 recognized him.

It was the same crispy demon captain that had led him up the mountain.

"Where is this place?" asked Exp 8, pulling his hands off the bars.

"The center of entertainment, the Crimson Coliseum!" The crispy demon pulled a lever that rose the iron bars up.

"Don't die, alright? You did a good thing in Respite, saving those kids. Beg if you have to. Strike a deal. Don't piss him off," said the charred demon commander.

Exp 8 stepped out of the prison cell and entered the Crimson Coliseum. The structure itself was made from bones, making it more durable than the fleshy buildings he had previously encountered. Tens of thousands of demons were stationed at the pews. Nearly all of them cheered when Exp 8 rose up his fist. There were only a few thousand that raised their fist in solemn silence.

Exp 8 got into a fighting stance as the bars of a nearby cell opened up.

The Baroness of Blades emerged, leaping onto the blood-soaked fleshy arena stage.

235:00

"What are you doing…?"

"As Etah's proudest warrior, I will strike you down, hero." She gripped the hilt of one of her rear swords and rushed up to her competitor.

"We can take him on together," said Exp 8, skipping back while using his jets.

"My pride will not allow it. *IGNITION!*" The Baroness unsheathed a sword, super heating it in the process. The blade missed Exp 8's head but sliced off one of his tendrils. She swerved out of the way of an orb directed at her face and slammed her bladed foot into her rival.

Exp 8 slid back, directing the momentum to get behind her.

The Baroness grabbed the hilt of a blade at her front and gouged it in.

Exp 8 ducked under her reverse jab and used the opening to stab his talons into her legs.

She ripped the dagger out of her head and jabbed it at his throat, blocked by his arm at each thrust.

Exp 8 gripped the arm holding the dagger and slammed his head into her face. "If this is some kind of ploy, best to end it soon. I don't want to kill you by accident." His turrets rose out from his shoulders.

The Baroness stopped all movement. "I may be incognito, but this fight is real. The winner gets to face Etah. This may be my one chance at taking him down. *IGNITION!*" She pulled out a dagger from her knee, set aflame by her boiling blood.

The blade slid up Exp 8's torso and sliced open his shoulder.

Exp 8 gripped onto the blade and twisted the talons he had imbedded in her leg.

The Hero of Sel Trailer

The Baroness collapsed to the ground alongside her rival.

Most of the protruding blades slid off Exp 8's armor, but two or three found the gaps and pierced his flesh.

"I don't believe you. You've had plenty of chances to fight Etah." Exp 8 twisted her arm, making her drop the dagger.

"Calling me a coward!" she yelled, biting into his neck.

Exp 8 slammed her against the bloody floor. "You want an audience! You need someone to see your victory. It's not tactics; it's your inflated ego!" He created an orb, gripped it with his gravity field and slammed it into her head repeatedly.

"That's right! Everyone is watching! I won't fail now!" She twisted one of her blades as she tore it out, blinding her rival with a gush of steamy blood.

Only able to see red, Exp 8 felt something slam into his chest. He was rolled onto his back. His vision adjusted through the blood to see a long slab of steel between his fingers. "Make it look good."

The blade slid through his fingers and into his chest.

The Baroness plunged the blade all the way through. "It's over." She stood up, yanked the sword out from his chest and raised it. "I won! I am the greatest warrior."

A few members of the audience cheered. Most were either silent or weeping.

Etah leaped off from his decorated podium.

The impact from his landing splintered the ground.

The Hero of Sel Trailer

The God of Hate backhanded the defiant demon lord. "What have you done?"

The Baroness slid back and jabbed a sword into the ground, slowing herself to a halt. "They're all watching. All of them! My pride is at stake!" She rushed at the Deva, wielding two swords in each hand.

"He was supposed to win! To triumph against an unstoppable force! How dare you deny these people their hero!" Etah's aura was sucked into his bulky body. "Death would be mercy. You shall be disgraced!"

The Baroness ducked under his fist and sliced his belly.

Etah's legs slammed into her body like battering rams.

The Baroness jabbed two blades into the Deva's knee and kicked off the ground. She rode the momentum, slicing the god's shoulders and positioning herself behind him.

Etah spun around. "All of it ruined! You want to be a hero so badly! Hmmhmmhmmmhuhuh! The job is yours!" He parried each strike with an equally powerful punch. His foot slammed down on hers, flattening it along with her pride. "Everyone behold! This is the embodiment of your hopes! She alone can save you from your judgment!" The god gripped her swords between two fingers each.

Nearly the whole stadium cheered for their new hero.

"You've taken up their dreams. You've stolen Exp 8's mission by striking him down. Can you live up to their expectations?"

"You will fall with all of Sel watching!" The Baroness dropped the swords and stabbed a dagger into Etah's throat. She twisted it as she ripped out the scorching blade. Lava gushed out of the deity's wound. "Never underestimate me!" she yelled in a frenzy, stabbing his throat with various daggers.

Etah knocked her off.

The Baroness rushed up to the Deva, her hands ready to unsheathe two more swords.

Etah's aura burst out and gripped her hands. His tattoos lit up once she was within range. His hands went around hers. "And so, the rebellion dies!"

"*IGNITION!*" The Baroness pulled her blades out halfway before they were pushed completely through her.

Etah twisted the blades and cleaved her body in two.

The Baroness joined the blood-soaked floor.

Moans, screams, and anguish from the pews blotted out all noise.

"This despair, it's superficial. Not nearly enough," said Etah with a clenched fist.

Exp 8 spat out blood.

Etah turned his attention to the fallen hero. His grimace shifted into a wide grin. "Still alive! Heal him!"

Four demons with white wolves and tigers on a leash came out from the sidelines. They went to Exp 8's side and placed their paws on him.

"I'm sorry, I couldn't free you," said Exp 8, tugging at their collar.

White energy poured out from the paws and entered Exp 8.

Within seconds his wounds had closed. Within half a minute, he was glowing with energy.

The Hero of Sel Trailer

Etah pulled the leader of the Freedom Forcers off the ground. "Residents of Sel! Your hero has returned from the dead! The battle you came for will now commence!"

The stadium shook, each cheer contributing to the quake of support.

"Come, hero! Fight me here and now in the Crimson Coliseum! End my reign, if you can," said Etah with a beckoning hand.

"No."

Etah took a step forward. "What?"

"I won't move a muscle until you heal her. I know you can do it," said Exp 8, patting his helpers on the head.

"You think a warrior like her would die so easily?" asked Etah, lifting up the demon lord's upper half.

The Baroness ripped out an arrow and jabbed into the tyrant. "Die! Die! I'm not done yet! I won't lose to you!" she yelled, unable to pierce his hardened muscles.

Etah flung her aside.

"Heal her or I'm out."

The God of Hate glared at the defiant hero. "You don't get to command me."

"Have it your way." Exp 8 flew off the ground. He slammed into a thin red aura.

"As if I'd risk letting you leave. Come down here and face me!" yelled Etah.

"Look everyone! See your ruler! Look how he struggles when things don't go as he plans. Marvel at his frustration," said Exp 8, flying circles around Etah.

The deity bit his lip. "Heal her." He turned his head to the demons. "I said heal her!"

The demons dropped their leashes and picked up the Baroness' halves.

"Wait. Stop." Etah looked at the hero and smiled. "I have a better plan. Either fight me…." His red aura shot out like a bullet. It exploded into the crowd like a grenade, killing seven demons immediately and injuring eleven more. "Or I'll dispose of the audience. It's your choice." The merciless tyrant gathered energy in his hand, aiming it at a group of child demons near the front.

Exp 8 sent a volley of orbs at the detestable deity while making circles in the air.

Etah redirected the blast at the Exp, followed by a volley of smaller bursts.

The Ultimate Exp enlarged an orb as he swerved around the attacks, all the while firing at the god's face to disrupt his aiming.

"Your hero will do anything to protect you! Come down, hero, or face the consequences," said Etah, aiming his aura at the audience.

Exp 8 swooped down and slammed into the deity. "I will take you down! BIG BALL SHOT!" He fired off the orb, sending his enemy back a few feet. After reengaging his thrusters, he pummeled Etah's chest, keeping steady fire on the god's face.

"Stop! I'm not done! He's mine!" yelled the Baroness, using her dagger to scale up the arena.

The Hero of Sel Trailer

Etah's aura gripped the orb and rammed it into Exp 8. He then grabbed onto the hero's leg.

Exp 8 slammed his talons into the arm holding his leg. He twisted out of the iron grip after firing a pebble-sized orb point blank at the god's face.

"Better hurry," said Etah.

The massive orb from earlier was now heading to a crowd that wasn't dispersing fast enough.

Exp 8 supercharged his jets and slammed his body into the orb, redirecting it to the ground. His jets flipped and backed him out, but he was still caught in the periphery of the blast.

Etah leaped off the ground. His massive hands grabbed onto Exp 8's torso. "You should pay attention."

The hero's jets flipped around again and blasted the god's face.

Exp 8 zoomed by, slicing Etah's back with his elbow talons. "Stop dragging this out. The longer it goes on, the more casualties there will be."

"Hmmhmmhmmmhuhuh. I'm well aware." Etah fired out heated blasts at the hero.

Knowing that a misfire would result in a casualty, Exp 8 slammed into each blast. The freedom fighter then crashed to the ground.

"Even when his life is on the line, the hero defends you! He protects people he has never met! Such valor!" Etah pinned down the mortal with his foot.

"These people aren't strangers. They're enslaved...like I was. We are made kin by our oppression!" Exp 8 struggled beneath the Deva's foot.

"Such powerful words! Though you could have picked a better time for them," said Etah, stepping on the hero's legs with his other foot.

Exp 8 punched the god's foot with great strength but it wouldn't budge. His tail smacked against the God of Hate's leg.

"What was that? Are you mocking me?" asked Etah, glaring down at the nuisance.

"Haven't quite gotten the hang of fighting with my tail, that's all," said Exp 8, struggling to push the god's foot off him.

"Behold: the Hero of Sel is unable to move! I could crush him at any moment! And if he dies! All of you die!" yelled Etah.

Exp 8 supercharged his jets yet again, sliding out from beneath the powerful legs and then quickly turning around to punch the god's face.

A stray arrow pierced into the gap in Exp 8's arm.

"I told you. I will kill Etah!" yelled the Baroness, ripping out another arrow from her body.

"How are you still alive?" asked Exp 8, rapidly dodging the tyrant's punches with properly timed jet-boosting.

"You know so little." Etah opened his fist and grabbed the hero's head. "Demons don't die, only suffer. Those children you failed to rescue. The ones you saw beheaded before your eyes, they are alive. I don't kill rebels, merely repurpose them! That's what happened with the Baroness! I break wills, not destroy lives. You are fighting to save them from nothing. What will you do now, hero?" asked the Deva, smearing Exp 8 with the blood of the wounded.

The Hero of Sel wrapped his legs around Etah's left arm. "Everyone dies. That's not what I'm against. Everyone suffers. Trying to stop that is pointless. What I fight for…what I died for is freedom! Slavery takes the meaning out of life and the purpose out of suffering! As long as living beings, whether sinners or saints, are trapped in a system of exploitation…as long as willful beings are treated as property, not people, I will keep on fighting! Until the system falls, I will stand and fight!" His jets went into overdrive.

Etah's arm twisted up and then back. The sound of it snapping ringed across the Crimson Coliseum.

Exp 8 careened into the ground and slammed into the wall of the arena.

Etah's left arm shook but he could not raise it.

The people cheered. They climbed out of their seats and charged into the arena, raising their blades, fists, and tendrils as weapons.

"Enough!" Etah's aura burst out from his body, melting anyone who entered it. He stepped up to the defiant hero who was still getting back on his feet.

"The people have stood up to you. You lost. The rebellion won," said Exp 8, gripping one massive orb in between his palms.

"Not another word!" Etah's aura burst out and slammed into Exp 8 from below.

Before the hero could reorient himself, the god gripped his arm.

Exp 8's eyes went blank as his left arm was torn from its socket.

Etah slammed the hero back and forth against the ground by flailing him around by the dismembered arm.

Exp 8's working hand disengaged his grip on the orb. He fell flat on the ground, his palm facing up.

Etah's aura crept out from his feet and held the hero's legs in place.

The Hero of Sel Trailer

Exp 8 stood up in a daze, his eyes fixated on the god. His still-attached arm was too weak to form a fist.

Etah's aura shot into the mob. It pulled them in and contorted them into a chair.

The God of Hate created a barrier between him and the mob with his aura. "Listen to your hero now. You'll find his words deficient in valor now that his life is in my hands," said Etah, his aura climbing up the broken mortal's body.

"I can't move," said Exp 8, tears dripping from his helmet.

"Hero. You may live yet." Etah sat down in his living chair and assumed a lax position. "I'm going to give you one chance. Abandon your ideals. Let go of your morals. Stand by my side as a new god of this world. All you have to do to rule alongside me, almost as equals, is lower your head. Bow down to me or perish," he said, staring at Exp 8 with his eyes aflame.

"In that simple gesture lies the injustice of surrender. I will not bow to anyone, neither mortal nor god."

Etah's fiery aura came out from his hand and pressed down on the hero's back.

The Ultimate Exp fought against the weight. He pressed off the ground and looked up at the tyrant, crouched on one knee.

"Ah, much better."

Exp 8 raised his head, his body still held in place by the god's aura. "I will not bow down to you. Even if you break my neck, my willful spirit will wholeheartedly oppose you," said the leader of the Freedom Forcers, his resolve firm and tall like a mountain.

The Hero of Sel Trailer

"A fool in the realm of the living and beyond. Such a shame. Your false hope has brought you so much determination, yet in the end, you had to surrender your life to be free."

"I chose to die. I did not surrender. I died for freedom! I am liberated now!" exclaimed Exp 8, raising a defiant trembling fist at the tyrant god.

"Utter nonsense! If you were truly free, you could have chosen to enter the portal of light like you desired. You were brought here by my willpower. Your freedom is an illusion. I own you, body and soul! You do not choose what path you take; I do," said Etah, clenching his fist.

"You may have sent me here, but I choose my path. I also decide what actions I take," said Exp 8, creating an orb in his fist.

Etah snapped his fingers. A figure in a clear cloak came out of the audience and rushed to his side.

"Such a blessed shame! You would have been perfect. You believe in this freedom so fervently you have deceived yourself into thinking you have attained it. Logic and reality have no power over your delusion. It matters not. By opposing me you have become a hero. All sinners, behold: the Hero of Sel stands against me even now! He values your freedom above his own life!"

Sinners throughout the arena raised their fists in solemn silence.

"By refusing me you have created a burning hope. A hope that is inextinguishable no matter what truths ram against it. You are a threat, a true threat. A psychopath who can deny the facts of life can only be tamed with insanity. Soon, you shall become like all the rest here, a brick supporting my foundation. All sinners, behold: I banish this hero to the realm of Absence! When your hero returns, he will be my new footstool!" Etah punched the Hero of Sel, his massive fist a blur.

The Hero of Sel Trailer

The legendary leader of the Freedom Forcers was sent flying back. He was gobbled up by an unseen portal and vanished from the Crimson Coliseum.

The Hero of Sel Trailer

TO BE CONTINUED IN THE HERO OF SEL RESURRECTION OF THE EXPS BOOK2

NOW AVAILABLE IN EBOOK AND PRINT FORMATS.

SEARCH *HERO OF SEL* @ amazon.com

RESURRECTION OF THE EXPS BOOK 2 The Hero of Sel. Copyright © 2016 by Alexander J. McCarty

ISBN 978-1-943733-033

If you enjoyed this story then you'll love the ***Of The Exps*** series (3 books currently available in eBook and print form in the link!).

https://www.amazon.com/gp/bookseries/B01N1P193D/ref=dp_st_1943733023

And subscribe to my website too!

https://sphereofcompassion.com

About the Author

Alexander McCarty is an animal born on Earth who actively seeks freedom for his fellow animals. He enjoys watching anime, playing video games, reading books by other independent authors, being an activist, writing anime-style stories, and living a vegan life. Having graduated from college with a focus on Asian and Religious Studies, he now spends his time as a writer and as an abolitionist vegan advocate. He listens to any and all comments, suggestions, reflections and criticism.

Please contact me with a link to where you placed a review for any of my books (Of The Exps/ The Main Character) and I will answer any single question as one of my characters for **FREE**. If you do a review (and point out where) in addition to submitting fan art, I will write a **FREE** short 2–4 page story (with my characters) in a scenario of your choosing. =(:3)*

Bloggers who wish to review *Exp 8: Rebellion of the Exps* or *The Main Character: The Hero's Epic Journey Begins Part 1* may request "Review Copies" at the links below.

authoralexandermccarty@gmail.com

alexanderjmccarty@facebook.com

Best Friend's Special Message

In this world there are the victims and the victimizers. If you believe it's wrong to harm the innocent, then don't do it. Animals of all species have cherished families. Freedom is their birthright. I don't want Main's fans to cheer on his heroic acts while hypocritically contributing to needless animal exploitation and death. Be your own hero and live with integrity. Live Vegan and inspire others to do the same!

If you seek resources, the ones below are the absolute best.

http://www.adaptt.org/

http://www.abolitionistapproach.com/

veganeducationgroup.com

www.ingramcontent.com/pod-product-compliance
Lightning Source LLC
Chambersburg PA
CBHW070916180626
46817CB00003B/1084